THE LAST LAMBS
ON THE MOUNTAIN

*A story of illness,
hope and despair at
Saranac Lake in the
New York Adirondacks*

FLORENCE MULHERN

Order this book online at www.trafford.com
or email orders@trafford.com

Most Trafford titles are also available at major online book retailers.

Printed in Victoria, BC, Canada.

ISBN: 978-1-4269-2364-7 (sc)
ISBN: 978-1-4269-2365-4 (dj)

Library of Congress Control Number: 2010900765

*Our mission is to efficiently provide the world's finest, most comprehensive book publishing
service, enabling every author to experience success. To find out how to publish your book,
your way, and have it available worldwide, visit us online at www.trafford.com*

Trafford rev. 7/12/2010

www.trafford.com

North America & international
toll-free: 1 888 232 4444 (USA & Canada)
phone: 250 383 6864 ♦ fax: 812 355 4082

PREFACE

Most people today are too young to know what tuberculosis was like before the breakthrough in 1954 with the miracle drug, isoniacid. Little more than a hundred years ago it was the second leading cause of death in the United States. For the first half of the 20th century, it was still a fatal disease that sent the ill to distant sanatoriums for lengthy, uncertain cures. The word held the same sinister meaning that cancer holds today.

It was an illness which had baffled mankind for centuries. Cough and fever, weight loss and fatigue—those were its symptoms. It was called consumption because, quite literally, it consumed the lungs. Sometimes, more dramatically, it was called the White Plague. There was a stigma attached to it and it was spoken about guardedly and in euphemisms. It was a disease of the young.

Tuberculosis has existed for at least 6,500 years. Anthropologists believe its ravages may be evident in skeletons that date back as far as the Egyptian Old Kingdom or even the Stone Age. Its victims included Chopin, Keats, Elizabeth Barrett Browning, Robert Louis Stevenson, Henry David Thoreau, Voltaire, the Bronte sisters, St. Francis of Assisi, St. Teresa the Little Flower—giving rise to the belief that sensitivity of feeling was a predisposing factor. Later names would include Frans Kafka, Bela Bartok, Anton Chekhov, Katherine Mansfield and Eugene O'Neill, perpetuating the myth that an artistic temperament heightened susceptibility to the disease. At the crest of the Romantic Movement in the 19th century, the illness was almost a mark of distinction, the pallor it caused becoming part of the standard of beauty. Women abandoned rouge and whitened their faces instead. The taste for wan, ethereal heroines was reflected in the art and theater of the times. Marguerite in La Dame aux Camelias and Mimi in La Boheme immortalized the consumptive.

Treatment for a disease about which little was understood amounted to guesswork and the concept of sanatorium care was itself a breakthrough. Although throughout history various types of institutions were created for the care of consumptives, most were hospitals. During the early nineteenth century a few English doctors came to believe that pure air, pure water and pure food were beneficial in the treatment of tuberculosis and thus began the journeys of the ill to health resorts at the seaside, in the mountains or the deserts, or even to the ordinary countryside. In the latter half of the nineteenth century a German doctor, Hermann Brehmer, founded an institution for the treatment of tuberculosis in the mountains of Silesia, the first of its kind that could be termed a sanatorium. Beneficial results were reported and other similar facilities followed though in limited number. None, however, was established in the United States.

In 1873, Dr. Edward Livingston Trudeau, suffering from tuberculosis and feeling he had only a short time to live, chose to move to the Adirondacks, a region he loved. Instead of dying he survived for forty-one years and not only resumed the practice of medicine but became internationally renowned as a pioneer in the treatment of tuberculosis. He advocated rest, good nutrition and abundant fresh air. Others before him had prescribed the same regimen but they combined it with exercise. Dancing, fencing, jumping rope, horseback riding—all were recommended, the idea being to improve the appetite and in turn the strength, but the fever such effort kindled caused a loss of both. Dr. Trudeau found in his own case that after periods of rest his fever abated. It was the first intimation of the value of rest in the treatment of tuberculosis. And while he continued to believe that the piney Adirondack air had some special virtue for the sick, he knew that sick men went elsewhere and recovered and so he concluded that it was not so much the climate or geography as how those factors were used.

For centuries the disease was believed to be non-transmissible. Medical students at the end of the 1800's were still being taught that it was due to inherited constitutional peculiarities, perverted humors and various types of inflammations. The sick huddled among the well. Fresh air was considered injurious, especially night air and windows were tightly sealed. Since rooms and often beds were shared by others in the household, whole families in time were infected. In the general hospitals of the day consumptives occupied beds side by side with non-contagious cases.

By taking patients out of their crowded surroundings and bringing them to his "cottage sanatorium" at Saranac Lake, Dr. Trudeau was unknowingly helping to prevent the disease from spreading. When in 1882 a German by the name of Robert Koch isolated the tubercle bacillus, the disease was proved to be contagious, an advance treated skeptically by doctors in this country for many years. After it was finally accepted, the segregation of the ill, already established by Dr. Trudeau's concept of sanatorium treatment, became of prime importance.

With the turn of the century mortality from tuberculosis slowly commenced to decline, mainly as a result of the routine of rest and good nutrition although some degree of success was being achieved by lung collapse, a therapy devised to tackle the problem encountered in the treatment of any moving organ. The first effort was a surgical procedure called a thoracoplasty and consisted of the removal of ribs—sometimes as many as nine or eleven—to inhibit the movement of the lung and give damaged tissue a chance to repair itself. However, the trauma and disfigurement, as well as an inability to realistically assess its value as a treatment tool, led eventually to its disuse. The more moderate pneumothorax, followed by the still more improved pneumoperitoneum, took its place.

Meanwhile, the search for a specific to combat the tubercle bacillus went forward on many fronts but success was elusive. In the mid-1940's streptomycin was developed and though it was not the long-awaited miracle drug, it radically changed the outlook of victims of tuberculosis everywhere. It had no capacity to cure but it eliminated cough and fever which in turn lent a feeling of well-being and, more important, it rendered the disease non-contagious. Of all the grief laid at the door of tuberculosis over the centuries ostracism was the worst. Patients were now free to make visits home and mingle with the well.

The cheering, however, was short-lived. The much acclaimed new antibiotic was found to have serious side effects, among them deafness but worst of all resistance. In 1949 another antibiotic, PAS (para amino salicylic acid), was developed which, when used in conjunction with streptomycin, alleviated most of its problems though it caused one or two of its own. In a glass PAS looked like straight bourbon whiskey but it had a peculiar, acrid taste and it resulted in nausea which, as dose succeeded dose, built up to heaving, wrenching proportions. At that point a respite of a day or two would be granted to give the stomach a chance to quiet down but then the dosage would be resumed and the cycle start all over again.

At the same time surgery remained very much in the arsenal of weapons and a technique called a resection came into fashion. It was intended specifically for cases where cavitation existed and consisted of the excision of the cavity and a surrounding wedge of lung, a procedure believed to be the most reliable means of insuring recovery and preventing recurrence. So much in vogue had it become that whether a cavity had closed or even existed, a resection was recommended.

So things stood as the long tragic history of tuberculosis moved into its final stages. Many patients after a lengthy sanatorium stay returned to normal life and remained well. Others, however, did not and it was just this threat of recurrence that clouded the future of every sufferer. The records are strewn with the names of those whose disease recurred, requiring another sanatorium stay with the chances of a successful cure reduced. The names of the dead over the centuries exceed the number of dead in all the wars fought in history.

Rumors of a cure, a miracle drug, peaked and subsided in the last years, unleashing hope and despair in turn. Finally they became a reality. The solution to the puzzle that had eluded the best minds in the field of scientific research for decades had been found. It didn't mean, however, that the disease would disappear as during the first halcyon days most people thought it would. Tuberculosis was not eradicated and probably never will be but its destructive impact was gone and it was no longer fatal.

At the close of any great disaster—war or famine, holocaust or plague—there are those for whom the end comes too late. So it was with tuberculosis. The new drug, as miraculous as an elevated host above an altar, pledged life from that day forward. A cure awaited all who came after but from those who fell short the old penalties were exacted—the grievous pain of banishment, love chilled by the cold breath of absence, lives wrenched askew. The people who moved across the final pages of that melancholy history were more to be pitied than the dead of twenty centuries. Shackled to the past by an accident of timing, scarred and set apart, they saw the wondrous new phenomenon and marveled. Beggars with faces pressed against the glass, they watched other beggars fed. No miracle dose could turn back time, restore the years, erase the grief, put right the disarray, undo the mischief done. The line between the fettered and the free was cleanly drawn and inalterably fixed.

The sanatoriums have closed, mobile X-ray units no longer patrol poor neighborhoods and skin tests for school children are a thing of the past. Modern treatment methods today make it possible for most of the ill to cure at home, the need for hospital care the exception rather than the rule. Nevertheless people continue to sicken with tuberculosis. After a dramatic decrease of the disease in the years that followed the advent of isoniacid, the number of cases in the United States and elsewhere has begun to inch upward due partly to the spread of AIDS. Its victims no longer are primarily the young, but comprise all age brackets and where once tuberculosis was found predominantly in the northern and temperate zones of Europe and America it is now prevalent in the tropical and subtropical regions of Africa, Asia and Central America. The battle lines have changed but the battle is still to be won.

For us, however, the disease whose shadow stalked the lives of our forebears has ceased to be and soon there will be no one left to remember the time when it was spoken of in whispers and the very word evoked dread. Its memory is ebbing, speeded by the urgencies of cancer, AIDS, Alzheimers disease, the afflictions of today which are as devastating and baffling as the White Plague of old. But the persistence that surmounted errors and follies, the doggedness that shed light on ignorance and sustained purpose in the face of bottomless discouragement sounds a ringing note of hope. What happened before will happen again. Let us remind ourselves that further conquests lie ahead.

The background of this story is authentic, the sanatorium described is Dr. Trudeau's sanatorium at the end of its mission, but the characters are fictional and any resemblance between them and persons living or dead is purely coincidental.

1.

They sat across from each other in a booth upholstered in peacock blue, the last one back in a small restaurant called The Silver Swan on 44th Street near Grand Central Station. A month ago they dawdled there over drinks and dinner, their world secure, their love a constant around which everything in Ellie's world revolved. It wasn't to be imagined it would ever change, yet it had, and now her recollection of that evening–the carefree laughter, the tight held hands, the bliss of love at the evening's end–rose up in her mind like a specter over a grave. A Scotch Mist stood in front of her on a paper napkin patterned with swooping silver birds.

"Take off your sunglasses, Ellie," Bob said. " No one can see you here."

"You can," she answered, frowning, but she took them off. "I hate for you to see me like this."

Earlier that evening when she dressed and put on make-up before they left the apartment, she barely recognized herself in the mirror. Her swollen eyes were a stranger's eyes and her face had a hectic flush. Between the final flood of tears and growing apprehension as departure time approached, her temperature had soared and she felt as if she were on fire. The air-conditioned chill of the restaurant after the blistering heat of the city streets turned her hands icy and she pressed bloodless fingers against her burning cheek. In her other hand she clutched a Kleenex which she put to her mouth each time she coughed—a soft almost gentle cough, the betraying cough of lung disease, the cough she did her best to suppress unless she was alone.

"I can't believe this is happening. I keep thinking I'll wake up and find that none of it is real." She looked into space and shook her head. Asleep or awake, however, it was all the same. The anguish pursued her even into her dreams.

Bob leaned across the table and took her hand away from her face. He held it tightly. "Listen to me, Ellie, it won't be nearly as bad as you think. You have to get well and this is the only way it can be done. Think of it in that light. Please try." He'd done his best to persuade her to see it rationally but she turned it all away. Again she disregarded his words.

"People look at me as if I'm different."
He shook his head. "That isn't so."

"No, it's true," she insisted. "They look at me as if I've changed and I haven't changed. I'm still the same. But they make me feel as if I don't belong, like I'm someone to get rid of."

It had happened so quickly—not the long series of indispositions which led to this climax, but the revelation of their cause. Looking back she could now see each ominous sign for what it was and she wondered for the hundredth time if somehow this catastrophe could have been prevented. If she had acted differently, if she had admitted to herself that something was awfully wrong and persisted in trying to find out what it was instead of letting it go on, if she hadn't wanted so desperately to believe it was nothing, would the nightmare then never have come to pass?

The awareness of being caught up in circumstances over which she had not the least control stripped her of her fond belief that she could manage her own destiny and left her with an unsettling fear. Never before had anything adverse happened to her which she wasn't able to counter in some fashion through her parents' indulgence, a teacher's leniency, or her talent for getting her own way. For the first time in her life she had no say in what would transpire.

A vision of Dr. Reiser's face, implacable as chiseled stone, rose up before her. He saw her not with the permissive approval she had come to take for granted but as a menace to the public health. He was a cheerless man and it wasn't his way to temper a prognosis with any words of comfort. He might have assured her she was being sent away in order to recover and that many people recovered. He could have mentioned the strides that had been made in the treatment of the illness and that it wasn't as bad as it used to be. He must have known how frightening it was for a girl of her years to be told she had a serious and often fatal disease. But long ago Dr. Reiser had built a wall between himself and his patients, his heart hardened by the toll the disease had taken among those closest to him and the impossibility of predicting who would survive and who would not. He did only what his professional role required which was to identify the ill and arrange for their segregation.

In a few days a faceless body called the Board of Health would come to the apartment to make sure she was gone. They'd talk to Joan and leave instructions about disinfecting the rooms and packing away what remained of Ellie's belongings. They'd tell her she must get chest X-rays without delay because it was possible she had caught the infection. She'd do so. And she'd boil Ellie's cup and plate, her glass and silverware, and remove the dabs of nail polish they'd painted on them to identify them as hers. Thinking about it flooded her with shame as if some unseemly behavior on her part had brought all this inconvenience about.

She lowered her swollen eyes. "I have such awful dreams. Dreams of being in a room with no windows and no doors, a room I can't get out of. Being in places where nobody knows who I am. Once I dreamed I was being sent away to prison. That's what this feels like—like I'm going to prison."

Bob tightened his grip on her hand. "No, Ellie, you're not going away to a prison or anything like it. You're going to a place where there are people who'll care about you and who'll do everything they can to get you well."

She appeared for a few moments to consider it, then her face turned stubborn.

"But I don't want to go away. Oh Robert, why can't I stay here?"

"I wish you could, kitten, but here in this air-polluted city it would take a lot longer to get you well."

"I wouldn't care," she insisted.

"But I care. I want you to get better. I want this to be over with and the best way to do it is to get you up in the mountains and let you breathe good clean air. That's half the cure, Ellie. It's been proven time and again."

The mountains and the piney air. When she and her brother, Larry, were children their grandmother had a balsam pillow which they loved to handle. It was covered in coarse burlap with a picture of a forest of pine trees stamped on the front and the words Adirondack Mountains printed above it. Inside were prickly needles that gave off a woodsy, aromatic scent and she and her brother would bury their noses in it and the aroma would linger on their hands and faces long afterwards. Once when Ellie had pneumonia her grandmother mailed it to her mother with instructions to keep it at the head of Ellie's bed. Something about the smell of pine was supposed to be good for the lungs.

"And they have streptomycin now," Bob went on. "That's been a big step forward. Until a few years ago they had nothing."

"But it's all the time it takes," she said despairingly. They talk about two years." She toyed with her drink which she'd barely tasted. Her deepest fear she left unspoken. Suppose he got tired of waiting? What if he wasn't here when she came back? She lifted unsure eyes and searched his face, longing for him to read her thoughts and reassure her.

"Time passes, Ellie, and you're not going to the moon. I'll be coming up to see you as often as I can." He reached over for her hand again and pressed it. "Won't that make it better?" She nodded and gave him a little watery smile.

A waiter came and bowing deferentially put menus in front of them. Ellie sipped at the Scotch Mist.

"You'll eat some dinner, won't you, kitten?"

"Not this minute. When I finish my drink."

In the center of the room, forward of their booth and in Ellie's line of sight, a half dozen young women sat at a flower-decorated table in the course of some sort of celebration dinner. When the girl at the head of the table got to her feet the reason for the occasion became apparent. She was very pregnant. From the hands of a silver-haired, approving waiter she took a proffered pink and white cake, all curlicues and buds of icing in the middle of which nested a small sugar cradle.

Ellie studied her carefully—the mane of blond hair and the radiant smile, the firm, sun-tanned arms that would soon hold a baby. They were probably the same age, Ellie concluded, but nothing else had they in common. The girl glowed with health. The man she loved was hers, her claim upon him legal, about to be bonded ever more lastingly by a child. She stood at a beginning with all the best of life opening up before her. Ellie, for all she knew, might be standing at life's end. A stab of envy went through her as sharp as the blade of a knife. A look of pain crossed her face and Bob, observing it, turned to see what had caught her attention. He took in the situation in moments and got to his feet.

"Come, Ellie," he said. "Sit over here."

He had her move to his side of the table next to the wall and he slid in next to her. He put his arm around her, expecting her to cry again, prepared to comfort her, but she shook her head. No words could lessen her pain. Her world, once so sound, had cut loose from its moorings, and the love which Ellie never had reason to doubt was now threatened by a foe she was powerless to fight—absence. Exhausted, coerced, she had no more tears.

She didn't eat dinner but she ate some strawberry ice cream and at seven-thirty they walked through the dusty heat-soaked streets to the station. Train time was eight o'clock.

2.

Winter comes early in the Adirondacks. Storms sweep in from Canada even before the last leaves fall from the trees and transform the world into a white image of itself. The ground is not glimpsed again till April. Not until June do lilacs flower. Three months at most of uncertain summer and the fingers of winter commence once more to curl into a fist.

It was considered ideal climate for tuberculosis. The cold was beneficial, they said, and the clear pine-scented air that distinguished the region was believed to have some special therapeutic value. The sick lay out on porches year-round— in patient hope or resigned despair—and even those who were cured continued the practice, convinced it had delivered them and would prevent a relapse. The houses in town were testimony to this belief, rows of porches across their fronts, each one holding a bed. Large three and four story boarding houses, catering to the ill who cured on their own, were built on the same plan because for everyone the remedy was the same. At the sanatoriums the sick were urged onto their porches, taught to lie prone, take shallow breaths and let the pure air help heal the lesions in their lungs. No image was more evocative of the disease than a bed on a porch.

Looking back to that time—World War II fought and won, a new confidence gripping the country as it moved into the second half of the century—there is a bitter sadness in recalling the dread and dismay the illness struck in every heart. It was feared much as leprosy was once feared and for the same reasons. It was contagious and there was no cure. Nor was there any defense against it. It was believed to be a disease of poverty and neglect which gave rise to the stigma against it but the belief was false. Anyone could be a victim. And if the afflicted rang no warning bell they were dealt with swiftly in the manner of the day.

Until the summer Ellie was eleven she had no more perception of the disease than its name. That year her parents were in Europe and she and her brother stayed with their grandmother in New York. She lived in a block of apartments on Riverside Drive, each one of which had a small stone balcony. On the balcony of an apartment close by a young woman lay out on a cot every afternoon. Ellie, her curiosity aroused, tried to see what she looked like but she could only hear her cough and she asked her grandmother what was wrong with her.

"She's in a decline," her grandmother said.

"Does that mean she'll die?"

Her grandmother nodded. "I'm afraid so."

The words gave her pause to think. Everyone knew they had to die but the day was far off and nobody worried about it. Suppose though you were young and the day was close at hand? When she saw her grandmother at Christmas she asked her about the girl on the balcony.

"They buried her last month."

Until then a cough had seemed so harmless a thing but now there was cause to believe it could be deadly. Questions were turned aside as if even to talk about it was to court disaster. A chance remark a year or two later only deepened the mystery. Old Mr. McGarry, a handyman who did odd jobs around town, had a lingering cough which may well have been caused by the evil little brown cigarettes he smoked. But one Sunday, after listening to the hacking during a church service, Ellie heard her mother say, "he sounds as if he's ready for Saranac." The words were spoken as if that would be the end of him.

What was this place called Saranac and why did the name have such ominous overtones? It was in the mountains, far up to the north where there was a lot of snow and freezing weather. It held the only hope of cure for people who had something wrong with their lungs but it seemed to be a flimsy hope at best, there being the implication that people who went there never came back.

The news that came one April day about Jerry Marshall settled the matter once and for all in Ellie's mind. He was the seventeen-year-old brother of Ellie's best friend in high school, a bony, large-eared, eager-to-please boy whose colds and coughs were finally diagnosed as tuberculosis after months of assurances that they were not. Three days before he was scheduled to go up to a sanatorium he hanged himself.

Ellie was twenty two when she was found to have tuberculosis, living in New York, working in Wall Street, ardently in love with a man who was forty years old and married.

3.

By November of that year enough snow had fallen to shroud the hills and bury the black-topped road that led from the town up to the sanatorium whose buildings sprawled over a mountainside. They dated back many years and those from its earliest period stood like rugged pioneers, heavy stone to their waists, tall stone chimneys and sharply peaked roofs. Among them, later buildings in less heavy-handed style seemed almost frivolous. All were anchored in the mountainside as firmly as outcroppings of rock. Inside they were broad and high-ceilinged, their tall, narrow windows tight against the worst of the winter storms that belabored the region.

Two square stone pillars marked the entrance to the grounds. Each supported half of an arched iron gate that was pulled back and had sunk of its own accord into the ground at either side. Not in anyone's memory had the gate been closed and whether its original purpose was to bar exit or entry no one could say. Someone claimed it as a symbol—a duel symbol of prison and refuge—and it could well have been for the sanatorium was both.

Past the entrance the road skirted the rising mountainside on the left while to the right the land fell away and revealed a splendor of peaks and valleys that moved back, fold upon fold, mile after mile until the most distant blurred into the horizon. The entire sanatorium claimed this view. The Administration Building and the medical buildings which constituted the heart of the complex beheld it with level eyes, the rest cottages and infirmaries scattered at random amid the pines that carpeted the slope, saw it from the vantage point of height.

The buildings were linked one to another by a single narrow, looping road that rose at an easy angle, curved across the upper incline and gently descended to become the access road leading in and out of the sanatorium. Only those who had reason to be there traveled its length. In summertime when visitors came, taxis and cars with out-of-state license plates were familiar sights but winter restricted traffic to delivery vans and workmen's trucks, the black limousine of one of the surgeons and occasionally a hearse.

Death was carefully orchestrated at the sanatorium. Because emotional upsets played havoc with precariously mending lungs, patients were zealously shielded from its impact. Agitation often caused a return of symptoms and could undo in an hour the laborious efforts of a month. In the intimacy of the infirmary where persons lived as close as neighbors in a small town, every happening involved all and a death could levy a costly toll. The staff did its best to handle these occasions in a manner designed to curtain every ugly detail. If, fortunately, a patient died at night the body was removed while everyone slept. Word would be permitted to filter out later, however it might. A door too long closed. A door open on an empty room. A question asked of a nurse and the answer given, calm-voiced. "He'd been sick for a very long time, you know." But if death did not oblige by night it was a trickier matter.

Monique died the first week in November at nine o'clock in the morning. Her door was closed and a Do Not Disturb sign hung on the doorknob. None the wiser, patients strolled their fifteen minutes in the hall or stood in the alcove looking out at the icy rain that glazed the fallen snow. Nurses passed through the hall on hushed white feet and smiled. Dr. Nichols stopped briefly and predicted the rain would turn to snow again by nightfall.

An alcove at either end of the hall commanded a view of the narrow road that rose out of the buildings at its base, served the infirmary and continued on beyond where it was promptly lost in a copse of trees. The alcoves were furnished with creaky wicker furniture covered by thin cushions of flowered cretonne worn to the shapes of the hundreds of patients who over the years had lingered and moved on to a life they'd known or to a grave. Along that side of the hall were also bathrooms and utility rooms and a few rooms for patients. Monique's was one of them. Rooms lining the opposite side of the hall were considered the most desirable because they looked out on the panorama of mountains.

"See," Miss Bodelle had said to Ellie the morning she arrived. "You have one of the loveliest views in the sanatorium."

From her bed on the porch she would study that lonely land, the mountains that rolled back in endless repetition, their slopes dense and secret, forests dark at noon. It could not have looked any wilder or more solitary a thousand years ago she used to think, and she would have preferred a room that overlooked the road even though most of the time it was empty.

That day the student nurses who served the lunch trays quietly closed each door behind them as they went out. A closed door, shutting her in, made Ellie uneasy but the girl was gone before there was time to ask her to leave it open. She started her lunch, trying to decide whether to open it or wait until she had finished eating. Halfway through she set the tray aside and got out of bed. She crossed the room in bare feet and started to turn the doorknob but stopped. A soft dull thud, a sound she couldn't identify, startled her and her hand froze. In the hush that followed she eased the door open just far enough to be able to see. A workman had wheeled a gurney out of Monique's room and apparently bumped it against the door jamb in making the turn. It now stood almost directly in front of her. Monique's body lay upon it hardly mounding the sheet that covered her, strapped down by belts across her chest and knees. Her head, from the contour of the sheet, was turned to one side as if she were lying in bed watching the snow drift down outside her window.

Miss Bodelle came out of the room carrying a small pile of her belongings and placed them at the foot of the gurney. Her white sweater, a blue flowered robe, slippers, the framed picture of her little girl.

"I'll come back later with a couple of boxes for the rest of the things," the workman said to Miss Bodelle.

"Wait till after one-thirty when everyone's napping," she answered softly. She closed the door to the empty room soundlessly and the Do Not Disturb sign set in motion, slid back and forth like the pendulum of a clock.

Ellie eased her door shut and got back into bed. Someone had said that Monique might not live until Christmas but it was hard to believe. Someone else said her disease had progressed beyond manageable limits but Ellie didn't know enough about death to make any judgments. Asked how she felt, Monique's answer was always the same. "Better, better than yesterday."

4.

Monique entered the sanatorium the previous July, shortly after Ellie, but she had been there twice before. She was a mild quiet person, often withdrawn, a Madonna-like quality to her face heightened by two wings of black hair she pulled back and tied at the nape of her neck. She came from a small town in Quebec where her husband, a boyish-looking diffident man, was a doctor.

They had come down again by car, making the trip leisurely as if to give it a holiday air, stopping along the way to take pictures, making little detours when something struck their fancy.

Monique loved flowers, especially wildflowers, and she knew a lot about them. On one of the detours she caught a glimpse of some small purple blossoms scattered across a slope and she had her husband stop the car.

"Claude, look" she exclaimed, and she pointed out the flowers. "They're what I've been looking for and never thought I'd find. Till now I've only seen pictures of them."

"Do you want me to get some for you?"

"Let me get them myself. I want to get roots and all so I can plant them." She'd already stepped down from the car.

"No, Monique, stay where you are! You can't climb that slope!"

But she was already ahead of him. "Only as far as the flowers," she called back.

He let her go and watched as she made her way up the incline, stopping to kneel every few feet and pull out clumps of blossoms. Halfway to the top she started to cough. When she got back to the car, her skirt full of purple flowers, she was coughing blood and by the time they reached the sanatorium she was hemorrhaging.

There was unmistakable commotion in the hall that afternoon when they brought her into the infirmary. Quick footsteps. Dr. Nichols' urgent voice. Another doctor coming on the scene. That evening Miss MacIntyre, the night nurse on the grounds, took over at the desk in order to release an infirmary nurse for duty in Monique's room. Miss MacIntyre was a pale, prim woman with snowy hair, easily scandalized. She was ablaze with indignation.

"Can you imagine," she said to another nurse in the hall after dinner. "He let her climb a mountainside! And he a doctor!"

Later Claude spoke to Dr. Nichols. "I know I shouldn't have permitted it. I was wrong. But she's missed so many things I couldn't refuse her."

It wasn't often someone arrived at the infirmary on an emergency basis and curiosity was aroused. Within hours Monique's story had spread from room to room, fueled by a patient who had known her before and who furnished details of her background. The nurses, pestered with questions remained calm, insisting there was nothing to be alarmed about. Claude's contrite admission to Dr. Nichols gave the story an extra dimension wherein lay room for individual judgments and it seemed as if everyone had his own opinion about it.

Until then Ellie had seen no one but patients in various stages of recovery and she had begun to believe everyone got well but it was apparent this wasn't always the case. What would it be like, she wondered, to think you were cured and then have the disease flare up again? They said each setback lessened the chances of an ultimate cure—like climbing a mountain and being knocked back within reach of the top, having to start all over again but with more pitfalls added. Monique would know. That was her history. And her husband knew and it was because of it that compassion moved him to let her make that fatal climb.

Standing at the window of her room that evening, watching the shadows darken and the sky dim, Ellie reflected on the day's events, seeing in her mind's eye, a girl on a hillside searching out flowers in a last harmless gesture of freedom before the walls and rules of the sanatorium closed her in. She saw her cough, her mouth become bloodied and purple blossoms fall around her feet.

The image faded and another took its place. Her own last hours before banishment slid into focus. Once more she saw the apartment's sunny windows, the prints on the living room walls, the glass topped table holding its collection of plants, the cat asleep on the windowsill. She heard the traffic noises from the street below and the chimes of the little gold clock on the bookshelf which inexorably marked off the hours of the day, the night and the one final day left to her to spend there.

Joan was gone when she awoke that morning but there was a note from her propped against the lamp on the night table.

"Good luck, Ellie. Write and tell me how everything goes and if you need anything let me know. I'll drop you a line when I get back."

Joan was a stewardess and they'd shared an apartment in one of the old brownstone houses on East 55th Street for three years. Much of the time she was away but when she returned she blew into the place like a gale force wind. She flung clothes around, let dishes pile up in the sink, monopolized the bathroom and the telephone. But she was generous-hearted, level-headed, capable. The day Ellie faced her with the news of her tuberculosis not a flicker of emotion crossed her face.

"My mother had tuberculosis all the time I was growing up. I took care of her, did everything for her, and I never got it. Not everybody does and I must be one of them."

"But this place is full of my germs. It will have to be fumigated the doctor said. And we mustn't use the same dishes."

"Yes, I know. We'll manage. Don't worry about it, Ellie."

In the kitchen Dulcinea lay stretched out full length on top of the refrigerator, her food set out for her on the floor beneath the window. Some coffee remained in the pot from Joan's breakfast and Ellie heated it on the stove. Beside the sink stood a bottle of drug store cough medicine, the last in a series she'd bought with the dogged hope that its persuasive promise of cure would prove true. Maybe for some it had but not for her. She unscrewed the bottle's top and poured what was left down the drain. Staring out the window, seeing nothing, she sipped at the coffee until it grew cold.

There were her bags to be packed. She pulled them out of the closet and opened them on Joan's bed. Riffling through underwear in dresser drawers, pushing through clothes on hangers, she made fitful choices and folded them in one bag or the other only to change her mind, take them out and put them back where they came from. An hour later, no closer to getting the job done, she abandoned it. She went through a drawer full of papers, determined to clear out most of them but ended by keeping them all.

She coughed carefully into Kleenex which she discarded into a plastic bag kept for that purpose as the nurse had instructed. She took her temperature 100.2. Too high for midday. The fever usually started in early afternoon, rose gradually and peaked in the evening. She shook the thermometer down and put it away.

It was another scorching day, the seventh in one of New York's typical summertime heat waves. The heavy air pressed down between the narrow streets as if a lid were crammed on somewhere overhead. The pavements shimmered. Only the fans in the apartment kept the place bearable. She showered to cool off and while it made her more comfortable for a little while, afterward she was warmer than ever.

She was brushing her hair when fatigue hit her—that curious, persistent symptom of the disease she'd struggled against so ineffectually all the preceding months. It would come over her without warning, a devastating feeling of exhaustion, and her hands would tremble and she'd be forced to sit. She lay down on the bed waiting for it to pass, willing her strength to return, but she fell asleep and didn't wake until she heard Bob's step in the living room. She called him and he came and sat on the edge of the bed and kissed her.

"When did you get here?" she asked.

"About an hour ago."

"Why didn't you wake me?"

"I was going to in another ten minutes. Do you know it's five o'clock?"

"That means I slept all afternoon." She sighed, "and I wanted to be all showered and dressed when you got here."

He put his hand on her forehead in a gesture that had become automatic. Her forehead was burning but he made no comment.

"What did you do all day besides sleep?" he asked.

"I tried to pack." She gestured at the open empty suitcases on Joan's bed. "I had clothes in and out of those suitcases half a dozen times. I don't know what to bring."

"We'll pack together in the morning."

"I suppose it's summer up there. They say it's cool, that it never really gets hot like here."

"It'll be good for you to be out of this heat."

"But I don't suppose I'll need clothes, will I? I'm going to be in bed." Her face sobered at the prospect. "It's so awful having to go away." Tears welled up in her eyes and spilled over. "It wouldn't be nearly so bad if I could stay here. I try to imagine what it's going to be like but I can't." She shook her head miserably.

"Ellie baby, people go there to get well and they do get well. It can't be all bad."

"I asked the nurse in Dr. Reiser's office how long people have to stay and she said usually about two years. Two years! I'll be twenty four!"

"You're going to be twenty four in two years no matter what happens."

A wave of desolation swept over her and she pressed her face into his chest. "You won't be there."

"It isn't a foreign country, kitten. It's just an overnight train ride. Only two hours by plane. Do you think I'm going to let you go up there and forget about you? I'll give you awhile to settle in and find out if you like it and then I'm coming up to see how it's all going."

"Do you mean it?"

"Of course I mean it. And if everything isn't just the way we think it should be I'll pack you right out of the place and we'll do something else. You don't think I'll leave you there if you're unhappy? But you have to promise me you'll give it a fair trial. Okay?"

Her face brightened and she nodded. "I will."

"That's better," he said. "Why don't I make us each a Tom Collins and afterward we'll have a turkey sandwich."

"That sounds lovely."

While he was in the kitchen she showered, put on lipstick and a thin blue dress and later they sat in the living room sipping their drinks.

"Do they know at the office what's wrong with me? That I won't be coming back?"

"Yes, Ellie, they do. Because I told them. The company isn't about to let you vanish without an explanation! I told them you had tuberculosis and were going up to Saranac Lake to cure."

She frowned, imagining the stir such news must have caused. Staring down into her drink, she poked the ice around with her finger.

"I wish everyone didn't have to know."

"It's nothing to be ashamed of, Ellie. Tuberculosis is a disease just like any other. Besides you can't hide these things and there's no reason why you should."

But she hadn't yet had time to see it that way. It was still the mysterious illness of her childhood, spoken about guardedly, a disease no one willingly admitted to though it might have claimed half a dozen family members. In spite of what Bob said it was still, for some reason she didn't understand, a disease with a stigma attached to it.

Bob got to his feet. "I'm going to make us another drink and then we'll eat our turkey sandwiches. How about that? Do you feel hungry, kitten?"

"I do. I'm really hungry." And she remembered that she'd eaten nothing all day.

They finished the drinks and sandwiches and Bob looked at his watch.

"It's bedtime, Ellie. It's cooler now. You'll be able to sleep. I'll sleep here on the couch."

He was standing in the center of the room and she went to him and locked her arms around his waist. "If I asked you something would you say yes?"

"Absolutely not."

"Why not?"

"Because you've trapped me that way before." He smiled. "I won't say yes unless I know what it is."

She hesitated.

"What is it?"

"Sleep with me tonight."

"No kitten." His face turned serious and he shook his head for emphasis.

"Please Bob."

"Baby, it can't be. You've got to be quiet. You shouldn't even be walking around."

"This is our last night. Don't make me spend it alone." She started to cry. "We don't know when we'll ever be together again."

"Ellie, be sensible. You hemorrhaged last Sunday. It could happen again."

"It won't happen again," she said heedlessly. "I know it won't."

He shook his head.

"Robert, I'll never ask you anything else ever. I just want one last night to remember."

"There'll be other nights, Ellie."

But she wept and pleaded and wouldn't let him go. And so he yielded. And he held her gently and his kisses on her contaminated mouth were soft.

Beyond the windows of Ellie's room the mountains were lost in darkness but overhead, pale and remote, every star in the firmament of heaven glittered. She stared at them blindly, seeing a girl on a hillside gathering flowers while an indulgent husband looked on. Then, like a second example in a textbook offered to illustrate the same point, she saw her stifling apartment, the droning fans, the waiting suitcases and she felt again Bob's arms around her, holding her close because she feared their nights together were ending.

5.

"How did your illness start?" The question was asked politely by one of three young, scrubbed-looking medical students who stood with clipboards in hand at the foot of Ellie's bed.

She tried to think of a straightforward answer to the question, one that wouldn't take an hour in the telling, so she said simply that it began with a cough that wouldn't go away. And the three young men dutifully recorded her words in their notes.

There was, of course, a lot more to it than that. She thought of Dr. Zeleny's X-ray and the blunder he made when he pronounced it normal. Had he read it correctly her disease would have been caught many months sooner, before so much damage was done and while there was still the possibility of an early cure. That really was where it all began.

Bob had been in Egypt for nearly the whole month of November and his return was cause for a special occasion. At the time Hildegarde was appearing in the Persian Room at the Plaza and everyone was talking about her. Ellie didn't know who she was. French? American? Nor did she know the songs she'd made so popular but she was the toast of New York that season and that was the place she chose for them to go.

She wore a filmy rose-colored dress with narrow rhinestone shoulder straps and a clinging bodice that fell to a cloud of skirt and the heels of her shoes were studded with rhinestones. Her hair was swept up on top of her head where it lent her face an improbable maturity. Bob was tanned from the Egyptian sun and looked so darkly handsome Ellie imagined every woman must envy her. When they walked together into that beautiful room, little tables at different levels, lamplight and flowers, muted music and soft rushes of perfumed air—it was another high point in what had become a luminous succession of them and proof to Ellie that it was possible to get anything she wanted.

She never ceased to be surprised at how readily it all came about but of course she had long ago set her goals and that seemed to her to be the key that opened every door. For reasons she could no more analyze than defend she wanted to be in the New York business world where she would become one of the smart, admired women who were part of the complex of people who ran it. She knew she would have to start at some humble level but it wouldn't matter as long as she got a foothold. The rest was sure to follow. Because she was quick and bright she easily learned the skills she needed to know and then just as easily was taken on by one of Manhattan's most prestigious firms. When she was catapulted from the obscurity of a stenographer's desk into its executive offices she didn't credit luck or chance or just the fact of being in the right place at the right time. She was convinced it was her own doing.

She hadn't foreseen, much less contrived, the love affair which followed and which now wholly absorbed her. That was a dazzling, astonishing development that wiped out all her early goals and left her with a single soaring aspiration to hold Bob fast, one day to marry him. Was it impossible? Deep within her was rooted the conviction that just as with everything else she'd wanted, this too would one day happen. She had only to wait. Young and prodigal of time, the future was forever.

"Do you know you're the best-looking man in New York?" she asked proudly when they were seated and served.

He shook his head, smiling, and lifted his glass. "Here's to love's blindness."

They were drinking champagne which Ellie didn't much like though the ceremonial touches of ice bucket and popping cork impressed her as did the regal manner in which it was poured. Besides, Bob liked it so she drank it with him glass for glass.

"Were there beautiful women in Cairo?" Whenever he'd been away she asked the same question and always he smiled at the artlessness which prompted it. Had she no idea of the extent of her hold on him. He looked at her across the table— the clear lovely face, lustrous-eyed, a girl who wanted only to please and be pleased. As if some woman, casually met, could blind him to that image, could hold him any longer than it took to sip a drink or share a taxi ride.

"No Ellie, nowhere. Only here. Only you."

"You did miss me?"

"Very much."

"I missed you terribly," she said and she closed her eyes against the memory of his absence.

He took her hand. "Let's dance so I can hold you."

In his arms he was conscious of how fragile she was. She had never been robust but now beneath the sheer fabric of her dress there seemed barely flesh enough to cover her bones. They danced only briefly and she asked to sit down. Though she wouldn't admit it she was exhausted. It was her cough. It wore her out. It drained away her strength. She'd had a chest cold in August and never really got over it. It left her with a cough that on a couple of occasions seemed to be clearing up but which came back again. All through the evening she coughed softly, intermittently, and Bob, observing her, grew quiet and speculative. Hildegarde came on at eleven after they'd eaten dinner and were on their third bottle of champagne. The room darkened slowly to pitch blackness, grew light again at the same slow pace, and there she stood glittering in the focus of a half dozen spotlights. She looked like a mermaid risen from the sea. She wore a dress of green sequins that fitted her body like skin down to her ankles, and rippled on the floor around her feet like the ruffled tail of an exotic fish. The songs she sang were sweet, sad, insinuative and Ellie listened as if caught in a spell.

Bob's face had grown more serious as the evening progressed and they left soon afterward. Joan was away and they taxied to the apartment.

"Would you like coffee?" she asked when they got inside and took their things off. "A drink?"

He shook his head. "I want to talk to you, Ellie. Come sit down."

She seated herself beside him on the couch.

"Before I left you promised me you'd see a doctor about your cough," he said. "Did you do it?"

She took his hand in both of hers remorsefully. "Honestly, Bob, I thought it was getting better."

"So you didn't."

"I was coughing a lot less and I thought why bother if I'm getting over it."

"That isn't the way the promise was made. Do you remember I asked you, no matter how you felt, to make an appointment and see a doctor before I got back and you promised faithfully that you would?"

She remained silent.

"I'm worried about you, Ellie. That cough started last summer. It's gone on too long and something has to be done about it. Tomorrow, without fail, I want you to call and make an appointment. Can I trust you to do it?"

She nodded, chastened. "But that was another thing," she said. "I didn't know what doctor to go to."

"You could see the airline doctor Joan goes to or the company doctor or anyone you like."

"Maybe the company doctor. Dr. Zeleny. That funny little man with the Charlie Chaplin feet."

"I don't care who it is. Just go."

"I will. I truly will."

It was a curious thing. After he'd gone to Egypt the tempo of Ellie's life slowed. She went to bed early, lay around the apartment on weekends and of course at the office with Bob away the days were tranquil. While the cough didn't disappear entirely, it subsided to a point where she truly believed it was letting go its hold on her and that by the time he returned she'd be over it. She was so sure this was the case that she didn't give another thought to seeing a doctor. But then Bob came back. And even before he did there were so many things to do to get ready for his return. The days were brimful of preparation. Then he was here and she abandoned herself to the joy of his homecoming.

She hardly noticed it at first, so insidiously did the cough creep back. But as the days passed it couldn't be ignored and soon it was just as bad as it had been before—a small, soft cough, constant throughout her waking hours, interrupting her sleep.

She phoned Dr. Zeleny's office the next day and got an early morning appointment for the following week. Once the commitment was made she rehearsed in her mind what she would say. She intended to describe every detail of the chest cold she'd had in August when it all started.

She'd never had a chest cold like it before and it frightened her. Three nights in a row she woke up drenched in sweat, her pajamas, the sheets and the pillow so wet she had to get up and change them. At the same time a sharp pain in her right lung caught her whenever she tried to take a deep breath. Joan was away, Bob was out of town. She stayed home a week, most of the time in bed because the least effort tired her and the pain when she breathed was slow to disappear.

Bob was still away when she went back to work. One day she had lunch with Mrs. Ramey, head of the Stenographic Department with whom she was friendly and she described the symptoms.

"Sounds as if you had pleurisy," she said. "Summer colds can lead to things like that. They're worse in some ways than winter colds."

Pleurisy. Of course. That's what it must have been. Just putting a name to it made it less frightening. But now she'd have a chance to tell a doctor about it and get a professional opinion.

Dr. Zeleny was the company doctor for three or four large corporations, Consolidated Steel one of them, which when added to his private practice made for a busy operation. His office was on 38th Street near Lexington Avenue in a building that looked as if it might have been a warehouse at one time. It was a warren of a place. The doctor's rooms were small cubicles strung out along two passages at right angles to each other and a steady stream of traffic moved through them.

Everything seemed much as it was when she'd gone for her company physical after she was hired. The same fat nurse and golden haired receptionist. The same plastic flowers and magazines with curling pages in the waiting room. Nor did Dr. Zeleny's private office look much different—a cluttered, musty-smelling room where the two of them sat almost knee to knee.

She was dressed again. He had listened to her chest, looked at her throat and taken a chest X-ray. He was a bearded man with a bushy mustache who wore a white jacket over shiny trousers and whose out-turned feet in scruffy brown shoes shuffled up and down the passages as if forever pressed to keep abreast of the tide of his patients.

"Your chest sounds okay and your throat looks normal. I don't see any signs of a problem. How long have you had the cough?"

"Since August. It started with a terrible cold, worse than any I ever had before."

But the doctor didn't seem interested in the cold. He interrupted her. "Do you smoke?"

"No."

"Lost any weight?"

"A little. Three or four pounds. I never got my appetite back after August."

He regarded her thoughtfully for a moment as if balancing the facts, then came down on the side of the favorable. "Eat an extra dessert once in awhile. Have some ice cream before you go to bed." He was casual, dismissive and it served to reassure her. If there were grounds for concern he would have made them known.

Nevertheless she persisted. "The coughing wears me out and then I'm too tired to eat."

"I'll give you something to relieve it before you go." He picked up the form she filled out when she came and studied it. "I see you're one of the Consolidated Steel people." Ellie nodded. "Do you know Bill Knox? Tracey Wyatt? Mac Saunders?"

"I know who they are," she said. Mr. Knox was the president. The other two were regional sales managers.

"They're great guys. You've got a great bunch of people down there." The form continued to absorb him. "You work for Bob Glynn?"

"Yes."

He tapped curved fingers on the desktop. "That may be your trouble."

She stared at him, wondering what on earth he meant and for a panicky moment she imagined he'd guessed their relationship. "He's a man with a lot of drive. He may be working you too hard."

"Oh no," she protested. "My job isn't too demanding. I enjoy it very much."

He continued tapping his fingers, mouth pursed. "Get a little more rest," he said. "Try to gain some weight."

"You don't think the cough is anything serious?"

"Let's see what the X-ray looks like. There's nothing so far to indicate it's anything more than an ordinary cough." He pulled his prescription pad to him and commenced to write. "Take a spoonful every four hours and call me Thursday."

He tore the sheet off the pad and handed it to her. The nurse stood in the doorway.

"Mr. Markoff is ready."

On Thursday when Ellie called he was cheerful and positive. "Perfectly normal. Nothing to worry about. Just take things a little easier."

She repeated to Bob what Dr. Zeleny had said word for word. Bob studied her face as she spoke.

"You look as if you don't believe me," she said and she laughed.

He smiled reluctantly. "No, I believe you but I wish Zeleny had explained why you can't get rid of that cough."

Nevertheless they breathed sighs of relief and went on as before. The time they spent together depended on Bob's schedule and his ability to be free. Ellie was always available, always ready to go along with whatever plans he might suggest. She never questioned or complained. She loved him and she had neither the wish nor the art to hide it.

It was March...

The company kept a limited number of rooms reserved at the Hotel Pierre for the convenience of its executives and sometimes when Joan was home between trips she and Bob stayed there. It was an elegant, exclusive place where he was known and not an eyebrow was lifted at their being there together.

The day had not been any busier than any other and it was only five-thirty when they left the office. In the pattern they'd established to avoid being seen together after office hours, Bob departed first, Ellie following a little later. He kept his car in a parking lot two blocks away and he intercepted her before she got there. They drove up to the Pierre, dallied over drinks in the bar and went in to dinner. As she sipped coffee at the end of the meal Ellie's hand started to tremble and quickly she set the cup down. A wave of fatigue so overwhelmed her she had to fight back the impulse to lay her head down on the table on the spot.

"Let's go upstairs early tonight, Bob, shall we?" she asked.

"Sure kitten, anything you say."

It puzzled and disturbed her that the evening, so looked forward to, had to be cut short on her account. It happened again not long afterward. And again. And once she'd been so full of life she'd dance till midnight.

It was April...

One morning, alone in the apartment getting dressed for work, she was seized by a paroxysm of coughing so violent she thought her chest would tear apart. She leaned over the basin in the bathroom to spit out what she coughed up and some of it was bloody. She stood back in shock. But then, trying to calm herself, she thought maybe it wasn't from her lungs. Maybe it was from her throat. The months of coughing had scraped it raw. Maybe she'd torn a blood vessel. Carefully, from then on, she watched for signs of blood when she coughed but there were none. Nevertheless she was alarmed.

It was May...

Mrs. Ramey had mentioned a doctor she thought she might consult about her recurrent back problems. He was an internist with an office on Park Avenue and although he was expensive he was reputed to be good. His name was Dr. W. Maximilian Buchanan. Ellie looked him up in the phone book one day and called and made an appointment. Ever since the episode of the coughed-up blood a sense of unease lurked within her and desperately she wanted her mind put at rest.

New York was at its loveliest that spring. Walking down Park Avenue in the early morning, the air against her face was as fresh as if it had blown across a country meadow. Flowers in window boxes made stabs of color against chaste stone windowsills. The streets had been washed and patches of them were still wet.

The doctor's office opened on the avenue—a pastel door flanked by tubs of white petunias and bearing a gleaming brass plaque with his name. To the left three waiting room windows, cottage-curtained, added to the calculated rustic charm. The receptionist, by contrast, was a perfect example of cool New York sophistication—sleek upswept hair, make-up that gave her face a doll's look and a clinging dress that outlined every curve. She took Ellie's name, gave her a form to fill out and directed her to the waiting room. The appointment was for eight o'clock and she was five minutes early.

There were easily a dozen chairs arranged around the room and all but two were occupied. She took this in with dismay. Ten or eleven patients ahead of her, fifteen or twenty minutes per patient. She did the arithmetic in her head and figured it would be nearly noon by the time she got down to the office. She told Bob when she left the day before she would be a few minutes late. But even as she sat down a patient came out of the inner sanctum and a nurse called a name. A man rose and went through the door held open for him. Less than five minutes later he was out and another name was called. Another patient entered the doctor's office and just as promptly came out again. Meanwhile arriving patients kept the population constant. The ten patients ahead of her were handled with such dispatch it was barely nine o'clock when the nurse called her name.

Dr. Buchanan was a tall, lean, pleasant-looking man with a southern accent. "Sit down, get comfortable," he said, and he indicated an armchair. Ellie was wearing a navy blue coat with wide, turned-back sleeves and long gloves that slid under them. No suggestion was made that she remove either.

The doctor looked at the form she'd filled out. "The trouble is a cough?"

"Yes," she said, "I've had the cough since last August. I cough all the time and it's wearing me out."

He put a thermometer in her mouth and continued his questions. "Do you smoke?"

She shook her head no.

"You cough all the time you say?"

She nodded.

"Do you cough at night?"

She nodded again.

"Well, then it's no wonder you're worn out," he said sympathetically. He leaned back in his chair and rested ankle on knee. "Coughs have a way of hanging on sometimes and they can be mighty unpleasant but we'll get to the bottom of it. Don't you worry for a minute."

He reached around, got his prescription pad and balanced it on his crossed leg. "I'll give you something to take that will let you sleep at night."

He wrote away diligently, finished and looked at his watch. He drummed his fingers on the desk while another minute went by. Silenced by the thermometer in her mouth Ellie sat with her gloved hands in her lap. He checked his watch once more before he removed it and squinted at it.

"A couple of points above normal but I don't think that's anything to worry about." He smiled. "It's a warm day."

He handed her the prescription. "Come in tomorrow morning at the same time." And he ushered her to the door.

Out on the street, the prescription in her hand, Ellie turned down Park Avenue, bewilderment flaring up into indignation. The morning wasted and she knew no more about what was wrong with her than she did the day before. She had set such store on the visit, hoping against hope that it would provide some explanation for the coughed-up blood, the lost weight, the persistent fatigue and now the night sweats which had come back. But the doctor had deliberately forestalled a recital of such details. Come in tomorrow at the same time, he'd said. How many visits would it take for all her symptoms to be described? How many more before he arrived at a conclusion?

At the corner of Park Avenue and 51st Street there was a trash receptacle. She tore the prescription into tiny pieces and threw it in.

It was June...

"Bob," she said. "Do you know what I'd love more than anything?"

They were strolling down Fifth Avenue, her arm linked lightly through his, the summer day ending in the usual rush of people homeward or pleasure bound. Women in pretty clothes sent little puffs of scent into the air around them as they passed. Smart-looking men, leather portfolios swinging at arm's length in the grip of curled fingers, moved along with purpose. Rockefeller Plaza was a glory of flowers. Banks of them all but buried the outdoor cafes and behind glittering shop windows that lined the avenue clothes and jewels, crystal, linens and lingerie were artfully strewn. To the west beyond the Hudson the sun sank in a splendor of pink and gold while against it walls of stone soared upward in long clean lines and a church raised a lordly spire.

"What would you love more than anything, kitten?"

"I'd love for us to go away somewhere together, some place we've never been before, where we'd have to take luggage and where we could stay for a whole weekend." Ellie looked up at his face as they walked along and she could tell the idea pleased him.

"I think that could be arranged. Any idea where you'd like to go?"

"I've never been anywhere except twice to Miami to visit my mother. Any place would be thrilling."

"After dinner we'll get some road maps out of the car and see what we can find."

It seemed to Ellie they had a hundred choices, there were so many directions and so many places with intriguing names. But after some thought Bob selected one of the maps and pulled it in front of him.

"How about Nantucket?" He pointed it out on the map.

Ellie studied it carefully. "It's an island. We'd have to take a boat to get there."

"There's a ferry that runs to Nantucket from Woods Hole. It's about a two hour ride but that's part of the fun."

"It sounds wonderful. Were you ever there?"

"Once a long time ago. I remember it as a delightful place. Beaches, boating, cobblestone streets, lots of history, nothing but ocean around you. I've always wanted to go back."

His words conjured up an exciting prospect. Beaches!

"Shall we bring our swim suits?"

"By all means."

She clasped her hands together in utter delight. "Oh Bob, won't it be heaven?"

It was July...

They made plans to go the weekend after the Fourth of July and just about then the weather turned hot. The Friday evening of their departure the city was in the first stages of a typical New York heat wave and they congratulated themselves that they were leaving it behind. It was a long ride to Woods Hole—over two hundred miles—and they drove that evening until eight-thirty. At a century-old colonial inn they stopped for dinner and the night.

The charm of the place and the graciousness of the staff was marred by a small but prescient incident. There were no elevators and Ellie, climbing the stairs more and more slowly, was stopped short of the top by a fierce spell of coughing. The gray-haired man who carried the bag slowed his steps.

"That's a mighty bad cough you have, little lady," he said and his voice was concerned.

Bob who was at the bottom of the stairs didn't hear the remark but it caught her up short. Back in the far reaches of her mind was a dim, fearful remembrance of coughs people spoke about in whispers, grave-faced, of coughs that sent the sufferer into exile. She resolved to do everything in her power to suppress the cough unless she was alone.

They got to Woods Hole at midmorning the next day and to Nantucket in time for a late lunch. Their hotel stood above a sea wall, a rambling place of weathered wood with sand underfoot and blowing curtains and the heady, pervasive smell of the sea sweeping around them. Their windows looked out on nothing but ocean except for a bayberry thicket directly beneath them and a pine grove to their left. Beyond the pines long stretches of white beach sloped inland to become dunes where tangles of blackberry grew. Beach plums and wild grapevines flourished along a rutted road.

Nantucket's main street was cobbled with stones more than a hundred years old, the same age as many of the stately houses that lined it. Strolling its length, Ellie set the pace professing to find everything worthy of scrutiny though the truth was it gave her a reason to walk slowly and conceal her shortness of breath.

They swam that afternoon at a curving beach deserted except for three or four couples stretched out on towels acquiring suntans and two old ladies in folding chairs under a beach umbrella. A sign read Nearest Land to the East— Portugal. They lay in the sun to dry, then moved higher into some shade where Ellie slept for more than an hour. She awoke revived. The cold sea swim, the sun, the snappy breeze, the sleep on the warm sand, all of it seemed to have restored her and she felt better than she had in weeks.

"Isn't this heaven? Positively heaven?" she exclaimed. They were sipping drinks on the hotel terrace. Her eyes sparkled, her lips were parted, not from shortness of breath, but from bliss. Never before had they so many hours at their disposal to use as they wanted. She studied the people around them, couples in casual dress, others in conspicuous resort wear, people there for the day or with on air of being on home ground, a young woman with brassy hair and a bored-looking man, an affluent older couple who exchanged not a single word. She amused herself by trying to pick out who was married and who was not.

"Bob," she said. "Do you think people think we're married?"

"Of course they do. And that we're here to celebrate our twentieth anniversary."

"No, seriously. Do you think we look as if we're married?"

"Absolutely. And that we just had a fight over the dry cleaning bill."

She laughed and he reached over and squeezed her hand. "What do we care what people think?"

"No, tell me. I want to know."

"I think we look too happy to be married."

Why was it taken for granted that one precluded the other? Yet she herself had been guilty of making the same assumption just moments before, sorting out who she thought was married and who not. One thing was certain, if she were married to Bob it would never be so.

He was pleased to see her so animated and so much like her old self again. She'd been so tired in recent weeks and then there was the little nagging cough she never seemed to be able to get rid of. Maybe a change of scene was called for more often. A waiter stopped at their table and Bob ordered new drinks.

Ellie gazed out at the great expanse of ocean, a red sun sinking behind it in the west, and sighed in contentment.

"It's so lovely here," she said.

"We'll do this again before the summer's over. We'll find some place else we want to see and take a weekend off and go. Would you like that?"

She drew in an ecstatic breath. "Oh Bob, I'd love it!"

And that night as they stood at the sea wall for a few minutes before going up to their room, Ellie slipped her arms impulsively around his neck, pulling his face down against hers.

"Robert, my dearest love, I'll remember this weekend as long as I live."

The ferry back to Woods Hole left the next day at four o'clock. By chance they were the first to board and the car was directed to first place in the center lane. There was a perfect view forward. The car seat was so wide and comfortable and suddenly Ellie was so terribly tired. Since morning, hour by hour, her strength had drained away though they'd spent the day in most leisurely fashion.

"We could stay right here, Bob," she said.

"Let's sit on deck. It's fresher up there. It's the last good air we're going to get for awhile."

There were comfortable deck chairs for the passengers and they settled themselves for the trip. While Bob went through the Sunday papers Ellie sat beside him, immobilized by fatigue. From time to time she coughed. All at once something seemed to loosen in her chest and she coughed more sharply. It snapped her out of her lethargy and she got quickly to her feet.

"I have to go to the ladies' room," she said and before he could answer she walked away.

It was in the middle of a dark passageway, a single electric bulb illuminating the door with its battered sign that read WOMEN. Mercifully it was empty. It was a tiny cubicle, hardly bigger than a closet, containing a toilet behind a partition and a wash basin. A filmy mirror was fastened over the basin and an ineffectual bulb beside it provided the only light. The door hooked with a primitive latch and she set it in place. Leaning over the basin she gave way to the wracking coughs that tore through her chest. Her eyes shut tight with strain, she groped for the water faucet. She turned it on to flush away the matter she coughed up but only a trickle came forth. When she opened her eyes the basin was bloody. She took out her handkerchief and wiped her mouth. Her handkerchief came away bloody. Then another spasm seized her.

When she was sure she'd finished, she cleaned the basin using some of the coarse paper towels from the dispenser on the wall. She buried them deep in the waste paper basket along with her bloody handkerchief. Then she looked down at her clothes. She was wearing a pale blue linen skirt with a short sleeved matching jacket, and the front of the jacket was splashed with blood. She tried dabbing at the stains with a paper towel soaked in cold water but it only made them worse. She took the jacket off. The sheer white blouse she had on underneath was unstained but she noticed blood on her forearms and she washed it away. The cloudy mirror did no more than return a ghost image of her face, too indistinct to warrant more than an indifferent glance. She was trembling so she stood a few minutes leaning against the wall until it stopped.

With her jacket folded inside out over her arm she walked back along the passageway to the deck. Bob stood up when he saw her, a look of alarm on his face.

"Don't sit down. We'll go back to the car."

He put an arm around her waist and they descended some steps that led to the parked cars in the dim center of the ferry. Still holding her as if she might slip to the floor if he didn't, he opened the car door and helped her in. She sank into the seat gratefully, resting her head against the back. He walked around and got in beside her.

"Ellie, what happened? There's blood on your face."

She turned her head toward him wearily. "I coughed up blood. A lot of it."

He took her jacket away from her, opened it and saw the stains down the front. Folding it again inside out he put it on the back seat. He took out his handkerchief and wetting it on his tongue—as one does for a child—he wiped the blood off her face.

"Are you all right now? Do you want anything?"

"Could I have a glass of water?"

He left and came back presently with a paper cup of water and ice. She drank it avidly to take the taste of blood out of her mouth.

All that long trip home the pain never left his face. It was six o'clock when the ferry docked at Woods Hole and long after midnight when they reached Manhattan. They stopped once some place where Bob bought her a milkshake and brought it out to the car. Sometimes she rode sitting up and leaning against his shoulder. And sometimes she curled up on the front seat and lay with her head in his lap. Then he'd hold his cool hand on her burning forehead.

Joan heard them come in and appeared in the living room in her pajamas.

"Is anything wrong?" she asked after she saw Bob's face.

"Let's get Ellie to bed first."

"I can manage, Bob, really I can," she protested. "I'm all right now."

But he and Joan undressed her and put her to bed. Ellie heard them talking softly in the living room before she fell asleep.

It was nearly noon the next day before she stirred. Foreboding, the undefined menace which haunted her during the long hours of the dark ride home, was waiting for her when she awoke. Slowly through the oblivion of sleep memory surfaced, the ghosts of night faded and left reality to be dealt with. Bit by bit the events of the weekend fell into their incontrovertible places—the brief, beautiful hours that ended in such a nightmare. She could fool herself no longer. Something was terribly wrong with her and whatever it was she knew that nothing would ever be the same again.

It was another hot day and the electric fan moved from side to side like a reproving head, sending currents of heavy air across the bed. Joan came into the room with a glass of orange juice.

"Feeling better?" she asked.

Ellie sat up and took the glass out of her hand. She nodded. "I hate being such a bother. I'm causing no end of trouble."

"If you think this is trouble you should see some of my passengers on the transAtlantic flights."

Ellie smiled. "I think I'll stay in bed awhile longer."

"You stay for the afternoon. I'll bring you toast and coffee."

"Thanks Joan."

"Bob called. He'll be here some time after five."

6.

In many ways Joan looked on Ellie as a younger sister and from this standpoint she was sorry to see her involved in an affair which was certain to leave her the loser. It was not that she didn't like Bob. She liked him very much but he was married. Sometimes when Ellie, flushed with love, confided snatches of a starry hour or repeated some laughing words, Joan would frown and remind her brusquely that she was wasting her time. These affairs go nowhere, she'd warn. How much pain it had cost her to learn that simple truth. When she and Ellie met and arranged to share the apartment, Joan was just getting over a disastrous love affair which had lasted four years. It was a searing experience and one she wanted to see Ellie spared.

Joan was the oldest of four children in a family whose history was a constant struggle against poverty. A sick mother and an ineffectual father forced responsibility upon her early and her years of growing up were a juggling act between school, care of the younger children and household chores. Nurses training followed by a grinding routine in a Newark hospital close to home was only slightly less exacting but she was still the family mainstay and her salary the one dependable source of income.

The day she learned that airlines were looking for young registered nurses to train as stewardesses, she seized on the opportunity as a chance to enter a different world and when she was accepted she promised herself she'd make the most of everything this new life offered. It was considered a glamorous, exciting thing to do at the time and the salary, compared to her pay at the hospital, was munificent. However, it was no sinecure. A lot of hard work was involved and there were many long, monotonous hours. The girls earned their money. They had to be tactful, patient, courteous, they had to have stamina and a cool head, and of course they had to be attractive. Joan, with her blond good looks, her slim, strong build and her years of doing for others was ideally suited to the job.

The airline Joan went to work for flew the route across northern Europe and during the years immediately after World War II, in the scramble to rebuild devastated areas and restore impoverished economies, traffic flowed steadily through the countries it served. Government officials on every level, diplomats, journalists, business men, all were among those involved in one way or another with getting the shattered continent once more on its feet.

Harley J. Ingersoll, on the evening flight from New York to London, was part of a consortium organized for the purpose of putting England back in the world's oil market. With offices in Houston, New York and London, the group had sound financial backing and as one of the first on the scene at the war's end it was eminently successful. Harley was a Texan, a millionaire at twenty-eight and now, in his mid-forties, worth ten times that much.

He sat in the first class section in the center seat of three, a briefcase on his lap, papers spilling over on either side of him. He was a massive, sandy-haired man in impeccably tailored clothes, a cigar jutting out of his mouth, a ruby ring on the hand that wielded an imperious pen. He was polite but demanding and by the time Joan had settled him to his satisfaction she'd had to short-change some of her other passengers. He made up for it afterward however, with a chastened apology and on leaving the plane in London thanked her graciously.

It wasn't until an hour later while passengers for Amsterdam were boarding that Joan found a manila envelope on the floor under his seat. It bore his name and an address on Fifth Avenue in New York. Ordinarily articles left behind by passengers were turned in to the nearest airline office but in this case it was too late. Joan tucked the envelope in the shoulder bag she kept in her locker, intending to leave it in London on the return trip but bad weather forced them to land at Prestwick, Scotland. Instead she carried it back to New York and mailed it to him with a brief note.

Once much later, after they'd become lovers, when intimacy had removed spoken as well as physical restraints, she said to him, "when I first saw you I didn't like you."

He gave a booming laugh. His ego was as impervious to criticism as a battleship to a BB gun. They were sitting in a rooftop cocktail lounge, sipping after-theater brandies and he clapped his broad hand across her slim one. "You didn't like me? Preposterous! Why not?"

"I thought you had too much money. That things had always been too easy for you."

He drew on his cigar reflectively. "Know what I thought when I first saw you?"

She shook her head.

"I thought I'd like to see you in satin. White satin with gold around your throat and on your arms. Things a queen would wear."

Her mouth melted into a smile and she locked her fingers through his. He'd given her things a queen indeed might wear. Beautiful clothes, exquisite jewelry. He'd opened charge accounts for her at the best stores. He'd taken her to the finest places in New York. They'd made impulsive, flyaway trips to the Caribbean whenever some of their free time coincided. And it wasn't just another affair. Their goal was marriage.

It had all gone slowly, step by step, the pace at which any serious relationship progresses. Theirs had been no precipitate leap into bed. One occasion led to another. Their first date, drinks at Peacock Alley in the Waldorf, was Harley's gesture of thanks for the envelope she returned. It was quickly followed by another which carried over into dinner. And another. And still others. Then finally, whenever they were both in New York at the same time, they spent most of the hours together.

Harley never attempted to conceal the fact that he was married but spoke of it from time to time in flat, bold statements. His wife was a good woman, hung up on religion. Her whole life centered around a little Baptist church in the Houston suburb where they lived, plus of course the raising of their sixteen-year-old daughter to whom they were both devoted. She'd never been willing to come up to New York with him and she'd as soon go to the moon as to London. There were few interests they shared. They'd had little enough in common when they married, he said, not much more than the circumstances which brought them together.

Reba's family was wealthy, owning tracts of oil-rich land in south Texas, and Harley, a poor boy with ideas and aspirations, had been taken on to help manage it. It was easy to see how the story unfolded—an ambitious young man with nothing but the clothes on his back and a plain, too-plump girl wealthy in her own right. Joan felt a little stab of disappointment but then, well, he wasn't the first man who had married for money.

They were still not lovers. Harley wanted her more urgently than he'd ever wanted any woman before in his life but Joan was not easily had. Her sights were set on marriage, a sound, substantial union which would refute all the starveling years of her growing-up. She put him off with the same easy grace, the same quick charm of manner that made her so infinitely desirable. But he'd waited a long time and he couldn't wait longer. He declared his intentions.

Reba was as disposed to a divorce as he. There was no hang up there. They hadn't lived together as man and wife for two, almost three years. The stumbling block was the matter of their daughter's inheritance. The family wealth was in the name of Reba's widowed mother, a woman of fanatic moral rectitude. Linda Sue, as the only grandchild, was in line to inherit the bulk of it provided Reba and Harley were married and living together at the time of her death. The old lady was rabid on the subject of broken marriages.

She'd never been overly fond of Harley and the rider she clamped onto her will was just an example of her pettiness, he explained, as he'd never given her the least grounds for suspicion.

But on the plus side, Harley said, the old lady was eighty-one and had had two strokes. "Hell, she can't live forever. With a little luck…"

Joan put a finger against his mouth. "Don't wish anyone dead, Harley. No matter what. Don't wish someone dead."

He gathered her in his arms, his mouth against her hair.

"Why do we have to wait? It can't possibly be much longer. Why are we wasting all this time?"

Joan's thoughts were in a turmoil. Married to Harley she'd have more than she ever dreamed of possessing. As Harley's wife she'd move in the best circles, sought after, held in an esteem she couldn't claim as her own but hers nonetheless. Wait, her mind told her.

"I love you, Joannie. More than I've ever loved anybody in my life. I want you. Not next year. Not next week. I want you now."

She wanted him too. Her tightened arms around him was her answer.

Harley had an apartment on the twentieth floor of a vast new apartment complex on the east side overlooking the river but Joan continued to share a crowded Greenwich Village flat with three other girls. Her mother was dead by then, her sister, the next oldest, was married. The two boys, though often they vanished for weeks at a time, still lived in the old house with her father. He was a decent man and it would have upset him had he known of his daughter's behavior but he wouldn't have wished it different. The check she sent him each month kept him comfortable and removed the need for him to look for work.

Time sped by, season nudging season, one year then another and nothing really changed. Intimacy deepened their relationship and made Harley more relaxed, more expansive. Joan who had been half in love with him before was now wholly so. Sometimes when colleagues came up from Texas and Harley took them out on the town she would like to have been included. But she was practical. It wouldn't do for any hint of another woman to get back to Houston. And much as she longed to be able to say to her friends, "Next spring I'm getting married," she was a realist. There was nothing to do but wait till the old lady died. She was eighty-three now. No, eighty-four, and in very poor health. It couldn't be much longer.

Only one thing was irksome. All too often their differing out-of-town schedules caused more separations than either of them wanted. Harley might get back to New York from Houston only to find that Joan was due out on a flight the next day. Joan might have a week free and Harley would be called to London. It was the only snag in an otherwise satisfying arrangement and because Harley wasn't able to do anything about it, it made him irritable. Joan, however, quietly explored her standing in Flight Operations and found she had sufficient seniority to qualify for the job of chief stewardess the next time it became vacant. It meant an office at the airport and a five day week. She told Harley about it and immediately his face brightened.

"How come you didn't do it before?"

"I didn't think I had a chance. But evidently I do."

"That's great, Joan. Great. When do you think it's going to happen?"

"It's hard to say. Anytime, I suppose. There's pretty much of a turnover. Girls who've had the job say it tends to get boring and they go back on flight."

"You won't find it boring, will you, sugar bear?" He gripped her hand and smiled at her meaningfully. She smiled back at him in return and shook her head.

But time went by, summer, half of fall, and nothing happened. Then one day in late October, coming in from a flight, Joan found a note in her box asking her to report to Flight Operations. To her delight she was told the job of chief stewardess was open and was hers if she still wanted it. Yes indeed, she said. She wanted it very much.

Tired as she was after the long hours of travel, she taxied home, showered and changed clothes, then taxied uptown. This was no news to be imparted by phone. This was news to be delivered in person. She could see Harley's face light up, feel the hug he'd give her. He wasn't a patient man and he'd been edgy of late. This would put an end to it.

Harley and a colleague shared a suite of offices in a lofty building of steel and glass a block south of St. Patrick's Cathedral. Joan seldom went there and mostly after hours when she did. It was not quite one o'clock. The reception room was empty, the secretary apparently out to lunch. The door to Harley's office was ajar and just as she was about to move toward it the phone from within rang. Expecting to hear Harley's voice she was surprised when it was answered in a clipped British accent.

"Malcolm Bracely here. No, he's not. I've come on from London to hold down the fort for a few days. May I help you?"

Some involved wordage followed having to do with British tax laws and the rate of exchange, then there was a pause and a shift to a lighter tone of voice.

"It's hard to say just when Harley will be back. I expect he's down there in Houston passing around cigars. Yes, a boy, and after three girls, a real cause for jubilation. I'll tell him you called. Indeed I will. I'll leave the message."

There was a click as the receiver was set back in place, then silence.

Joan stood as if turned to stone, her face drained of color, her limbs like lead. The Englishman came out of the office and saw her. Her presence surprised him. Furthermore she appeared to be ill.

"Is there someone you want to see?"

She shook her head. "No. No. I'm sorry. I must be in the wrong office."

After she left, it crossed his mind that she looked like the girl he once met with Harley.

Blindly Joan made her way out of the building, jostled by people she didn't see, accosted by street noises she didn't hear. She walked a block and it started to rain and she moved into the entrance of a store whose double windows displayed expensive, imported shoes. They appeared to engross her but she might as well have been staring at a blank wall. Her mind held nothing but the magnitude of Harley's duplicity.

For days she went about in a trance, zombie-like, emotionless, vaguely aware that at some distant point the wound would start to heal but unable to foresee it. Another woman might have wept but Joan remained dry-eyed, the lump in her chest which tears could have melted a constant, remindful pain. Years ago her mother had taught her that tears solved nothing. And who had greater reason to know? Two babies she never had strength enough to hold, a bumbling husband, the knowledge that she'd never see her children grown. Across the years Joan saw her mother's face—worn, white, sad, yes. But never stained by tears.

Harley phoned, again and again and again, until finally, in order to put an end to the calls, she agreed to talk to him. "Joan baby, listen to me. Give me a chance to explain. That's all I ask. Nothing has changed. It's just a goddamn shame this happened, that you had to find out about it that way."

She interrupted. "Please don't go on, Harley. There's nothing you can say that I want to hear. I just don't want you to call again."

"I've got to see you, Joannie. I love you, believe me. I can't let this end. I swear to you everything's the same."

"Just don't call me again. Do you understand?"

"Please baby, if you'd just let me explain. That's all I want, just a chance to talk to you. Let me come down and pick you up and we'll have dinner. Please Joannie. I love you. Joannie, are you there? Joannie?"

Softly, decisively, she would not have recognized the gesture in herself but exactly as she used to close the door of a patient newly dead, she replaced the receiver.

She stood at an ironing board set up in front of the bookcase in the living room, pressing her uniform skirt. Ellie, pajama-clad, sat on the couch painting her toenails while she described the evening she and Bob spent together the night before—dinner at a French restaurant on 57th Street, the Broadway musical, Oklahoma, and finally the elegance of the Hotel Pierre. Just the telling of it recaptured the magic. Her words were studded with superlatives and her eyes were dreamy.

"Bob said I should think about what I want to see next and he'll get tickets."

Joan had said nothing throughout the recital and her silence finally got Ellie's attention. "You're awfully quiet," she commented.

Joan shifted the skirt on the board. The iron thumped and hissed. "I don't know whether you'll like what I'm going to say, Ellie, but I'll say it anyway." She paused, weighing her words. "This is all very glamorous and exciting but there's another side to it you should consider. It's one thing to be in love and have a future but nothing can come of this affair with Bob. It doesn't seem to me from anything you've said that he plans to get a divorce and marry you. If you want to play, by all means play, but just remember time is passing." The lesson she learned at such cost was one she'd never forget and it disturbed her to see Ellie go so carelessly down the same road with no one to warn her of its perils. As if love never changed but burned forever at the same white heat, as if the flame would never dim. In the past when Joan had spoken to that point Ellie just laughed and shrugged it off. Don't worry, she'd say, I know what I'm doing. But did she? Time was going by and she was nowhere except deeper into a relationship that was bound to end unhappily. Though she knew her words would go unheeded Joan felt compelled to continue.

"Just stop long enough to look at this realistically. Take time out to consider your own interests. Where will you be and what will you do when this ends? It will, you know. It has to."

"For heaven's sake, Joan, you'd think I was thirty and about to go on the shelf." (Joan was twenty nine.) Ellie held the little nail polish brush in midair as she studied the foot she'd just completed. "You make such a big thing of it."

"And isn't it? You don't see anyone else. You're not interested in meeting anyone else. You go no place unless it's with Bob. Ellie, it can't last and when it ends you'll be the loser. You can tell me it's none of my business, of course, and you'll be right but I don't want to see you get hurt."

Ellie started on her other foot. "The reason I don't see anyone else is because there's no one else I want to see. I haven't met anyone I'd even be remotely interested in."

"Well it's up to you but unless Bob has some plans for the future that include you I think you're wasting your time."

Ellie heaved a deep sigh as she dipped the brush into the polish. She would never admit it to Joan but she knew very well she had no valid place in Bob's life. He told her at the outset that he couldn't marry her and her answer had been that she didn't care which wasn't the truth. She cared very much. Being married to Bob and having him completely hers was her most blissful dream, and she didn't by any means think it impossible. It was just a matter of waiting and being patient. Things happened, circumstances changed, what seemed inconceivable today was matter-of-fact tomorrow. She'd seen it happen time and again. Hadn't she already proved to herself that the way to get what you wanted was to want it badly enough? That was her cardinal rule. But there was no point trying to explain this to Joan. She'd say anyone waiting for something like that to happen might just as well wait to win the Irish Sweepstakes. She'd say Ellie was out of her mind if she thought any man would give up a comfortable, established life style for something he already had. That would be Joan's response.

"Who knows how this will turn out? I'm just going to wait and see."

"Don't wait too long."

Ellie let her have the last word. Joan was goodhearted and she meant well but her advice was nothing but the old clichés. The trouble was she equated everything with that unhappy experience with Harley, convinced that every other affair was basically the same and doomed to end as badly as hers. This was different. She and Bob loved each other truly, totally, living for the present because for now there was no other way but who knew what might happen in the days ahead? Meanwhile there was no one on earth she'd change places with. His love had changed her life, transformed her into someone she hardly dared hope to be. Because of him she'd become part of that lofty New York scene where successful people mingled at the smartest places, ministered to, deferred to, made much of—not for any talents of her own but because with Bob she stood at his level. Never had she felt more buoyant, more confident. With untroubled soul she walked through the office corridors, high-hearted, prideful, heels clicking, hair flung back, hugging to herself the avowed conviction that nothing she wanted was beyond her reach.

7.

Dusty streets, a blinding sky, sun-saturated pavements. Ellie looked again at the slip of paper in her hand. Dr. Bruno Reiser, the Chandler Building, Madison and 49th Street. One of the best chest specialists in New York, Bob had said.

Maybe, just maybe, she'd be told it wasn't serious at all. As frightening as it had been, the blood, the coughs tearing out of her chest, the time span the cough now covered, maybe there was an innocuous explanation. She studied her face in the mirror. It wasn't the face of someone mortally ill. Maybe it wasn't as bad as they thought. But yesterday when she put the suggestion to Bob, his face remained grave.

"Let's see what the doctor says."

"I hate it that this happened," she'd answered and her voice was resentful. "I never wanted you to see me sick or crying. I just wanted you to see me well and happy. And look at the way things turned out." Tears filled her eyes.

"There's no such thing as trouble-free living, Ellie. No one gets a free ride. Sooner or later everyone gets the ground knocked out from under him." He put his arm around her and she pressed her head against his shoulder. "We've got to find out what's wrong, kitten. That's the only way we can start putting it right." She remained silent.

"Do you want me to go with you tomorrow?"

"I can go alone."

The taxi left her at the corner and she walked in a narrow lane of shade to the middle of the block. The building was old, substantial, given to offices of architects and exporters. A carpeted stairway with brass stair rods seemed less formidable than the elevator cage with its heavy door but by the time she reached the top the exertion had set her heart thudding in her chest and brought on a fit of coughing.

Dr. Reiser's offices consisted of several large, high-ceilinged rooms, gloomy as a mortuary, one with a closed door, the others empty. She appeared to be the only patient. There was no receptionist, just the nurse, a thin, gray haired woman who met her at the door and led her to an examining room. Her solicitude underscored the gravity of the visit.

"Would you like to sit quietly for a few moments before we start?" Her voice was kindly. "There are a lot of questions I must ask you."

Ellie shook her head. All she wanted was to have it over and done with and so while she sat in an armed chair, the nurse on a stool across from her read from a form on a clipboard. The questions were much the same as the ones found on forms in all doctors' offices but these were more detailed and covered more ground. By the time she finished they'd brought out a full history of the complaint from the time it started the previous summer up to the present.

"Have you had a chest X-ray taken within the last year?"

Ellie thought a moment. "Yes." And she gave her Dr. Zeleny's name.

"Has anyone belonging to you ever had tuberculosis?" The word was out in the open for the first time.

"Yes." And Ellie named as many as she'd heard of. The specter of the disease had haunted her father's family as far back as it could be traced but with his mother's death when her father was a boy it was believed to have ended. There was a picture of her grandmother among the family photos and she'd often studied it. A dark-eyed girl with a wistful, pretty face. She was in her twenties when she died but for a long time no one mentioned what she'd died of and when they did it had no particular meaning. She was the last to come down with the disease.

The questions finally were finished. The nurse rose ."Please take off everything above the waist and put this on, open to the front." She handed over a short white garment.

"Now," she said, "why don't you lie down? It will be a little while before Dr. Reiser sees you and you might as well rest." She fixed a pillow under her head on the examining table and left.

Dr. Reiser was a dark, cadaverous man, as somber-looking as the offices he inhabited. One couldn't imagine a smile on a face so stern. He was niggardly with words. His greeting was a nod.

"Sit up," he said.

With the clipboard before him he studied the nurse's notes. Two or three times he asked for elaboration, observing, silently, his face devoid of sympathy or involvement. He wanted to know about the family history of the disease.

"Does anyone in your family now have tuberculosis?"

"No."

He put the form aside and listened to her chest, front and back, with scrupulous care. "Breathe in, breathe out, hold it, say ninety-nine." A dozen times, two dozen times the exercise was gone through. He looked in her throat with a light. He took chest X-rays. Three of them.

"Get dressed."

He left and the nurse came in. "It will take awhile to develop the X-rays. You'll be more comfortable in the waiting room." She smiled one of those professionally indulgent smiles reserved for the seriously ill and helped Ellie down from the table.

Back in the waiting room she settled into a soft chair, her handbag tucked down beside her, a wad of Kleenex in her hand to cover her mouth when she coughed. Between times she dozed, her head against the chair's tall back. After a long wait the nurse reappeared and ushered her into Dr. Reiser's office.

The room was crammed with books and old-fashioned furniture that looked as if it might have been inherited from a previous generation. He sat at a dark wood desk and indicated a chair at its side for Ellie. In lighted frames on the wall were the three X-rays.

Even before he spoke she knew what his pronouncement would be so that when he uttered the word she felt no emotion except a mild surprise that she accepted it so submissively. Tuberculosis. She hadn't the will nor energy to register the slightest protest. On the contrary there seemed a certain solace in having it recognized and labeled at last, and she listened with a sense of detachment.

"Upper lobes of both lungs are involved, moderate in the left, advanced in the right. There's also cavitation in the right lung." In neither his voice nor manner was there the slightest trace of commiseration.

She looked at the X-rays on the wall, thinking he might get up and point out to her the shadows that carried such ominous meaning, but he didn't move from his chair.

"You will, of course, have to be institutionalized."

She winced at the word. Surely, she thought, there is none uglier in the English language.

He sifted through some papers on his desk. "There's not much space anywhere in Saranac right now but Trudeau Sanatorium might be able to take you."

She made no comment nor was she expected to. No longer had she any voice in what was to happen to her. He reached for the telephone, asked for the long distance operator and placed the call. There was a long wait and they both sat still and mute. Then unexpectedly he leaned back in his chair and sighed wearily.

"If we can't get you into a sanatorium within the next few days you'll have to be put into the isolation ward at Bellevue."

If she'd been struck by a bullet she could not have been more stunned. She stared at this man who spoke words so freighted with horror in so bland a voice. Put into the isolation ward at Bellevue? Someone to be feared? To be shunned? No leper of old, given his bell and begging bowl and cast out of society, knew a more consuming anguish.

The call came through. She heard his words clearly but she was too stricken to take in their meaning. For long moments she sat frozen, her mind paralyzed, until slowly reason reasserted itself. She breathed deeply and let her mind focus.

"They can take you at Trudeau. They'll expect you Saturday. Get a roomette on the Friday night train and you'll arrive in Saranac at eight the next morning." He didn't look at her as he spoke but kept his eyes fixed on her papers. "Meanwhile you're to remain absolutely quiet and in bed. There's danger you may hemorrhage again. Stay away from people and don't let people come near you. You have a communicable disease."

A brutal summing up but an accurate one.

Dulcinea, in sphinx pose, rested motionless on the windowsill and Ellie stood beside her mechanically scratching the top of her head. She heard Bob's key in the door, heard the door open and close softly behind him and she halfway turned to watch him walk to her across the room. He waited for her to speak but she remained silent.

"I talked to Reiser awhile ago," he said finally. "He gave me the whole picture."

She nodded, detached, as if she were far away.

"It won't be as bad as it seems now, Ellie." Actually the way it came through from Reiser, Ellie's condition was a lot worse than he expected and furthermore the doctor refused to commit himself on any aspect of her cure. All manner of imponderables came into the picture, he said, and all he could do was speculate. "The main thing is to get you well."

She looked past him into the street with dazed eyes. "How did this happen? How could such a thing have happened?" She put her face in her hands and wept.

He held her against him, murmuring, kissing the edge of her hair, soothing her. Dr. Reiser's final words slid into her mind and reluctantly she stood back from him, holding him off. "You shouldn't come near me. The doctor said I wasn't to let anyone close to me. I have to stay away from people."

"You don't think it's going to make any difference at this point, do you?" He held up her face. "I've got all your germs, kitten. It's too late now." He gathered her close to him again and kissed her but once more she pushed him away.

"You have to have your chest X-rayed. Everyone who's ever been near me has to have chest X-rays because," she faltered for a moment, but went on, "I may have given them my disease." Her face contorted as the full impact of her words struck her. How would she ever live down the guilt of it if someone became ill because of her?

"That's no big deal, Ellie. Most people get chest X-rays taken on some sort of regular basis."

"Oh Bob, it's all so awful."

"You shouldn't be on your feet," he said gently. "Do you want to sit here in the living room or will you lie down?"

"I think I'll lie down."

He adjusted the fan in the bedroom to get a better circulation of air and put a cold cloth on her forehead. "Where's Joan?"

"She went to dinner with Frank but she'll be home early. They're both going out on the same trip Thursday and they have a lot to do tomorrow."

"I'm going down to Washington tonight," Bob said, "but I'll be back Thursday. I'll come here as soon as I can."

"You won't be here tomorrow?" Seldom if ever did Ellie question his priorities but the devastating events of the day left her yearning for the comfort of his presence. She reached for his hand and clung to it weakly. "There's so little time left."

He looked at her—the flushed face, the heavy eyes, the white fragile wrists—and a wave of pity, akin to the emotion he felt when one of his children sickened, washed over him. Once again he considered postponing the trip. The men he wanted to see would be as accessible next week as this but to conclude his business with them sooner rather than later was in keeping with the way he handled all his dealings . He decided it best to stay with the original schedule. He'd come Thursday as soon as he was able. She'd be all right.

He sat on the edge of the bed. "I know it, kitten, and I wish I didn't have to go but it can't be helped."

"I'm taking up an awful lot of your time."

"No Ellie, no, you're not." And after a pause. "Will you eat something? A sandwich if I make it for you?"

"Maybe later."

But she fell asleep and quietly he let himself out of the apartment.

8.

She didn't really cry until it was time to take Dulcinea away and then it seemed as if she couldn't stop. The problem of what to do about her once Ellie knew she'd have to go away quickly became critical and Joan solved it in the best possible fashion under the circumstances. She knew a woman in Greenwich Village who loved cats. Joan contacted her and explained the situation and although Mrs. Spencer already had three cats of her own she agreed to take her.

To be forced to part with her and send her to strangers was almost more than she could bear. She found her on her way home from work one rainy evening shortly after she and Joan moved in together, a thin frightened kitten huddled in a doorway, mewing. Ellie carried her home inside her coat and in the warm apartment fed her and fixed her a bed. She'd grown into a sleek, beautiful cat and repaid her a hundred times over with her devotion.

It was Friday afternoon. They let it go till last. Bob had helped her pack her bags and they stood next to the door in the living room, locked and ready to go. Dulcinea's carrier stood next to them. Dulcinea herself dozed on the windowsill as if this day were exactly like any other. "It's three o'clock, Ellie. I guess I'd better take Dulcinea down now and on the way back I'll drop the bags off at Grand Central."

She nodded, too grief-stricken to speak and brushing past him she fled to the bedroom where she threw herself down on the bed weeping. She was still weeping when he returned an hour later. He pushed the hair back from her wet face.

"Please get control of yourself, Ellie. You're tearing yourself apart. She'll be all right. She's in a good home."

"My poor little cat," she wept. "Why does she have to suffer for this? It isn't fair. It isn't fair."

He held her in a tight embrace and kissed her burning forehead. "Ellie baby, nobody ever promised that life would be fair."

9.

Each morning Ellie woke and stared out at the same lonely mountains, now dense with summer green. Her eyes had already memorized their profiles. Only the sky changed, clean-swept or fog-bound, adrift with lofty clouds or full of rain. Whatever the weather, each morning after breakfast a couple of workmen, long cured patients themselves, came through the halls. They went from room to room pushing beds through the double doors that gave onto each room's porch where the occupants commenced another day of breathing the prescribed healing air. Beyond the porches thick stands of evergreens sloped sharply downward and sometimes when chill gusts of wind blew out of the north they ruffled and whispered.

She knew his footsteps. Sitting up, listening with held breath, she counted them starting at the hall moving across her empty echoing room and before he quite reached the porch, she slipped out of bed in order to throw herself into his arms. Ecstatic, hugging him, she pressed herself against him. He held her gently and tilted up her face and kissed her.

"Hold me tighter," she said, "so I'll know you're for real."

He held her a little more closely. Her body under his hands felt as frail as a bird's. "Are you supposed to be out of bed?"

"This one minute isn't going to matter. Hug me some more."

"Are you feeling all that better?"

"Ever so much better, honest."

"You look a lot better, that's for sure." He studied her face and saw a notable change for the better. The fatigue that had altered it like a mask was gone and her skin had a healthier tone. "Now get back in bed and tell me what's been going on up here." He settled himself in the chair beside her.

"Nothing, absolutely nothing."

"You mean it isn't as horrible as you were convinced it would be?"

Ellie smiled. "It's just, well, different." Her face sobered a little. "To tell the truth in some ways it's better."

"Oh?"

"I don't feel like the outcast I was in New York those last days. Everyone here is sick, not just me. No one's afraid of me. Millie, the librarian, even ate the chocolate eclair from my lunch tray the other day when I said I didn't want them."

Bob smiled. "You'd better start eating some chocolate eclairs yourself. You've got no more flesh on you than a sparrow. Tell me, besides trying to fatten you up what have they been doing?"

"Like I said, Bob, nothing. I just lay in this bed and eat and sleep and breathe all this fresh air. Miss Bodelle stops in once in awhile to see if I want anything and the student nurses run in and out. They giggle a lot and we compare movies we've seen. Oh yes, and once a day Dr. Nichols comes by. He talks about the fishing up here. He says there are beautiful trout streams in the mountains and nice places for picnics. And he tells me about his golden retriever named Fancy. He hardly ever says anything about tuberculosis. It's strange. You'd think we were all up here at a resort. Do you know he had tuberculosis too? Most of the doctors and nurses here have had it."

"Well, that figures," Bob said. "After you've had an illness like this you're bound to have a lasting interest in it and to know a lot about it you didn't learn from books. For a doctor or a nurse that must be a tremendous advantage."

"Oh yes, they took some X-rays. One morning one of the student nurses helped me get dressed—as if I couldn't do it myself—and I rode down to the X-ray building. Rode, Robert, can you imagine? It's no farther away than a slide down a banister but I wasn't permitted to walk."

"Enjoy the easy life while you can, Ellie."

"But that isn't all. Do you know we can't even wash our hair. Once a week a lady from the beauty parlor in town comes up and does everyone's hair. She's got a basin on wheels that's the silliest looking thing you ever saw and a hair dryer on wheels and she pushes them from room to room. All we do is get out of bed and sit in a chair."

"Sounds like the life of Riley."

"But I hate the way she does my hair and after she goes. I comb it all out."

Ellie took a few sips from a glass of chocolate milk that stood on her bedside table. "I'm supposed to finish this before lunch. I just hope I don't get fat."

"I wouldn't worry about it if I were you."

"And do you know, Bob, at first they weren't sure whether I should be permitted to get out of bed to use the bathroom across the hall. There was a lot of discussion and finally they decided I could. But if they hadn't I would have had to go to the bathroom in bed." Ellie's face registered horror. "Can you imagine?"

"Sure. It happens to people all the time."

"Oh Bob, you're not being the least bit sympathetic."

"Ellie baby, I can't see that you've got any cause for complaint. What about the X-rays they took? Did you get a report on them?"

"Not yet but I'm not surprised. Everything here goes as slow as molasses. The morning I went down to the X-ray department I was there for two hours because no one would dream of hurrying. They took some regular X-rays and some planigrams. The planigrams will give them a three dimensional picture of my lungs so they can see how big the cavity is. It's a gloomy place, the X-ray department, but Tommy, the man who's in charge of it, is a nice little man. He told me he cured here twenty years ago and stayed on. His wife was a patient too and they have children and live in town. It's funny. A lot of people around here once had tuberculosis and never wanted to go back to where they came from."

"That isn't so surprising, Ellie. There are lots worse places to live than here. This is magnificent country." He looked out over the great sweep of landscape approvingly. He loved mountains. Some of the happiest days of his boyhood were spent in the mountains of his native Colorado.

It was a perfect day, clouds as soft as lambs low-floating against a pure, bright sky. Their shadows stained the green-gold slopes to match the dusky valleys while beyond them the mountains stretched back for miles in a retreating succession of peaks, their color changing so that the farthest ones were palest blue.

"I wouldn't mind living here for awhile," he went on.

"Oh it's beautiful," she conceded though inwardly she didn't agree. To her this isolated, land-locked country was alien and held little charm. It would be easier to get to Albany, she thought, than to a peak twelve miles away. "But it's always the same. I look out at all these tons of mountains and I like to imagine that they're all smoothed over into streets like Fifth Avenue, 42nd Street or Rockefeller Plaza where every minute things are happening. And I see us walking along, belonging there, going to all the places we used to go."

He laughed. "My incorrigible New Yorker!" He picked up her hand and squeezed it. "Don't look so sad. It's all there waiting for you."

She brought his hand up to her face and pressed it against her cheek. "That's what I think of most of the time."

"We'll do it all again, Ellie, but first things first. Concentrate on getting better. The sooner you're well the sooner we can make it all happen." He was right, of course. She'd try.

"Who works for you now?"

"No one on a permanent basis. I haven't needed anyone. Every once in a while Mrs. Ramey sends someone over from the Stenographic Department to take care of things that have piled up and Marge Foster or Mrs. Cooper answer my phone. It isn't the best arrangement but it works out well enough for now."

"But you'll have to have someone permanently, won't you?"

She hated the thought of someone else sitting at her handsome desk, in charge of all that was once hers, privy to all the pursuits that made up Bob's busy days.

"Not right away. I've got a trip to South America coming up soon. Till then I can make do with one of Mrs. Ramey's girls. After that we'll see."

"How long will you be away?"

"I don't know, Ellie. The company wants to take a real hard look at some of those Latin countries. Things have changed down there since the war. There's a lot going on, government projects underway, expansion in private industry, foreign investors coming into the picture. Things are really on the move. We want to be in a position to take advantage of all these new developments."

"We have people down there now, haven't we?"

"Yes, but they're agents and they're nationals. What the company is considering is setting up a South American office and heading it with someone from New York. There are a lot of pros and cons, of course, and what I have to do first is find out if there's actually enough business potential to make it worth our while. If that's so then being on the scene will put us in a much stronger position than we're in at present, having to deal from the United States. It's going to take awhile to put it all together so it's hard to say how long I'll be there."

Ellie sighed. "I wish you didn't have to go."

"I won't be going right away. There are things that have to be settled in New York first." He looked at her clouded face and paused. "Come on, kitten, smile. That's better. Which reminds me." He got to his feet. "I brought you something. Where did I leave my briefcase?"

He retrieved it from the bedroom, took out a flat rectangular package wrapped in white paper and handed it to her. She opened it slowly. It was a photo of Dulcinea in a silver frame. Tears sprang to her eyes and she tried to speak but couldn't.

"Ellie baby, I didn't mean to make you cry."

She pressed the picture to her heart as if she had the cat in her arms. "Where did it come from?"

"I phoned Mrs. Spencer one day and asked her if I could stop by and get a picture to send you. She said yes."

"Oh Robert, what a wonderful thing for you to do. Is it a good home? Does the woman love her?"

"I think she's got a very good home, Ellie. I saw a couple of other cats around. Everybody seemed happy."

She studied the picture. Dulcinea's sweet face looked squarely into hers. Her gray fur glistened and her white-mittened paws were placed modestly side by side. It was one of her most endearing poses.

"She's wearing her silver bell," Ellie said, her eyes bemused by the photo. "Remember the day we bought it?"

Bob nodded, smiling. They'd gone to a craft fair one lovely autumn afternoon where all kinds of intriguing things were spread out on tables under trees on the road to Tarreytown. Bob said she was to buy anything she wanted for herself. She looked at everything twice over and chose the little bell.

"For Dulcinea."

He'd shaken his head. "I don't know how long I'm going to be able to afford a woman with such expensive tastes."

Lunch and naptime took the whole middle out of the day and visiting had to break off until it was over. One of the sanatorium rules most strictly enforced was the afternoon nap and nothing was permitted to interfere with it.

"This is one of the things I hate," Ellie said as he was leaving to go down to the main building for lunch. "All this regimentation. Being told how to spend every minute of every day. Here you are for only a few hours and we can't spend the whole time together." She sighed in exasperation. "Come back at three-thirty, not a minute later. I'm not going to sleep. I'm just going to lay in this bed and keep telling myself that you're here and that I'm not dreaming."

But when he came back at three-thirty she was asleep, her soft heavy hair spread wide on the pillow, and she didn't wake up till he kissed her.

She slid her arms around his neck. "Oh Robert, if I could wake up this way for the rest of my life."

He kissed her again. "I missed you Ellie more than you know. I want you to get better fast."

"If only we could run away together now, this very minute. Wouldn't it be heaven?"

"Not yet, kitten, but there's reason to be encouraged. They tell me you're doing very nicely."

After his lunch he'd sought out Dr. Nichols and had a long talk about her. "You know, Ellie, they've got a whole different slant on time up here. And maybe they're right and the rest of us wrong. Nothing is done in a hurry. He said you were exhausted when you got here and what you needed more than anything else was to be left alone to rest. They're only now talking about treatment for you. He said there was a review of your X-rays last week and you'll probably be going on the drugs soon. Streptomycin and PAS. Apparently all the patients take them and they've had good results. Dr. Nichols was very encouraging when he spoke of the rate of cure."

"Did he say how long he thought it would take?"

"No, baby, he didn't. No one can say that."

She frowned, staring out at the mountains. "That's what makes it so hard. Not knowing. If I had some idea of when I'd be getting out of here it would be a lot easier to bear." She paused, then turned her head and looked at him. "Do you know there are patients who've been here three and four years?"

"Ellie, you're not going to be here three or four years. Now put that out of your mind."

"But there's no way anyone can tell and it scares me. For some people it isn't easy to get better and I don't think anyone knows why."

Bob got up from his chair and sat on the edge of the bed. "Look kitten, make up your mind you're going to get well. You have an illness that takes time to cure and you have to learn to be patient. You're going to make things worse if you don't. This thing happened. Nothing can change it. Will you just try to concentrate on getting better and not worry about how long it's going to take? For me?"

He put his arms around her and she nodded her head against his chest. For him she'd do anything. But he didn't know it was the fear of losing him that destroyed her best-intentioned resolution to be patient.

10.

Once in a subway in New York Ellie saw a woman whose back was so misshapen it was hard to imagine what might have caused it. Side by side they clung to straps, rocking back and forth as the train sped underground, two of only a half dozen people standing. Gusts of hot, fetid air swept through the car, pressing their thin summer clothes against them and when the woman turned Ellie saw that one side of her back was caved in as if it had been crushed. If indeed that was the case it was done in a uniquely uniform manner because the other side of her torso had a normal contour. Ellie couldn't guess how such a peculiar malformation might have come about.

At the sanatorium a month after she arrived she discovered what had happened to her. Fernando, the Venezuelan boy down the hall had a similar deformity.

On the lower floor of the infirmary a couple of rooms were assigned to lung collapse therapy and patients undergoing the treatment gathered there a half dozen at a time on appointed days. Dr. Connor who was in charge of it used to explain it to them. He was young, newly married, barely a year over his own cure.

"The difficulty healing diseased lung tissue," he'd say, "is the same difficulty found in healing any moving organ. Imagine you have a cut on your elbow and you want it to heal but you have to bend your arm several times a minute. The cut would take a long time to mend. It's the same with your lungs but if you can inhibit their expansion the lesions have a better chance to heal."

Pneumoperitoneum, the lung collapse therapy then in vogue, was designed to do exactly that. By means of a hollow needle, air was introduced under the diaphragm forcing the lungs upward and limiting their expansion. The pressure under the rib cage was uncomfortable, often painful, and Ellie along with most of the patients complained frequently and because the air dissipated it was necessary to repeat the procedure every week or ten days to maintain collapse. But it was one of the few treatment tools that seemed to produce results. When the complaints got too much for him, Dr. Connor told them how lucky they were.

"Six or seven years ago," he'd say, "they were still doing thoracoplasties to get lung collapse."

The evidence was all around them. Wherever there was a misshapen back the chances were a thoracoplasty had been done. The surgery consisted of removing ribs and permitting the caved-in back to inhibit the movement of the lung which in turn gave the lesions a chance to heal. So it was believed at the time.

One morning as Ellie and a few others waited in the anteroom for their lungs to be checked by fluoroscope, the conversation turned to the past—the primitive methods, the negligible rate of success. To make the point Fernando rose, took off his robe and pajama top and revealed his back. Ellie was horrified. Into her mind flashed the memory of the woman in the subway with her flimsy dress clinging to the scooped-out half of her torso. So that's what it was. Then someone repeated Dr. Conner's words. They were lucky. Thoracoplasties were a thing of the past.

Nearly as bad to Ellie's way of thinking was the resection, a surgical procedure developed a year or two earlier which had come into widespread use. Its purpose was to prevent recurrence by removing the diseased portion of the lung and it was hailed as a great advance since the ribs were left intact.

When Amy Cannon came back from the general hospital on the other side of town where all surgery was performed she showed Ellie her scar. It extended like a whiplash from the top of her right shoulder to the left side of her waist and notched along its length were dozens of small, embroidery-size scars from the stitches. Ellie was so taken aback she was speechless. This was the surgery that was said to be moderate, a vast improvement over what had been done before. Compared to a deformed back, yes, it was an improvement but still an appalling disfigurement. She thought of all the pretty clothes that could never be worn, the backless dresses, the swimsuits. She thought of embraces slowed, halted by the feel of that ugly incongruity furrowed into the skin of an otherwise smooth back, a thing to be lived with for the rest of a lifetime. No. That she wouldn't submit to. Surprisingly, Amy's attitude was casual.

"With a little luck I'll have only my left lung to worry about now." she said.

She was nineteen and she'd been sick since her fifteenth birthday. Long ago she'd come to terms with her illness, forced to it by seeing setbacks follow rebellion, stabilization the reward of compliance. There were many others like her at the sanatorium, patients who dutifully swallowed extra-curricular eggnogs, accepted all the restraints passively and wiled hours away doing handwork, watching birds at feeders rigged up outside their windows, engaging in all manner of harmless, inconsequential activities to help time pass. Ellie regarded them curiously, skeptical and unconvinced.

Sometimes, however, there were patients these diversions didn't satisfy. While strict control could be readily maintained in the infirmary it was not all that easy to do in the cottages and those who wanted to take advantage of the situation could do so. Some patients took to drink, smuggling in supplies from town. Since drinking to excess was strictly forbidden they were first warned, then expelled. More serious, however, were the love affairs that got out of bounds. Nothing was made of them provided they stayed within certain limits but if an after-hours rendezvous in one cottage or another was discovered, both parties involved were sent on their way within hours. The sanatorium was tolerant, certainly there were no moral sanctions brought to bear, but patients were there to cure, not party.

Sometimes in late afternoon, after the naps and the chocolate milk and before beds are rolled back into bedrooms, Fernando visits, sitting on the porch beside Ellie's bed with his back to the fading mountains. He wears an ancient wool robe in which his frail body seems lost and his slippers have trodden down, flattened backs. His skin is delicately white and his eyes, as dark and liquid as a doe's, glisten with animation as he speaks. Other young men his age excel at sports, can swim, bowl, play baseball, tennis. They roar around and party, chase girls and dally with the willing. Fernando can do none of these things but he knows all about tuberculosis. It is his one claim to distinction and it bolsters his self-esteem to educate Ellie. His English is good though heavily accented.

She listens with rapt attention, sitting cross-legged in bed, her chin on her fists. The air is chill with the feel of a season about to change and the blanket is pulled across her chest and under her arms. It seemed as if he'd never been well. He was sickly as a child. In his teens he was prone to fevers which were thought to be caused by malaria and he was dosed with quinine until a shrewd, self-effacing Indian doctor discovered the true reason for his symptoms. At a sanatorium in the hills outside Caracas he underwent the standard treatment of the times—fresh air, fattening food and rest, but rest carried to near-immobility. The germs in the lungs were thought to be like water in a glass—easily spilled, invasive, quick to spread to new ground. Even a raised arm was considered risky. At the end of a year he was dismissed with congratulatory handshakes. Six months later he returned and was greeted with frowns. And so began a perplexing cycle of setbacks and recuperation until at last the specialists advocated surgery. As radical as it was, as much hope as it held out, it achieved nothing. His disease went on as before, unabated, and the doctors shrugged and lifted their hands palms upward. There was nothing more they could do.

At that point his family resolved to send him elsewhere, either to Switzerland or to Saranac Lake.

"It was less expensive to come here," he explains. His mother is a widow. His four sisters, all unmarried, work at whatever they can do. One is a school teacher, two are store clerks, the other like his mother is a seamstress. "They're in debt because of me," he confesses regretfully. "I hope some day I can repay them."

He describes his arrival. "They carried me off the plane on a gurney. It was raining, a typical Adirondack spring day. Someone walked alongside holding an umbrella over my head. All I could think was that when they saw how sick I was they wouldn't take me and I was so scared. And then at the sanatorium I just lay in bed day after day. Everyone was nice but no one did anything. They didn't even X-ray my chest. I thought they were getting ready to send me home." Fernando laughs. "Afterward Dr. Nichols told me they didn't think I'd live and they wanted to find out first whether or not I would."

That was four years ago. The lung the doctors in Caracas tried so hard to save not only proved useless but turned out to be a focal point of infection, spreading the disease to the other lung, and it was being removed in three stages, two of them accomplished, one last round of surgery to go.

Ellie shifts position and hugs her knees with her arms, sobered by the recital. Throughout the sanatorium are people like him, many of them, people whose illness goes back years and who are still battling to regain their health.

"But hasn't the streptomycin helped?" she asks.

"Oh yes, it's a lot better with it than without but it doesn't solve everyone's problems. Like Mr. Myers for instance."

Mr. Myers had died the week before. He'd been one of the first patients to go on streptomycin after it came into use and there was such speedy, striking improvement that it was felt an eventual cure was almost a certainty. Then he became resistant and all the progress slipped away. In long established, chronic cases of the disease other difficulties showed up, forlorn evidence that recovery was not to be taken for granted.

Fernando becomes aware of Ellie's somber face and makes a switch.

"But for people like you, Ellie, sick for the first time, it's different. You won't have any of these problems. Look at all the patients who are going home now after only a year or so."

It was true. Every month, it seemed, there was a farewell dinner in the dining room for another newly discharged patient.

"You don't have anything to worry about," he went on. "You're lucky."

That word lucky again. She wished people wouldn't use it. Like Dr. Connor telling them they were lucky because there were no more thoracoplasties. Dr. Nichols saying how lucky they were to have streptomycin. What they called luck wasn't luck at all. It was just the lesser of one or more evils. Luck was something you didn't know you had until you lost it.

11.

They led an odd but by no means unpleasant existence in an atmosphere deliberately keyed to tranquility. Nothing was permitted to ruffle the even tenor of the days. There were no strident voices, no undo haste, no pressures. Patients were humored, permissiveness was the rule rather than the exception. Professor Palmer was served his Scotch and soda every afternoon at five o'clock prepared by one of the nurses exactly according to his wishes. Mrs.Trevelyan had her glass of sherry at bedtime. Patients who smoked were permitted to smoke although some who smoked a pack of cigarettes a day were urged to try to cut back.

And every so often when the confinement of the infirmary became intolerable a patient would be given a pass to go in to town for dinner. Amy Cannon stretched the privilege to its limits but in her case, as with other patients who were young and had a long history of illness, the staff was especially lenient.

She came from Springfield, Illinois, the only child of well-to-do parents, her father a state senator, her mother a decorating consultant. Circumstances made their visits infrequent but they phoned her regularly and gifts and cards came on a steady basis. Seeing them with her it was obvious they doted on her, forever trying to make up to her for everything her illness had robbed her of and, in their presence, Amy acted with the certainty of pleasing no matter what she did or said.

She was small with a narrow face delicately freckled, clear blue eyes, pretty eyes, but because the lashes were so pale they seemed lash-less. Her one claim to beauty was her hair. It was red-gold, worn clamped to the back of her head with a thick shining coil of it resting across her shoulder. Red-gold tendrils brushed her temples and fringed her forehead. To Fernando she was as exotic as a Persian princess.

He was always at her disposal. He borrowed magazines for her, did errands. He'd sit patiently in her room, a skein of yarn across his wrists while she wound it into a careless ball.

Sometimes he'd bring his guitar and play Spanish love songs but she'd soon tire of them.

"I don't understand the words, Fernando," she'd complain. "Don't you know anything in English?"

He did everything he could think of to amuse her but she was easily bored. Secretly, however, his attentions flattered her and she was very much aware that his devotion could at times be put to good use. The date he finally succeeded in making with her came about because somebody else stood her up.

Harry worked at the radio store in town and he came to the sanatorium frequently to rent radios and record players and, to patients who chose to sleep out on porches year-round, electric blankets. He was blond, broad-shouldered, with a blustery manner and a loud laugh. Amy was taken with him and one day in town he bought her lunch at the sandwich shop on Main Street. Out of it she managed to extract the promise of a dinner date. She was given a pass for the agreed-upon evening but Harry phoned the day before and said he couldn't make it. Disappointed and embarrassed and with a pass in hand she didn't want to go to waste, her only possibility was Fernando. When she asked him if he wanted to take her out he was overjoyed.

She stopped by Ellie's room dressed for the occasion in ski clothes, looking more resigned than happy. "Can I use your lipstick? I like the color better than mine."

"Help yourself."

She rummaged around the dresser top until she found what she wanted. "I told Fernando to meet me here. He's down the hall calling a taxi."

"Where are you going?"

"Probably Luigi's. That's closest and cheapest."

"He doesn't have much money." Ellie thought of his few belongings, most of them hand-me-downs, and wondered how he'd scraped money enough together to take Amy anywhere.

Amy didn't comment. She finished her mouth and studied herself critically in the mirror.

"Oh well, I'm going out. That's something."

Fernando's footsteps in the hall ended their conversation and moments later he was in the doorway. To Ellie who had never seen him before in anything but pajamas and robe his appearance caught her off-guard. In a dark suit of foreign cut, an oversize shirt whose collar was held together by a purple tie, and with a black borrowed overcoat hung over an arm, he looked like an underling from some obscure foreign legation though it was obvious he considered himself properly attired for the outing. His face was aglow with anticipation and his eyes, resting on Amy, were filled with admiration. She made a pretty picture, the glistening hank of red-gold hair draped across a shoulder of her powder blue jacket. Fernando smiled and sighed at the same time.

"Ready?" he asked and he crooked his elbow to take her arm.

They started out of the room and at the doorway he turned.

"We're going to Luigi's," he said proudly.

The next day in Ellie's room and for her benefit he re-lived the evening. There was accordion music, he said, and the wonderful smells of Mediterranean cooking. The waiters joked in loud voices and nobody minded the smoke or the noise or spilled drinks. He was sure Amy had enjoyed it every bit as much as he and in the taxi on the way home he held her hand. A deep sigh of contentment summed up the memory of it all.

But to Ellie, Amy shrugged off the evening impatiently. He didn't speak English well enough to suit her and his odd foreign courtesies disconcerted her. Harry's glib manner and fast talk were more in line with her standards, standards Fernando could never hope to meet.

12.

The original purpose of Bob's trip was to explore the feasibility of setting up a headquarters in South America. Events, however, moved more swiftly than expected and by summer's end it had acquired larger dimensions. The postwar upswing reflected to some degree everywhere, brought about a swelling tide of demand in the steel industry and Consolidated was positioning itself to respond. To date, the company dealt abroad only through agents but now a decision was made to go ahead with the establishment of a South American office without further delay. No one who attended the many meetings held to discuss the various angles of such a move doubted that the man best suited to spearhead it was Bob Glynn. The handling of foreign projects had been his sphere of expertise since he'd connected with Consolidated several years earlier. Thus it came as no surprise when Bob was given the task of setting the mechanics in motion.

Walking out of the final meeting with Knox, the company president, Bob was surprised to hear him ask if he intended to bring Sally with him.

"No," Bob answered. "I hadn't considered it."

"Why don't you? I know it isn't customary to take wives along on business trips but this one is rather special. Give it some thought."

Speculating later on the exchange Bob could only interpret it as a straw in the wind. Already there were rumors that the organization chart was under revision and that the creation of new executive positions was being studied, one of them said to be vice president in charge of foreign affairs. In light of Knox's suggestion it wasn't outside the realm of possibility that Bob might be the one chosen to fill it. In such circumstances a man's wife was considered part of the equation. Sally Glynn was very well thought of by those in the upper echelons of the company, not only because she was attractive and knew her way around but she had a presence that set her apart from the general run of company wives. On the occasions that lay ahead when there would be business leaders and government officials to meet and entertain, Bob was well aware as were others that she would be an asset.

At first Sally was less than enthusiastic about the proposal. She had never been keen on foreign travel, feeling that the drawbacks far outweighed the enjoyments and the prospect of an extended trip to South America did little to stir her interest. Besides she was loath to be away from her work for any length of time. However, as she listened to Bob's assessment of this turn of events she agreed that it might well be the forerunner of an important step forward in his business career and she was as hopeful as he at such a possibility.

And so a period of harmony and mutual purpose followed as they prepared for the trip, leaving in a flurry of farewell drinks and good wishes. Only by small degrees did this spirit dissipate, undone by Sally's dismay at the squalid slums between airports and cities, beggars tugging at sleeves, cripples on street corners selling lottery tickets, the primitive level at which the great masses of poor lived out their lives. Her greatest indignation, however, was reserved for the personal inconveniences, the unexplained lack of hot water as she was getting ready to shower, telephones that did not work, the dozens of small annoyances that resulted from societies far behind hers in the technological scheme of things. Bob did his best to put it in perspective, pointing out to her all that existed of consequence and diversity, but she saw only what she wanted to see. That Bob took everything in stride and refused to get unduly upset only added to her resentment.

On one score alone she was mollified and that was in the wealth of art and artifacts to be found in the museums of the large cities. Endless rooms offered to the discerning eye centuries of history recorded in ceramics and sculpture, scraps of weaving, gold and silver ornaments. Professor Macaulay for whom she did research was an art historian and the author of four esoteric tomes on ancient cultures. He was indefatigable in his quest for little known material, no description too sketchy, no detail too obscure for his consideration and Sally knew her notes would be of much interest. Thus while evenings were given to socializing with Bob's business contacts, in the course of which she played a faultless role, she spent her days filling her notebook with the particulars of objects of legendary antiquity.

In Peru she left Bob in Lima and flew up to Cuzco intending to spend four or five days examining all she could of its ruins and artifacts but she had no sooner arrived when she was stricken with violent dysentery. Early on the third day she flew back to Lima when after a week of doctoring she was no better, Bob agreed she should return to New York. Once back on home ground she was so charmingly contrite for having to cut her stay short that she gained more sympathy than she earned. She sighed with relief and in the comfort of familiar surroundings she got full marks for what she accomplished, as little as it was.

While Bob regretted it, for after all her social skills were useful, he felt a sense of relief. He was able to move more quickly, more directly, without having to consider Sally's likes and dislikes. A hotel didn't have to be four star or a restaurant given top rating in her guide book. The purpose in having her come with him had been served. She proved herself to be the asset everyone thought she'd be.

13.

The smallest unit of time at the sanatorium was a month. In a world revolving around a disease which ran a long slow course, time was pulled out of shape, elongated and days and weeks were seldom used as measures. Ellie, who in New York chafed at an hour's delay, at a day's postponement, who ran up moving escalators, who got out of taxis and walked if it appeared to be faster, she had come to accept this curious deceleration of time.

"Two months more and I can go on to a rest cottage," someone would say.

"Next month I'll be on morning and afternoon exercise."

"Six months from now I may be going home."

But if at the sanatorium the time frame was distorted, beyond its walls time moved in the usual implacable divisions.

Bob was in South America on the trip he warned would be a long grind. He left not knowing when he'd return but he assured Ellie he'd stay in touch. Subsequently a postcard came from Quito. She cut the stamp off and gave it to Fernando for his collection promising him more but nothing further arrived.

The company published a quarterly news bulletin for its employees and when Ellie went up to Saranac, Mrs. Ramey put her name on the mailing list. The fall issue arrived one morning and before reading it Ellie leafed through it, glancing at the usual pictures of employees promoted or transferred, the company bowling team, somebody's new baby. All at once she froze. On an inside page there was a picture of Bob and Sally Glynn seated at a restaurant table in the midst of a group of smiling people. The particulars beneath it read:

Friends hosted a farewell dinner party for Bob and Sally Glynn prior to their departure on an extended tour of South America. The trip is in conjunction with a survey Bob is making to assess business opportunities in that part of the world. Sally who hasn't been to South America before says she looks forward to having a look at it.

Ellie was stunned. Bob traveled a good deal in his job but not since she worked for him had Sally gone any place with him. It never occurred to her that she would. Why didn't Bob tell her? What did it mean? Until now Sally had posed the least threat but obviously that conclusion would bear re-thinking. Ellie dredged up out of her mind the few images she had of her. On two occasions she came by the office in late afternoon after a stint at the library, a bulging leather portfolio in the crook of her arm, a handbag slung over her shoulder, cool, smart, distant, the same bland smile for everyone. One knew without being told that she was important in her own right. The cocktail party at which Sally, socially prudent, moved smoothly among the guests, pleasant to everyone but focusing attention on guests who mattered. Her voice on the phone the times she called and asked for Bob—tinged with the same overtones of aloofness. How foolish she'd been, Ellie thought, to assume theirs was a spent, run-of-the-mill marriage. How preposterous to imagine that she might one day take Sally's place.

Dead and dying love affairs were commonplace at the sanatorium. Examples fell with dismal regularity out of its narrow skies, the grief betrayed by silence, the numbing pain laid bare by distant eyes. More often than not the links which led events to their sorry conclusion were similar. Letters and visits that tapered off, bonds that weakened and finally broke under the corrosive action of absence. Just as often the endings were alike, shaped not in hurtful explicit words but by the lethal wound of silence.

Thanksgiving came and went. Each morning Ellie waited tremulously until eleven o'clock when one of the student nurses brought the mail around. There was nothing. Why didn't he tell her Sally would be with him? Why didn't he mention it when he phoned the week before he left instead of saying he'd stay in touch, which was one thing if he was alone but quite another if his wife was with him. How likely was it she would hear from him? Still, he'd sent the postcard from Quito. Maybe there'd be another from someplace else. Hungrily she watched but nothing came.

She worried Miss Bodelle. On any pretext she stopped by Ellie's room to borrow a chair, to bring it back, to water her African violet and chide her for neglecting it. Once a day Dr. Nichols came by, sometimes just to put his head in the door but other times he stayed on. Once he said, try to eat a little more, Ellie. Your weight's going down. Another time he asked if anything was troubling her. He knew, of course, what was wrong. There was little that escaped the doctors and nurses. He thought she might feel better if she talked about it but no, she said, nothing is wrong, I'm all right. And so he smiled agreeably, squeezed her toes through the blanket and left.

As often as Ellie had considered the possibility that one day for whatever reason her affair with Bob might end, she was never able to convince herself that it would really happen. It couldn't happen. Their love was meant to endure forever. Now, however, she had to face the fact that very possibly it was over.

The infirmary was built long before telephones became an indispensable part of daily life and whenever the concession was made to provide one for the patients it may well have been considered a fad that wouldn't last. The telephone for their use clung to the wall in the far alcove midway between a tangle of fern in a ceramic planter and a wicker armchair. Ellie forever strained her ears to catch its ring. A faint peal, another and another, then silence as one of the nurses answered. Another silence while footsteps tapped along the hall and stopped at the chosen door.

Dinner was over. An hour to go before lights went out at nine o'clock. Down through the corridor came the telephone's faint peal. Ellie sat up in bed and leaned forward to catch the sound more clearly. It rang again. A third time and a fourth. Then silence while it was answered. Footsteps clicked along the hall. Ellie held her breath. All of a sudden Jenny, a student nurse, plump, starched, her country-girl face grinning, materialized in the doorway.

"Ellie, it's for you." She flew out of bed, grabbing her robe and pulling it on as she went out the door. One of the nurses caught sight of her as she sped down the hall.

"Walk, Ellie, walk! Don't run!"

"I can hardly hear you, kitten. Are you all right?"

"Yes, I'm all right. I'm fine. The hand holding the receiver was shaking. When did you get back?"

"Last night. Late."

Returned yesterday. Calling her today. Light flooded the darkness. "I was worried about you. You've been gone so long."

"Didn't you get my letters?"

"I only got a postcard from Quito."

"You never got any mail from Peru?"

"No, nothing."

"I wrote and told you I'd be back after Thanksgiving."

"I never got the letter."

"Damn it, Ellie, I'm sorry. Most of the time I was in the boondocks but I wrote you twice from Lima. They had a postal strike going on there although foreign mail was supposed to be getting through."

"It doesn't matter. Just as long as you're back safe."

The wretchedness of the weeks before vanished like fog before sun. Nothing was changed. Everything was just the way it had been before. But it was strange. Bob talked as if he'd been alone. Where was Sally?

His voice took on a different tone. "Look baby, your birthday is a week from Saturday."

"I know."

"How would you like me to take you to Lake Placid for the weekend?"

She gasped. "Oh Bob, don't say things like that. I might believe you mean them."

"I do. I phoned Dr. Nichols this morning and asked him if he didn't think you could take a little time off. You've been there five months and you need a break."

"What did he say?"

"He agreed."

"I think I must be dreaming." She leaned back against the wall, clutching the receiver to her ear with both hands.

"I'll come up on the Friday night train and rent a car when I get there so we'll be mobile."

"Can you stay till Monday?"

"Even if I could, Ellie, Dr. Nichols wouldn't permit it. He wants you back in the sanatorium by eight o'clock Sunday night."

"Damn."

"Look kitten, you be good now."

" I just may die of pure, sheer, unadulterated joy thinking about it."

"Don't you dare."

What did it matter that Sally had gone with him? Nothing at all. Didn't he call her almost the very minute he got back? Didn't he immediately make plans for a weekend together? What more could she want? He was hers and nothing else mattered.

14.

The day before Ellie's birthday a card arrived from her mother. On the front was a pretty picture of some flamingos at the edge of a tiny man-made lake and the message inside read Have a Beautiful Birthday. It was signed with love, Mother. A letter written on her heavy, creamy stationery, twice folded, was tucked within. It read:

My darling child:

Just these few lines from sunny Florida to say that you are, as always, in my thoughts and prayers. May your birthday be as happy as possible under the circumstances. How I wish I were near to hold your hand and comfort you! How I wish I could send you some of our glorious sunshine! Our weather is perfect and there are flowers everywhere. Your Aunt Dorothy and I spend a lot of time at the beach, mornings mostly, because afternoons are too warm. The new swim suit I so extravagantly bought is still a little snug despite all my efforts to slim myself into it. I must cut down on my calorie intake.

The Charletons were in for bridge last night and we had an enjoyable evening though I find Harriet a little trying. She has a skin allergy from the sun and she harps on it constantly. You'd think it was the end of the world. She should have some of the crosses I've had to bear in my lifetime. I often wonder what I did to deserve them.

It breaks my heart to think of you in all that dreadful snow and cold. The minute you are well I'm going to insist you come down here to live. I should never have permitted you to stay on in New York in the first place. That crowded, dirty city! I hope I never see it again!

Received a postcard from Larry from North Africa. All he says on it is that it's hot. Isn't that just like him? I'm not sure when his ship is due back and must look again at the schedule.

Well, my darling, I've chatted on long enough and I mustn't tire you. Please do everything you're told to and try to get well. I pray you will never know anything like the sorrow your illness has brought me, my only daughter coughing her life away in a sanatorium.

There is a little package in the mail for your birthday and I hope it arrives in time. At least that's what I intended.

Heaps of love,

Ellie returned her mother's letter and card to the envelope and pushed it to the back of the drawer in her bedside table, wishing it was as easy to push aside thoughts of her. Coughing her life away! That was typical of her passion for melodramatics. Ellie burned with indignation. Within two months of her arrival at the sanatorium the doctors had stopped her cough. In fact, very few patients coughed. She had written this to her in an early letter, saying how vastly improved she was to have just this one symptom of the illness eliminated. Had it slipped her mind? Or would it minimize the blow she'd suffered were Ellie to recover too quickly?

Just as with every calamity that had befallen the family, Ellie's mother had seized upon the illness as if it were her own. She had a talent for laying claim to another's trouble and focusing it on herself while the sufferer stood in her shadow, enduring not only his own grief but somehow responsible as well for hers. She played a major role in every family misfortune though, as families go, they had far fewer than most.

During the years that Ellie and her brother were growing up they lived in Oyster Bay on the north shore of Long Island which at that time was a small town tucked into a wooded shoreline. Miles of unspoiled meadow and woods surrounded it and furnished an exclusive haven for many people of wealth who sought escape from the city. They dominated its small society and while the Stuarts were not one of them, they were comfortably off and blended easily into the social affairs of the town. Ellie's mother was an extremely pretty woman, blonde and petite, with a gregarious manner and an engaging smile. Her father was a quiet, kindly man and together they made an attractive and popular couple.

Larry was the first tragedy. All through childhood Ellie listened to her mother lament the loss of her son's good looks. He was older by four years and though she was too young to remember what he looked like before the accident, pictures showed a strikingly handsome little boy with magnificent eyes. When he was seven a sling shot, widely off mark, hit him squarely in the left eye, destroying the sight and damaging the muscle in the upper lid so that afterward his eye remained half closed. He was still a handsome child and he grew to be a handsome man but his mother could see the mishap only as a disaster and herself the victim of an unjust fate. As a result, she caused Larry to become overly sensitive to what was at most a minor disfigurement while at the same time the truly serious after-effects of the accident she missed. Because he couldn't see properly he did poorly in school. His mother railed and carried on and couldn't understand why a child of hers would be left back, blaming teachers, changing schools, all to no avail. It was one more cross, she told her friends, she would have to learn to bear. All through the early years Larry carried his double burden while his mother swept onstage, pink-tipped fingers pressed to heart, asking what she had done to deserve it.

Ellie was sixteen when her father died. The accident happened in Connecticut—a speeding van on a narrow road making a too-wide turn. His car was pushed over a fifty foot embankment and so badly demolished the license plates were barely decipherable, his body so tangled in the wreckage it took workers hours to cut it free.

Ellie's mother fainted when she got the news. Lifted solicitously to a couch by rallying friends, she lay with an arm thrown across her eyes, begging to know what she had done to merit this catastrophe. Onlookers spoke in hushed voices to calm her and sat in uneasy silence while she wept floods of theatrical tears. The violence drained her and she shifted into a less demanding role, one of acquiescent resignation. Garbed in black, a dainty black veil on her shining hair, she moved through the funeral services with the submissiveness of a medieval saint. But the question she put to heaven was always the same. Why did this happen to me?

It infuriated Ellie. How was it her mother didn't wonder why fate had chosen her husband for such a tragedy? He was only forty-five years old, successful, a man who loved his wife and delighted in his children. Did she think he wanted to die? Why had it happened to him?

Quickly she made the decision to sell the house and move to Florida. Her sister had settled there some time before and urged her to come. In no time she commenced to dispose of his things—clothes, books, tools, his personal papers. And his sailboat.

He loved to sail and all the years Ellie and Larry were growing up he had one boat or another in which the three of them sailed on Long Island Sound from early spring to late fall. He taught them all there was to know about small boats, how to tack and go before the wind, how to tie knots and pick up a mooring. A couple of years earlier he'd bought a thirty-five foot ketch secondhand and most of his spare time after that he spent restoring it. It was in commission a month before he died and he and Ellie went out together on its first voyage. The day, in early April, was cold and rainy with a blustery northeast wind whipping the seas into choppy whitecaps. Dressed in foul-weather gear Ellie huddled beside him in the cockpit, feet braced against the starboard seats to keep from sliding downward while seas washed over the cockpit combings and burst across the bow. She was both terrified and thrilled.

"It's a fine boat," he announced at dinner after he and Ellie together had described the afternoon's sail. "We'll have some good times in her."

To Ellie's surprise her mother responded with a degree of enthusiasm. But then the boat had bunks, a galley and a head. It wasn't the primitive kind of thing they'd knocked around in during previous years. Yes, she agreed, it might be fun.

He got to sail it one more time before he died and now it was to be sold.

"You wouldn't, mother, would you?" Ellie asked.

"Wouldn't what?" her mother answered, puzzled.

"You wouldn't sell daddy's boat?"

She looked at her daughter with a favorite expression of hers—a mixture of fondness and exasperation. "But darling, what would we keep it for?   We're moving to Florida."

"Couldn't we have it down there?"

"Ellie, we won't have waterfront property. And besides who would sail it?"

That was the question and she was justified in asking it. Larry, after some fumbling starts trying to find himself, seemed to be aimed in a satisfactory direction at last. He was making a modest reputation for himself playing drums with one of the swing bands then popular out on the island. He was totally involved with music now. He had no interest in boats. What else was there to do but sell it?

The day the boat changed hands to a small fat man with a small fat ugly wife, Ellie went down to a lonely part of the beach and cried as she hadn't cried since her father died. She couldn't bring herself to watch her mother signing papers, handing over keys, smiling her bright smile and wishing the new owners many happy voyages. Thinking of all his loving work, the care he took to have each detail perfect, she felt as if they were betraying him. But again, what else was there to do?

When the move to Florida was made Larry went along. He had recently established a connection with a small orchestra that sailed out of Miami on the cruise ships. Ellie stayed behind. She had no desire whatsoever to live in that part of the country and besides she felt she had to cut herself free.

Her mother didn't object nearly as much as might have been expected. By that time Ellie had met Joan Wiley who was looking for a small apartment in Manhattan and someone to share it with; it was what she too wanted and so they joined forces. Mrs. Stuart was most accommodating. She gave them carte blanche to take whatever they wanted from the house before she put it on the market. Only a few things were to be sent down to Florida.

"It's a whole different way of life down there," she explained at one of the many farewell parties given for her. "Besides there's too much pain for me living among all the things Alex and I shared for so many happy years. I must try somehow to make things a little easier for myself."

And she had. She and her sister dawdled the days away over bridge tables, sipped tall drinks beside swimming pools, bought clothes, changed hair styles, drove to Key West for a special lime daiquiri. Once in awhile, motivated by an urge for self improvement or boredom she took a course in some undemanding subject or attempted to learn a craft.

Now, into the placid waters of her rightful ease, there was about to drop the bombshell of her daughter's tuberculosis.

Ellie and Joan sat in the bedroom of their apartment that stifling July evening, each on her own bed, the telephone on the night table between them.

"I don't know how to tell her," Ellie explained. "No matter what I say she'll carry on, have hysterics as if I've done this on purpose." She shook her head miserably. "I don't think I can take it."

"Look Ellie. Do this," Joan said in her down-to-earth fashion. "Call her. Give her the word however you see fit. I'll stay right here and if she goes into one of her acts let me have the phone and I'll finish off the conversation. She's got to know she has to quiet down. That you can't be upset."

Ellie's temperature was 101.9 and a clammy film of sweat covered her chest and back. Her hands shook. She picked up the phone and dialed the Miami number. It rang and rang and rang some more. Just as she was about to hang up her mother answered, her voice gay, anticipatory.

"Darling!" she said when she recognized Ellie's voice. "What a lovely surprise! How are you?"

"I guess I'm okay. How are you?"

"You called at just the right time to ask that question! The truth is I'm miserable. We were out in the Evans' boat yesterday and I'm afraid I got a little too much sun. My skin is quite badly burned and I spent an agonizing night trying to get comfortable enough to sleep. You know I'm so fair. I just burn and burn. Not like you. You're so lucky to tan so easily."

Ellie held the phone a little distance away from her ear so Joan could hear the voice going on and on. She looked across at her helplessly.

"Cut her off," Joan whispered urgently. "Say you've got something to tell her and let her have it."

"Mother," Ellie interrupted. "Mother," she said again. The voice at last halted. "I've got some news and I'm afraid it isn't good." A pause while the words sank in. "You know I've had a cough for a long time."

"No, I didn't know you had a cough for a long time."

"I mentioned it in a letter awhile back. Well, anyway, I found out that it's more serious than just an ordinary cough. A chest specialist told me yesterday that I have tuberculosis." Silence. Than a sort of muffled scream. Joan grabbed the phone away from Ellie but there was no one on the other end.

"Mrs. Stuart!" she said sharply. "Mrs. Stuart!"

Another woman's voice came on the line. She said she was a friend visiting and she asked what had happened, what was wrong. Joan gave her the facts tersely. "Ellie's going up to Saranac Lake Friday night. Please tell Mrs. Stuart and tell her that unless she's able to talk to Ellie calmly she mustn't call. Ellie can't be upset." Joan hung up. Ellie wiped her sweaty face with Kleenex, her hands still trembling.

"Lie down, Ellie," Joan said. "Put it all out of your mind. She had to know and now she knows. Period."

She went out to the kitchen and came back with ice in a towel. "Put it across your forehead." She turned off the light on the night table, leaving just the lamp on the dresser burning.

"Sleep a little if you can," she said and she left the room.

Ellie lay between dozing and waking before drifting into sleep and a little later when the phone rang it startled her. It was her brother.

"What's cooking, kid?" His voice was anxious. "Is it as bad as they say?"

"It is, Larry. It's about as bad as it can get."

"Is there anything I can do? Do you want me to come up? I won't be able to stay long because I've got a trip to Rio the middle of next week. But I could come up for a couple of days."

"Thanks, Larry. No. It isn't necessary. Everything's arranged. I won't be alone. Has mom gotten over the shock yet?"

"You know how she is. She's carrying on like you'd expect. She wants me to tell you she won't be able to come up."

"That's good."

"She says it's too much for her right now but she'll try to get up to see you in Saranac."

"Please discourage her. I don't want her to come."

"I wouldn't worry about it. She probably won't."

There was an awkward pause. Then Larry said, "Look kid, try to get better fast, won't you?"

"I will, I sure will." She wanted to tell him she'd miss him but she started to cry and had to hang up.

Wide awake she got up, showered and went back to bed. Dulcinea was stretched out across the foot where a current of air from the fan ruffled her fur. She doubted that her mother would actually make a trip to Saranac but nevertheless she took comfort from Larry's assurance that it was nothing to worry about.

The birthday gift was in a large sturdy box, carefully packaged, probably by Larry, and when Ellie opened it she found it contained a little willow basket. A card was inside it. "An example of your mother's very dubious talent, nonetheless sent with love." She examined it carefully and it looked to be nicely done until the top edge where Ellie could see her growing bored, she had hurtled to a conclusion. The rim was tightly pulled in one place, loose in another and there was no handle.

Looking back across the years it was typical of everything her mother had ever got involved in. Great initial enthusiasm followed by an abrupt loss of interest. It was a pity because she was clever in many ways but it was beyond her to stay with any one undertaking until she reached an appreciable level of skill. Either the novelty wore off or she found more effort was demanded of her than she was prepared to expend. Later she'd discover something else which was really what she'd been looking for. And all would be repeated.

Like the weaving. She got the notion that she wanted to weave and she went to some classes where she saw examples of beautiful hand-loomed fabrics. She was carried away. She'd weave new living room drapes and what a conversation piece they would be! She acquired a loom, she ordered boxes of every kind of yarn, instruction books and all she ever made were four place mats and a cushion cover.

And the sculpture classes. The instructor was a small, pop-eyed man with a thick German accent who'd had a successful exhibition of his work at a Madison Avenue gallery. He turned up at one of the local cocktail parties and he argued that everyone had latent talents, that it was just a matter of seeking them out. Ellie could still remember how taken with him her mother had been. She bought clay, armatures, a sculpture stand and she rode into New York to class every Saturday morning for all of two months. But then she admitted it was rather tedious and that was the end of it.

The truth was she had no patience with what she considered to be petty details. There was an amused edge of scorn in her voice when she spoke of someone who struggled through a long apprenticeship, who stuck to his guns to accomplish what he set out to do. That wasn't for her. She looked for achievements that came about in one wide easy sweep, a little gem of a painting turned out while the tubes of paint were still new. To her it was the sign of an artistic temperament to spurn trivia and that included just about all the homely mechanics of a project except the end result.

She felt the same way about orderliness. She saw nothing amiss in her disorganized dresser drawers, scattered jewelry, a perfume bottle whose stopper she couldn't find and unanswered mail. On the contrary she seemed to take a certain pride in it as if tidiness, like patience, was a banal virtue, found only among those with little imagination. Luckily there was always a woman who came in to clean and straighten up, even after her husband died, so her carelessness didn't spillover into the appearance of the house. But she often regarded Ellie quizzically when she sorted out her clothes or pasted pictures in albums instead of heaping them in a box. My little apple-pie order girl, she'd call her.

Ellie studied the basket she'd sent, wondering what use could be made of it. Then she discovered it was the right size to hold her African violet so she put the flower pot inside it and set it back beside the window.

15.

The heavy snow that fell all during the first part of December threw Ellie into despair. Suppose the trains weren't able to get through? Suppose Bob couldn't get here? Her mind reeled at the awful possibility and she listened to every weather report on her radio in desperation or hope as the case might be. But then the snow tapered off, a pale sun appeared, and with her birthday came a forecast of cold, clear weather. She nearly wept with relief. When Bob arrived shortly before ten o'clock that morning she was dressed and waiting and a smiling Miss Bodelle said they surely had the weatherman on their side.

There was almost too much joy to handle. "How long has it been?" She hugged him as she spoke. "I had it all worked out in days but now I've forgotten. And it doesn't matter, does it?"

"It's been a lot too long but no, Ellie, it doesn't matter." He held her face in his hands and kissed her long and deeply.

"Oh Robert, I'm so glad you're back. What about South America? How was your trip?"

"Frustrating. It's impossible to get anything done down there in a reasonable length of time but I managed to cover all the bases so that stage of the work is done."

Somehow, some place, during this weekend Ellie was determined to learn more about that trip, about Sally going with him. If a likely opportunity didn't present itself she'd have to make one.

Bob went on. "But let's talk about you. You're looking good, much better than when I saw you last. How's it all going?"

Really very well, she assured him, elaborating as they walked through the hall to the entrance and down the snowy steps to the car parked out front. Oh it was boring, monotonous, all the regimentation and being in bed all day but now she was permitted fifteen minutes exercise in the hall morning and afternoon. So there was progress. Her chief complaint was everyone's complaint—not getting better fast enough.

She settled herself in the car and stroked the leather upholstery with her gloved hand, her face radiant. "Do you know this is the first time I've been in a car since I came here last July?"

On this bright cold morning everything thrilled her. The road down through town to the lake at its end where the road to Lake Placid began was full of wonder.

"Can you imagine, Bob? All the months I've been here and I've never seen any of this. I haven't been out of the sanatorium since the day I arrived."

She gazed in fascination at everything they passed. The stores that sold guns and boots, the bridge over the Saranac River, the single movie house on Main Street, a ramshackle wooden hotel that looked so ancient there might have been horses hitched to posts out front. Everything, in fact, seemed so old-fashioned

"It's such a funny little place," she said. "It's hard to believe it's in the twentieth century."

"I don't know. I think it's got a lot of character. It's tough country up here, yet towns like this keep right on going in spite of blizzards and ice storms and weather that'd bring New York to a standstill in a day. That says a lot for them."

"Do you know, Bob, most of the people here have all had tuberculosis?"

"That means a lot of people got better."

"But they're afraid to leave. They think as long as they stay here in this climate and breathe this air they'll stay well but if they go back to a city they'll get sick again."

"I don't think that's so, Ellie."

"And do you know something even stranger? There are people at the sanatorium who are cured, who could go home, but don't want to. They've been here for years and they don't have to be."

In some cases patients who regained their health were unable to adjust to normal life and found it impossible to return to family and friends. They chose to stay on, abiding by all the rules and limitations of sanatorium life in exchange for a cocoon-like security they wouldn't find outside. They became permanent invalids, making a fetish of their health, basking in the solicitude the sanatorium staff extended to everyone within its walls. Sometimes brief excursions were undertaken but inevitably they ended in a litany of dissatisfactions—crowds, haste, germs, polluted air—and the ever firmer conviction that the insubstantial world they inhabited was their only choice.

"Millie, the librarian, is one of them," Ellie went on. She had cured years ago, she was attractive, she was still a young woman, but she had no inclination to live a normal life. "The man in the drug room is another. And there are more. Did you ever hear of such a thing, Bob?" It was something Ellie found impossible to comprehend.

"I don't think we have to worry about that happening in your case," he said.

Ellie just shook her head. "I won't stay here one minute longer than I have to." She sighed. "Bob, you don't know how I dream of being back in New York again. Shopping in Saks and Lord & Taylor. Do you know how we shop here? Out of the Sears Roebuck catalogue. Yes, honest, can you imagine?" She laughed and hugged his arm. "I dream of us going to all the lovely places we've been before and I say to myself maybe a year from today it'll happen."

"It will happen one day, Ellie, I promise you."

She rested her cheek against his shoulder and he patted her knee. All the old intimacy between them was back. He was as entirely hers as he had always been.

Between Saranac and Placid the road was a level twelve miles of highway plowed narrowly to two lanes. It cut through forests of snow-burdened evergreens, curved past snow-blanketed meadows that rolled away to distant snowy hills. It followed a frozen stream that lay at the foot of a sheer fall of rock and farther on it skirted a wide frozen lake. A rugged little house stood alone on a slope, smoke pouring from its chimney and Ellie wondered who would live in such a solitary place.

Lake Placid was a year-round resort but the unpredictable weather discouraged most visitors except those who came for the winter sports. Their hotel had few guests. It sheltered in a copse of trees at the end of a long driveway that divided at the entrance and went on around each side to meet at the back and continue on down to the edge of an icy lake. Fir trees lined the drive, standing at attention like soldiers to hold back the forest.

Thick, sand-colored wall-to-wall carpet. A king sized bed. Six feet of mirror. Music at the touch of a fingertip. After the bare floors and monastic beds in the infirmary it was wildly luxurious. They left the drapes in place across the windows to keep it dim and savoring each other's closeness like a prize hard won, they stood in the center of the room in a lengthy embrace. Pushing Bob's necktie aside Ellie undid some of the buttons on his shirt, then pressed her face into his chest.

"I want to breathe you," she said, inhaling deeply. "you always smell so good."

"It's a special formula I make up myself from honeysuckle flowers and ground elephant toenails and it's guaranteed to drive girls named Ellie crazy."

She laughed delightedly. "It works," she pulled her sweater off and tossed it over her head, unzipped her skirt and let it drop to the floor. And still laughing she threw herself into his arms.

It was nearly two o'clock when they went down to the dining room for lunch and Bob insisted they not dally. "We have to get you some proper clothes. You don't have the right things to wear up here."

"I haven't needed them. I haven't been anywhere but in bed."

"But you're going to start needing them. You're going to be out of bed more and more now as things move along. At least that's what Dr. Nichols tells me."

There were wonderful shops along the main street, small branches of the smartest New York stores. They had never shopped together before and it thrilled Ellie to ask his advice and have him help her select things to wear. Ski clothes were the standard attire of sanatorium patients and so they bought ski pants and a ski jacket, two angora sweaters and one from Iceland, ski gloves, a lacy blue scarf to match one of the sweaters, fleece-lined boots and wool socks. Back at the hotel, tumbling things out of boxes and tissue paper, Ellie tried them all on again, one after the other, exclaiming and enthusing. Suddenly the old familiar sensation of fatigue struck her and she sat down abruptly, her hands shaking. Bob stopped short, alarmed.

"Come on, kitten, get back into bed." His eyes were filled with concern.

"I'm all right, really, Bob," she insisted. The possibility that something, anything, might be permitted to spoil the weekend was unthinkable. "This happens every once in awhile. It's nothing."

But even as she protested he took off her shoes and stockings and her outer clothes and when finally she acquiesced out of sheer fatigue and lay back in bed, he covered her and sat beside her for a minute.

"This day has been too much for you."

"Don't say that. Please don't."

"It's taken a long time to get you this far, Ellie. I don't want anything to set you back."

"Loving you won't set me back."

His eyes were still troubled. "Sleep awhile. Sleep as long as you want. I won't make a sound."

"Kiss me," she said. She fell asleep before he took his mouth away.

At first she thought the house she approached was her childhood home in Oyster Bay but it was Bob's home. Summer flowers edged the walk and grew in profusion below the open windows through which came sounds of music and people talking. Apparently a party was in progress and she started to go back but as she turned she heard a voice asking her what she wanted and she saw Sally standing at the front door garbed in a beautiful evening gown. Ellie said she had something terribly important to tell Bob at which a crafty look came over Sally's face. Holding her glittering skirt aside she swept the door open and gestured her into the hall. Immediately the hall became a stage and Sally a magician's assistant. As if preparing for sleight of hand she pulled a table forward and covered it with a black cloth, shifted black drapes until only a staircase and a small portion of stage was left unenclosed. Her movements were exaggerated, theatrical and her eyes burned with malice. She called up the stairs, "Bob, that Stuart girl is here." Bob's answer, seeming to come from far away as if she had used some magic to distance him, was clear and unequivocal. "Tell her I've gone to North Africa."

The dream wrenched her out of sleep and onto a blurred level of wakefulness where portions of it remained vivid while other portions began to ebb. Fully awake at last there lingered still the malevolence in Sally's eyes, the denial in Bob's voice, and she wondered was the dream a forewarning? Was it meant as a sign that she could take nothing for granted? The reason Sally went with him on the trip to South America and why Bob hadn't told her about it beforehand wasn't touched upon, much less explained, giving it in Ellie's mind a much weightier meaning. Two or three times she'd been on the verge of asking him about it but then the opportunity somehow slipped away. She switched on the bedside lamp to look for him but the room was empty. A rim of light outlined the bathroom door and, shaking, she crossed the room in her slip and pushed it open. He was sitting on the floor on a chair cushion reading Time magazine. He looked up and started to smile but stopped.

"Ellie, what's wrong?"

She dropped down beside him and buried her face in his chest. "Oh Bob, I thought you'd gone! I woke up and switched on the light and you weren't there."

"But honey, I only wanted to leave you alone so you'd sleep."

"I know, but I had such a terrible dream." She shook her head from side to side against his chest as if to dispel the last remnants of it.

"What was it? What was so terrible?"

She hesitated. "It was about you and me and Sally. I can't put it together anymore but it was awful."

Bob stood up and pulled her to her feet. "Look Ellie, dreams are only dreams. They have no meaning whatsoever and it's silly to think they have." She said nothing, leaning against him, arms around him. "Come on now, don't you agree?"

"I guess so." But her voice was unconvinced.

"You're not going to let something like that spoil our weekend together, are you?"

"No." Was now the time to ask him about Sally and the South American trip? She started to frame the question in her mind but before she could put it in words Bob lifted her face.

"Do you know there's something you're forgetting?"

"What?"

"Today's your birthday!"

In the bedroom he opened his bag and took out a small Tiffany box. It held a pair of antique Spanish earrings—dull gold, carved and dangling, with fierce little hooks to go into her pierced ears. She lifted them up and drew in a deep breath of pleasure.

"Oh, Robert, they're beautiful, simply beautiful."

Standing in front of the mirror, still in her slip, she put them on and then stood back to admire herself. "Thank you, thank you." And she hugged him.

Her question would have to wait.

They slept late the next morning and by the time they'd dressed a pale but valiant sun was spangling the snow in the white world outside their window. Their room overlooked a lake—a small, platter-shaped stretch of solid ice with dense pines crowding its farther shore. Beyond it a slope rose sharply, dove into a hidden valley and rose again to join a tier of blunted peaks behind which successively smaller fainter peaks, like echoes, moved back a hundred miles to meet the sky.

Bob stood at the window studying the view. "I think I like this country even better in winter," he said. "You'd have to go far to find anything more beautiful anywhere."

Ellie stood beside him and he put his arm around her waist. It pleased her that he found this region to his liking and she agreed it was beautiful but such great reaches of empty land, no visible roads, no lights at night to rout the darkness, chilled her. She thought of how it would be to be lost in that wilderness, struggling to find a vantage point from which to guess direction, and it seemed as terrifying as being adrift in the middle of the Atlantic.

Much more to her taste were the ski jumps. The brief afternoon was bitterly cold and they sat in the car with the heater going, a blanket tucked around their legs, while they watched breathtaking dives down slopes like glass. It was incredibly exciting at first, but after awhile a dull ache of envy throbbed inside her. A lot of the skiers were women, glowing with youth and health, not much younger or older than she. Their bodies were superbly functioning machines, their lungs were sound, things they looked upon as their right, not anything to be grateful for. Once she too had taken those things for granted.

How far away they seemed, the carefree days when everything she wanted slipped so readily into her hands, when wishes came magically true. How long ago and lost the charmed destiny she once believed was written in her stars. Life then had stretched before her, a shining road with marvels unfolding all along the way, hers for the taking. Who could have guessed it would ever change? Who would have believed her taut young body flawed, that it harbored a foe who would stalk her, snare her, make a shambles of her ambitions and in the end re-write her life?

Bob guessed her shift in mood because he turned and put his hand over hers. "I think it's time for a drink," he said. "The day is getting away from us and I don't want to get you back to the sanatorium late."

"I wouldn't care."

"But I would. They might not let you out again."

"They wouldn't dare."

A fieldstone fireplace took up half a wall of the bar at the hotel, its leaping flames and the pungent smell of burning pine logs giving the room a cozy intimacy. After the stark cold of the waning day the warmth was as comforting as an embrace. Except for two men talking to the bartender at the far end of the bar the place was empty.

"It's been a wonderful weekend, Bob. It's been everything I knew it would be." They sat close to the fire and its glow gave her hair a golden sheen.

"I wish I could say we'd do this soon again, Ellie. I wish I knew when I'd be able to come up again but I don't."

"Hardly anyone comes up in winter. The weather is just too bad and if it isn't it can be."

"I wasn't thinking about the weather. I'm going to have to go down to South America again."

She looked at him in surprise. "But you just got back."

"Not right away. Sometime early in the year and things are going to be busy till then."

"You never really told me about the trip you just made."

"There wasn't much to tell, just the usual long grind, always on the move, setting up meetings, trying to nail down government people. You know the routine."

"That isn't what I meant." He waited for her to continue. "You never told me Sally went with you." The silence became a wall between them. "I saw the picture in the company news bulletin."

He reached over and took her hand. "I didn't tell you. because it wasn't that important."

"But she never went with you before."

"It wasn't my idea or even hers. Knox proposed it. He thought it might serve a purpose to have her on hand for after-hours when local wives would be on the scene."

"And did it?"

He knitted his brows as if considering it, as if wishing to give an accurate answer. "Yes, I think it did. Very much so."

It wasn't what Ellie wanted him to say and her face reflected it.

"What difference does it make?" he continued. "It has nothing to do with us."

But for Ellie it had. To her it was evidence of a closeness that up to now she had convinced herself didn't exist. Time and again she wondered what their marriage was like and long ago had reached the conclusion that any real intimacy between them was a thing of the past. She saw them as two people held together by a bond they accepted but ceased to cultivate. It seemed she was wrong. She must force herself to take a new look at her carefully manufactured assessment of their marriage.

"Anyway as it turned out she only lasted two weeks. She got a bug and had a really rough time of it so she gave up and went back to New York."

"Is she going with you again?"

He shook his head. "No. Sally isn't keen on traveling and she didn't think much of what she saw of South America. But that's not the point. Whether or not she goes with me doesn't matter. It isn't going to change anything between us. Don't you know that?"

Defeated, she nodded. "How long will you be gone?"

"It's hard to say. Consolidated wants to open an office in Lima, Peru, and I've got to go down and get it in the works.

It's a time-consuming job but we'll do it in stages. I don't plan to be down there any longer than I have to at any one stage. I'll be dividing my time between New York and Peru."

"Who will head it up? Not you?" She blanched at the thought of his being in South America on a permanent basis.

"No, I won't be the one. We'll send someone down from New York to take over when it's ready to go."

"I hate for you to be going away again, Bob." Ellie put her hand over his. "It's bad enough with you in New York and me up here. But when you go so far…" Her voice trailed off. It was different when she sat at her polished desk, answering mail and phone calls, tracking his travels, counting days, waiting for his return with secret anticipation. To the others now in her place none of it was anything more than routine.

"I won't be leaving for awhile. It'll probably be March before I can get away. And whether I'm in New York or Lima remember every week that passes you'll be that much better."

She stared into the fire, the headway he predicted of little consequence seeing instead all the stir attendant on his going, the busy eventful days, and it was as if she looked into a lighted room she could not enter. The silence lengthened. "The time will go quickly, you'll see."

"You'll write, won't you?"

"Of course." He put a hand under her chin. "Smile, Ellie. You don't want me to remember you frowning, do you?" Her face softened and she shook her head.

"It's getting late. What shall we do about dinner? Would you like to eat here or shall we go out?"

"Let's eat in our room."

Alone with him again for one last little while, the prohibited world retreated and in the fastness of his arms she envied no one.

16.

She used to like to imagine that they'd met on a ship or on the steps of a French cathedral or in one of the dusty, smoldering Moorish cities of southern Spain. Her mind would play with the scene from the first flash of mutual recognition—for in her imaginings they knew instantly they were meant for each other—to the tentative touch of hands and on to the glorious, ever-binding finale. It seemed a sorry oversight on the part of destiny that they came together in so mundane a fashion.

Bob Glynn was a smart, aspiring engineer on the executive staff of Consolidated Steel Corporation, a company whose dealings were worldwide and whose headquarters were in Wall Street. Ellie was assigned as his secretary after an apprenticeship in the Stenographic Department although Mrs. Ramey, its' supervisor, was not at all sure of the choice, feeling that an older person would be more suitable. She may well have been right. None, however, was available.

Ellie had presented herself just as Mrs. Ramey was on the verge of contacting an employment agency and she asked to be considered for the opening. The request came as a surprise and she looked at the girl in front of her as if seeing her for the first time. A slender figure in a navy blue dress, standing very straight as if wanting to make herself look taller. Shining honey colored hair brushed smooth to the shoulder, serious hazel eyes, a child's purity of skin. Most attractive, no doubt about it. Her work was good too. She was quick and accurate, clearly better than many of the girls in the department who had been there longer but though she might have all the basic skills needed, she lacked experience. Her age was the drawback.

"How old are you now, Ellie?"

"Twenty. Twenty and a half."

That was it. Much too young for a job in one of the front offices where nearly all the secretaries were mature women. She thought briefly of Mrs. Wilson, Mr. Glynn's secretary for eight years whose husband's terminal illness caused her to resign. A vision of that sturdy woman, able and vigorous from years spent in business offices, superimposed itself momentarily on the young girl standing in front of her and she hesitated. Ellie spoke up.

"Can't I take the job on a trial basis and if it doesn't work out I'll go back to the Stenographic Department?"

Mrs. Ramey was a sympathetic woman, the widowed mother of three, her oldest about Ellie's age. How were these youngsters to make anything out of themselves if nobody gave them a chance?

"I tell you what, Ellie. I'll talk to Mr. Glynn and see what he has to say. We'll let him decide."

When Mrs. Ramey was finally able to get in to see him it was at the end of one of his long busy days and it seemed wise to be brief. Unlike many of the other men Bob Glynn wasn't given to small talk so she got right to the point. She described Ellie's qualifications, saying she considered her one of the brightest girls she had. There was only the matter of her age. She was quite young.

"A little over twenty."

He leaned back in his chair and rubbed fingers across his eyes. "How long has she been here? How well does she know the company?"

"She's been here a year and she's done work for every department. She has a good grasp of what the company's all about." There was a silence and Mrs. Ramey added, "I've found her very reliable and quick to learn." He appeared to consider it—or was he just weary, Mrs. Ramey wondered.

"Send her around Thursday. I'll be in Washington tomorrow. By the way, what's her name?"

"Ellie Stuart."

He nodded. Mrs. Ramey went on, "Of course it will be on a trial basis. If it doesn't work out we'll get you someone else."

"Fair enough." And the interview was over.

For Ellie it was a major triumph. The leap from ordinary stenographer to an executive secretarial position was something she hardly dared believe would happen but it proved there was nothing lost by asking. It scared her a little too. Suppose it was too much for her? Suppose she turned out to be a dismal failure? She made up her mind she wouldn't fail for lack of trying. She'd do everything in her power to insure her success.

She knew next to nothing about the man she had asked to work for though she knew who he was, of course, and saw him occasionally in the halls. He was a tall, good looking man whose quiet manner downplayed a quick mind and a lot of drive. He'd come far in the ten years he'd been with the company and there was a general feeling that he'd continue to move ahead. He was in charge of the company's foreign projects, initiated many of them, saw them off the ground and followed their progress through to completion. He was away a lot and when he returned he was the center of meetings where his opinions carried a lot of weight. All this added to the challenge Ellie faced and tended to intimidate her but she resolved to go slowly and take things a day at a time.

She was thrilled with her new surroundings. The executive offices were spacious and beautifully appointed throughout. Bob's office was one of three in a section he shared with the company treasurer and the director of marketing. The section faced south and from their vantage point on the 52nd floor one glimpsed a part of the Statue of Liberty and on sunny days the sparkle of waters plied by the Staten Island Ferry. The secretaries sat at desks within little railed enclosures in front of each office and facing a reception room which ran its length. It was furnished with couches, heavy chairs for visitors and coffee tables that held wide glass ashtrays and technical publications. Tall plants in majolica pots made splashes of green against the beige and cinnamon color scheme and were tended with spinsterish care by one or the other of the two secretaries. Seated in her own little railed enclosure between them—the wintry visage of Mrs. Cooper on one side and Marge Foster with her untidy hair and orthopedic shoes on the other—Ellie's glowing presence was as arresting as a neon sign. Neither of them thought she'd last very long in the job and for a while neither did she.

The first week was easy. After two days Bob went to Pittsburgh and in his absence she had time to study the files and read all the Projects Pending stacked up on a table in his office. She found out where everything was kept and reorganized her desk.

When he got back, however, one flurry of activity followed on the heels of another with scarcely breathing space between. Telephone calls came in, some of which were to be put through, others held off. Men from different departments stopped by and either saw him or had to be scheduled for a later time.

One afternoon there was a closed-door meeting in his office involving six or seven men. The buzzer on Ellie's desk sounded and she got up and went in. Bob nodded toward Mr.

Herrman, a beefy, red-faced man who asked her to bring him the Cerro de Pasco file. She went back outside, found it and brought it in. Mr. Herrman dismissed it.

"This is only part of the file." Ellie had brought just the current year. "I want the whole thing!"

Flustered, she went back and dug out the files for the previous two years—all there was on Cerro de Pasco—and returned with them. Mr. Herrman flipped through the pages impatiently.

"Where are the financial statements?"

"We keep those separately," she replied.

"Well go get them!"

It took her an inordinate length of time to find them and then make sure they were complete but finally she was able to present them. He brushed them aside with on irritable hand. "Never mind. I don't need them now."

Disconcerted, flushed with embarrassment, aware that every eye was on her, she stood for an indecisive moment or two before taking them back. She had one swift glimpse of Bob watching her, his face expressionless. Outside at her desk she went over her inept performance and resigned herself to dismissal. Mrs. Ramey was right to have misgivings about her. Someone more experienced would have handled the situation with more finesse.

The meeting ended, the men filed out and dispersed. The buzzer sounded. She got to her feet and with a heavy heart went into the office. Bob was lounging back in his chair, relaxed, his feet on a corner of the desk. He dug into his pocket and extracted some coins. "Go get us each a coke, Ellie."

She stood for a moment transfixed while relief flooded through her and as she took the money from his hand her face softened into an expression of tremulous gratitude.

He felt sorry to see Ellie the target of Herrman's rudeness that afternoon but the world was filled with all kinds of people and all of them had to be dealt with. The sooner one learned to do so the better. All things considered she was doing nicely in the job, in spite of the doubts he'd had when she was first introduced. She seemed then like a child who had strayed into the adult world and he wondered at the time if Mrs. Ramey was getting her recruits from slumber parties.

But he was glad to be proven wrong. He really had no fault to find, on the contrary there was about her a touching eagerness to please which he found rather novel remembering the sure-footed Mrs. Wilson. She had a way of waiting to smile until he smiled, laughing only if he laughed first after which her eyes would light up and monopolize her face— clear, beautiful eyes with long sweeping lashes. Davie, his younger son, had had the same mannerism when he was small and each time Bob saw it repeated in Ellie a recollection of those halcyon days was tugged out of memory.

Inevitably the appearance of a girl as young and pretty as Ellie in the front offices where visibility was high and where the women in most of the top jobs were staid, mature types, gave rise to a certain amount of facetiousness. Most of it was harmless but occasionally there was a speculative or salacious observation. Bob took it all in stride and countered none of it. Everyone knew where he stood on the matter of involvements among company personnel. He'd witnessed the fallout of people hurt, marriages on the rocks, careers side-tracked, and he'd have none of it. It wasn't the moral aspect of the thing that concerned him. There were transgressions in his past. It was simply a matter of good policy.

He readily admitted Ellie made an appealing picture but admiring didn't imply desiring and while it pleased him to have so attractive a secretary it went no further.

The reverse was not quite true. Ellie used to study him in the pauses when he was dictating, examining at her leisure the clean-cut profile, the lift of dark hair above his forehead, wondering what it would be like to have him regard her as someone other than the girl who typed his letters and handled his telephone calls. And while other secretaries were delighted to have their bosses out of town, she was happiest when he was there. She'd never had a romantic involvement of any depth although she'd gone to dances and out on dates from the time she was sixteen. There just was never anyone she cared enough about to see on a steady basis. Joan chided her about it and tried to remedy it by arranging dates for her with flight crew members but none of them ever came to anything. Now for the first time Ellie found someone to daydream about.

She was aware, of course, that Bob was married and that he had two sons, eleven and thirteen. It was difficult, however, to guess what his wife was like. They said she was very much part of the art scene, very knowledgeable in the field of art. She was presently engaged in research for a Harvard professor who was an authority on Stone Age art. But obviously no conclusions could be reached on the basis of such meager information and Ellie would have given a lot to know what she was really like.

In October John Sutton, the company vice president and general manager, was selected by the administration in Washington to fill a prestigious government post, an honor duly noted by the news media to the credit of Consolidated Steel. To mark the event the company arranged a farewell dinner for him at a country club in Greenwich and Bob and Sally Glynn, who were longtime friends planned a cocktail party at their home to precede the dinner.

Mr. Sutton was a handsome, genial man, well liked in all circles, and a large number of company people were invited to attend the double affair. To Ellie's surprise she found herself included. She was in the job only two months at the time and had no such expectation but she suspected it was more a matter of not knowing how to exclude her. After all, she was Mr. Glynn's secretary and all the executive secretaries had been invited.

The appointed Saturday was an Indian summer day, the sun strong, the air so mild everyone dressed as if it were

September. Ellie wore a soft, water-green dress and a gold chain her father had given her shortly before he died. Marge Foster organized the transportation and arranged for Ellie, Mrs. Cooper and Kitty Adams, another secretary, to drive up in her car. All the way there, sitting in back beside the quiet Mrs. Cooper, Ellie wondered what kind of house Bob lived in and what his wife would be like.

The first thing that struck her about his home on the outskirts of Greenwich was how much it resembled her old home in Oyster Bay. It backed on the water, a haphazard lawn tipping down to where a couple of small boats were tied. Trees grew at random and flower beds were casual. The house itself, however, was much larger and grander and it was impossible to guess how many rooms it had but there was the same off-hand charm, the same prodigal use of space which marked so many homes of that era. At the rear facing the water was a large stone terrace where many of the guests had already congregated, drinks served them by a crew of white-coated waiters.

John Sutton and Bob and Sally Glynn greeted people as they arrived and later mingled among them. Drink in hand, Ellie watched as Sally moved through the gathering, practiced, self-assured, skillfully paying attention to guests in the order of their importance. Assessing the wife of a man she was so drawn to, Ellie's feminine eye missed nothing. Sally appeared to be in her mid-thirties, tall, trim, brown hair cut in a casual fashion, a straight nose, firm jaw line and large, dark-rimmed glasses which gave her a rather scholarly look. She wore a tailored blue and gray print dress, little makeup and no jewelry except for pearl clip earrings. Although her manner had a certain contrived charm she was the perfect hostess. There was nothing she could be faulted with. Toward the end she came to where Ellie was standing and said how glad she was she could come.

"You're the new secretary," she remarked. Ellie smiled and nodded.

"I hope you'll be happy in the job."

"I'm sure I will."

She murmured something to the effect that she hoped Ellie was enjoying the party and moved on. It was a meaningless exchange, a small social ritual ordained by the occasion, nothing more, and if Sally had any reservations about so young and pretty a girl in daily contact with her husband, she gave no indication of it. Later Ellie saw her joined by a suave, bearded, fair-haired man she introduced as Professor Martin Macaulay and until the cocktail party ended she gave him a lot of her attention.

At the edge of the terrace, looking across the lawn, Ellie was struck again by the memories of her childhood that the setting evoked. Two boys were down on the narrow beach throwing sticks into the water for a black Labrador—dark-haired, bare-footed youngsters and she assumed they were Bob's sons. The only time she exchanged conversation with him was when she arrived.

"I'm glad you made it, Ellie," he said. "I was afraid you might not come."

Once later he smiled at her across the terrace and started toward her but people intervened and waylaid him and he never reached her.

Dinner at the country club was an elegant affair and at the end there were speeches and presentations. Shortly afterward guests began to leave. Ellie was halfway down the drive with Marge when she remembered her scarf left on a chair at the dinner and she hurried back. Departing guests saying last goodnights were still exiting the building and she looked for Bob as she wove her way among them but there was no sign of him. Then as she came out on the drive a second time she almost literally bumped into him.

"I thought you'd gone," he said.

Out of breath she explained adding that Marge and the others were waiting for her in the car down on the road.

"I'll walk down with you. This place should be better lighted." And taking her hand he went the length of the shadowy driveway with her.

All the way home her thoughts drifted around those few minutes walking beside him, her hand in his. The silent Mrs. Cooper sitting next to her and Marge and Kitty chatting away in front might have been part of another world. She thought about Sally, attractive, coolly competent, self-possessed and she admitted to herself reluctantly that Sally was just the kind of person she would expect Bob to be married to. And she wondered about Professor Macaulay

At the office on Monday Bob made only a single reference to the occasion. "Did you all get home okay Saturday night?"

"Yes, we did. We made better time than going up."

"Good." And that was the end of it.

Late in November he went to the Philippines and his return set off a period of increased activity at the office. So many reports had to be written and so many specification lists typed up that Marge was pressed into service to help out. They worked on after hours one night and at six-thirty Bob took them downstairs to a little restaurant off the lobby where they had something to eat. Back upstairs they continued to work until finally he came out of his office looking at his watch.

"It's eight-thirty. Let's call it a day."

He drove them uptown, letting Marge off at Grand Central and continuing on to 55th Street where Ellie thanked him and said good night.

The next night they worked late again but Marge left at six, pleading a previous engagement. This time they didn't eat downstairs.

"How about putting our things on and going out some place to eat? Would you like that?"

Ellie smiled. "That sounds lovely."

It was a clear cold evening and they walked through silent, almost deserted streets. The hordes of people who descended on the Wall Street area for the working day and abandoned it at the day's end seemed to her like the tide—sweeping in at early morning and spreading to the farthest reach, then as purposefully retreating at nightfall, ebbing, leaving streets as silent and solitary as a distant tide-drained beach. Their steps clicked on the empty sidewalks and the street lights threw their faces into glow and shadow as they advanced upon them and left them behind. From a foreign ship in the East River came the pungent smell of coffee, conjuring up visions of lush, exotic places.

At a small, half-empty Spanish restaurant on a nearby side street they were greeted effusively by its plump Latin proprietor and seated with elaborate courtesy. On the table between them an earthenware bowl held gaudy red and yellow flowers and the walls around them were set with tiles decorated in cobalt blue. The foreignness of the place thrilled her and made her want to exclaim but she behaved sedately, the lessons of her early schooling having been well-learned. At Bob's recommendation she ate mussels—something she never dreamed she'd eat—and an omelet Valencia style, both of which she found delicious. During dinner he talked about foreign countries he'd been to and Ellie drank in every word. Once when she was unsure whether or not a story he related was to be taken seriously she waited, her eyes riveted on his face. Then he smiled and she smiled too and he looked at her with unexpected softness for having reached back across years and brought into startling clarity a little boy who was all too quickly growing up.

Back at the office business demeanor was resumed and they worked another hour before calling it quits. Then as he had on the previous evening he drove her home and as she got out of the car she put her hand impulsively on his.

"Thank you so much. I had such a lovely time." She was thinking of their dinner in the Spanish restaurant.

He laughed. "On the contrary. Thank you, Ellie."

The week before Christmas brought a festive air to the office and there were parties and lunches and extra time allowed for shopping. Marge Foster decorated a small tree and set it on one of the coffee tables and fastened a sprig of holly to her lapel. One morning at ten o'clock she was delegated to make reservations for six at Delmonico's. Bob, Mr. Steele and Mr. Loring were taking their secretaries to lunch. Ellie was hard put to hide her pleasure.

The first snow of winter was falling when they came out of the building and it added a perfect holiday touch to the occasion. In the cozy warmth of the restaurant Ellie watched it descend outside the tall windows, thick flakes that drifted, stalled and sometimes seemed to float upward. Nearby the lights of a huge tree flicked off and on amidst ornaments and tinsel and silver rain. Christmas carols, sweet-sounding and muted, came from somewhere around them. They had drinks—Ellie ordered Scotch and soda when she saw that was what Bob ordered—and afterward they had lunch. They talked about things of no consequence and they laughed a lot. Even Mrs. Cooper smiled once or twice. Two hours flew by.

Nearly an inch of snow had accumulated by the time they left and the sidewalks were slippery. Bob looked down at Ellie's flimsy high-heeled shoes and shook his head.

"You'd better hold on to me," he said. He drew her arm through his and anchored her hand with his own. It was as she sometimes dreamed he and she might walk, and all the way back to the office she was silent, the better to store it away in her memory.

March was a wet and dreary month. Dressing for work that Tuesday morning, Ellie deplored the need for yet another day of rainy-day clothes—oxfords and the wool skirt and cardigan she wore under her raincoat for warmth. But during the afternoon the rain stopped and looking upward into the sky from their lofty windows she saw the cloud masses part to let shafts of sunlight through. The weather turned fair.

Five o'clock, her desktop cleared, the files locked, she was about to leave when Bob came to the door of his office and stopped her.

"Would you mind very much waiting, Ellie? There's a call coming through from Ecuador and afterward I'd like to dictate a letter."

"I don't mind at all," she said, and while she waited she did some odd jobs at her desk. The call finally came through, the letter was dictated and typed. As he had done before when she stayed on after hours he offered to drive her home. They walked the couple of blocks to the parking lot through drying streets and the wind that had blown the rain away nudged their faces. It came from the south, mild, tantalizing, hinting of change.

"It feels like spring," she said. "My favorite season."

"Mine too," and he glanced her way approvingly.

The drive uptown was leisurely, the traffic rush over, and when she thanked him for the ride and started to get out in front of her brownstone, he held her back. Quite suddenly the prospect of a solitary meal at home—Sally was out of town—seemed depressingly uninviting.

"How about having some dinner together, Ellie, shall we? Unless you have something better to do."

"That sounds lovely," she said and her face lit up.

"No, I don't have anything else to do." But she looked down at her shoes and raincoat. "Would you mind if I took a minute to change my coat and shoes?"

"Of course not."

"Won't you come in?"

"I'll wait here."

"Oh no, please come in."

As soon as she said it she wondered what prompted her words. Never before had she issued such an invitation to anyone when Joan was away. Yet the truth was she'd daydreamed of just such circumstances—the two of them alone together secure against intrusion, heedless of rights and wrongs. All the experiences of her growing up, the boys she'd dated and dismissed, the occasional crushes that came to nothing, all of it seemed to be no more than marking time until their paths so inevitably crossed. That he was mature, experienced and worldly-wise quickened her pulse and the fact that he'd fathered two children stirred her inexplicably.

She led the way up the single flight of stairs and once inside switched on the lamps at either end of the couch. Dulcinea, curled against a russet cushion, blinked her eyes at the light and yawned. Ellie put away their coats.

"Can I fix you a drink? Scotch?"

"Fine. Make a drink for yourself too. I don't like to drink alone."

She got glasses out of the kitchen cupboard, ice from the refrigerator, measured and poured the Scotch. Bob leaned against the kitchen doorway watching her. She topped each glass with soda and handed him one. He took it but didn't drink.

"You shouldn't have invited me in."

"Why not?"

For answer he set his glass down on the kitchen counter, took hers away from her and set it down alongside. Then he held her face up and softly kissed her mouth. It was with no more design than a head is bent toward a flower to inhale its scent.

"That's why," he said when the kiss ended.

"I wanted you to kiss me," she said guilelessly.

She studied the mouth that moments before had been pressed against hers, then putting her hands on either side of his face she kissed him back. The hunger of it caught him unaware and provided the spark that set the fire blazing. He had spoken lightly, playfully, and he'd imagined if he kissed her at all they would draw apart laughing and maybe tease a little about it afterward. He hadn't suspected the kiss would lead to a lengthier kiss, and to another deeper kiss. He hadn't intended his arms to tighten around her. Nor could he have anticipated the fervor of her response.

Swept along on a tide she made no attempt to hold back, she nevertheless became conscious of the enormity of what she was doing. They were standing in the bedroom and it was as if the floor suddenly shifted under her feet. All through her formative years she had been warned of the perils of such conduct and she had absorbed the teaching without question. Yet here she was in the very circumstances she'd been counseled against, caution thrown to the winds the first time it was put to the test.

When she let him lead her to the bedroom (no, that wasn't quite the truth—she lit the way), she gave her tacit consent to what would follow. To retreat now would surely be to lose him forever. Yet might not so ready a surrender invite the same loss? To the backward glance at ignored injunctions was added a more immediate confusion and she wavered. But what would he make of such behavior, bold and timid by turn? What would he think of her? No. She had yearned for him, dreamed of him, despaired of anything ever coming of all her longings. Now it had happened. It might never happen again. And even as Bob told himself that this was the place to stop, to let her go, she put her arms around him and held her mouth up to his.

Later, much later, drowsy and relaxed, their heads on a shared pillow, he raised himself on his arm and tipped up her face.

"You never made love before, did you, Ellie?"

"No."

"Why did you do it?"

She closed her eyes. It never occurred to her she'd be asked to explain. And what was there to say? Because he smiled at her in a certain way? Used a softer tone of voice when he spoke to her? No, there was much more. He seemed to be someone she'd searched for, someone she'd known and lost and found again, someone she knew instinctively, half memory and half dream. But how could she explain a thing she scarcely understood herself—much less say why it had led to this hour? She groped for the telling words but like a dream that fades before the mind can fasten on it they slipped away beyond her reach.

"Why, Ellie?"

"Because I love you." It was all the answer she could think to make, and it was true, even though as she said the words she questioned the wisdom of so sweeping an admission so precipitately made. He might shrink back from something he hadn't bargained for, might shy away, wary of ties he didn't seek. The words hung between them in unsteady balance. Then he bent his head against her shoulder and silently kissed her throat. There was something of surrender in the gesture that refuted all her fears and she felt suddenly wise, as if she'd stumbled on the secret of conquest.

They were dressed.

"You must be hungry, Ellie. I know I am."

"We don't have to go out," she said earnestly. "I can make peanut butter sandwiches."

He smiled, hesitated. "I'd like nothing better."

He sat at the kitchen table and as she got out plates and spoons, cups and saucers, he set them down in places across from each other. He folded two paper napkins. He poured milk into a saucer for Dulcinea who was meowing around their feet.

She cut the sandwiches in threes to make them look pretty and she arranged them on a porcelain plate that had belonged to her grandmother, a plate bordered with roses and rimmed with gold. He took it out of her hands and set it down in the middle of the table.

"Elegant," he said and she flushed with pleasure.

Sitting opposite each other they ate—he as composed as if this had happened a dozen times before, she in a trance, her mouth swollen from his kisses, her mind giddied by the memory of his weight on her breast.

From ecstasy she plummeted to despair. In the following days not by the least word or glance did he acknowledge that anything had happened between them. They went about their usual daily routine the same as always and even when they were alone in his office he said nothing he would not ordinarily have said, looked at her no differently than he had all the months before. It puzzled her at first, then plunged her into scorching, shame-filled misery. He regretted it. It was a mistake. To act as if it had never happened was as close as he could come to undoing it. Where in the beginning the recollection of that hour lifted her to towering heights, now she cringed, seeing herself through his eyes—impetuous, awkward, foolishly saying she loved him. Was ever love more bungled? She thought of all the beautiful, sophisticated women who would be his at the snap of a finger and she wondered what impelled him to kiss her that first time.

For Bob the memory of that evening blazed with guilt. He viewed what had happened as an aberration for which he was solely to blame and a departure from his normal standards of conduct he found impossible to account for, much less excuse. She was a child, an innocent one at that, not much older than his oldest son. He was nearly twice her age. It was he who should have stepped back, put her aside, teased her and turned the fateful moments into light-hearted play. How could he have let it go full circle? His mouth tightened remembering the times he'd aired his views about just such matters. Short-sighted, unwise, foolish, senseless. Those were some of the words he'd used and each now had a crushing, private meaning. To say nothing of the consequences should the episode ever come to light. His career, built upon single-minded dedication and filled with promise would be ended. Involvements such as this were given short shrift by the top office. No, nothing could erase that hour but he was determined it would never be repeated. Somehow his relationship with Ellie had to be put back on its former basis.

He might as well have tried to divert Niagara. Meeting her clear, candid gaze across his desk, seeing the supple form, the slim young arms, he couldn't help but remember. And remembering stirred desire. To push him further into retreat was the bewilderment he sometimes glimpsed in Ellie's eyes. It was obvious she expected him to acknowledge by some least smile or word what had happened between them and as time passed and none was forthcoming the bewilderment turned to pain. It was more than he could endure. There had to be a middle way.

A week went by and part of another and then at five o'clock on a Friday afternoon he stopped her as she was taking the signed mail from his desk. The day had been sunny and a last glow filled the office with bright, reflected light. He stood against it, his back to the window.

"Would you like to have dinner at the Hotel Pierre tonight, Ellie? There are Flamenco dancers from Spain, I'm told."

Her heart leaped. "That sounds lovely," she said and her face became radiant.

He took his car keys out of his jacket pocket and slid them across the desk. "Why don't you go on ahead and wait for me in the car? You know where I keep it. I'll be about ten or fifteen minutes."

His voice was casual, the expression on his face noncommittal, but the intimacy implied in that simple act struck her with such force she trembled. She picked up the keys from his desk and carried them outside as if he had given her a gold ring.

The Hotel Pierre was on Fifth Avenue at the lower end of Central Park, built at the same time and along the same massive lines as many of the mansions that gave the avenue so much of its elegance. Inside it was beautiful in a dim, understated fashion, and the cocktail lounge where they went first for drinks appeared to be a reluctant concession to a contemporary vogue. They sat in deep chairs whose size precluded closeness.

How badly she had misjudged him! All the pain and puzzlement of the preceding days were swept away in a flash leaving her light-headed with joy and anticipation. But oddly enough as the evening progressed there was no return in either talk or gesture to anything that could be construed as intimacy. They might have been good friends amiably dallying over drinks, engaged in pleasant conversation, enjoying each other's company, and while he was attentive and approving it was as if a wall had been built around that wondrous hour they'd shared, sealing it away.

Driving up from Wall Street they had talked about the most commonplace things, he directing the conversation and she responding. And aside from helping her out of the car and steering her through the hotel lobby to the cocktail lounge he didn't touch her. Her hand lay within reach on the broad arm of her chair but it was left undisturbed. She was mystified and when they finished their drinks and he asked if she'd like another she said yes. She thought a second drink might break down his reserve but it did nothing of the sort. He talked about a variety of things in delightful and amusing ways so that she hung on his words, laughing and serious in turn but not by even the most indirect reference was anything personal alluded to.

They went in to dinner. Throughout the meal and afterward the conversation followed the same pattern. When they got up to dance Ellie was sure there would be at least an unspoken admission in the way he held her but there too she was wrong. There was nothing to be interpreted from his arms around her, only a sort of teasing once when he chucked her under the chin but that was like something her brother might have done.

The Flamenco dancers whirled onto the floor in an explosion of guitars and castanets, staccato heels and spinning scarlet ruffles. The women were exotic creatures, black hair, penciled eyes, dagger-length earrings, the men sleek and arrogant. The music they danced to was strange, the melody one of intricate melancholy and when a woman sang it was a haunting cry out of Africa. She stood with arms akimbo, face up-tilted, and her voice was as clear and sharp as glass. They were such a commanding troupe of people, so aggressively skilled, so stirringly provocative, that it caused a sense of her own inadequacies to take shape inside her and grow into sharper and sharper focus. Sitting in mute admiration she was woefully conscious of her pale dress with its narrow belt, the modest silver bracelet on her arm, and she wished she had dark eyes and strong brown shoulders. Her hand, resting on the table still untouched was all the proof needed of her shortcomings.

The entertainment over, Bob asked for the check and when it came he signed it. He turned to her then.

"Shall I take you home, Ellie? Shall we have a last drink in the bar? What would you like?"

She looked at him with wide steady eyes and slowly shook her head.

"Let me stay with you," she said and she took his hand in both of hers and held it tightly.

The words, so direct and unanticipated, stunned him and an emotion he would have believed himself incapable of caught him in its grip. He clenched his hands around hers and lifted them to his lips.

That was how it began and once started there was no turning back. His initial resolve melted away. One part of his mind urged him to remember the risks he ran. He could lose all he'd worked for as well as Sally and his sons. The thought sobered him but only for a time. It could be handled, he decided. He had only to remember Ellie's lifted face, the words she spoke and all prudence slipped away. It would take the utmost caution and judgment but it could be done. The sweep of her love overwhelmed him. What did she know of him to love him so blindly? How had he earned such love? There was a sweetness about her, an artlessness that touched him profoundly yet beneath her innocence lay a womanliness as ancient as Eve. The ardor of her embraces kindled passion in him that matched the passions of his youth and left him rapt and possessed. It was unlike anything he had ever known or expected to experience.

Discretion dictated the pace of their meetings and prevented an extravagance which in the first great rush of love they might easily have succumbed to. Their behavior toward each other on all occasions was circumspect and no place was any suspicion aroused. Because Bob was away a lot, the nights they could spend together were not all that many and though they chafed when the time between was long, it heightened the ravishment of the first returning kiss.

No, he couldn't give her up but as time passed a basic integrity forced him to consider their relationship from Ellie's standpoint. It was grossly unfair to her. He was a married man with a wife and two sons and nothing would change that irrevocable fact, nor did he have any reason or wish to change it. The road they were on for Ellie led nowhere and as long as he preempted her time he thwarted her chances of meeting someone who could give her all the things that he could not.

He steeled himself to tell her that for her sake the affair must end. In all decency he could do no less. At least the circumstances must be set out before her and she must understand them. To the wrongs already assembled he wouldn't add the wrong of leading her on. But the night he faced her with the facts he had so reluctantly prepared, she burst into a storm of tears and clung to him.

"I know all that you're telling me," she wept. "I know it and I don't care."

He held her close. "But Ellie, you have to care. You have to think of your future."

"It's mine to do with as I please!"

"This can't go on indefinitely. I can't let you go on wasting your time."

"Wasting my time? Is that how you think of it? Oh Bob, how can you say these things? We love each other. How can you want this to end?"

Relief made him bold. "I don't, kitten, I don't but it must. You should be going out on dates with boys your own age, thinking of getting married and starting a family. I'm taking time out of the best years of your life and there's nothing I can offer you."

"I'm not asking you to offer me anything."

"The day may come when you'll bitterly regret this. I don't want that to happen."

"I'll never regret loving you, Bob. Never." She pressed her wet cheek against his face. "Don't put me out of your life, I beg you. I don't want anyone but you."

He sighed deeply and stroked her hair, soothing her. His mind was at ease. He'd done his best to persuade her but she refused to consider it. Whatever the future held, it couldn't be said he deceived her. His silence was his assent and finally, tears still clinging to her lashes, she smiled at him.

It wasn't wise, it wasn't smart, but in his case and hers they weren't dealing with choice. It was done. All that remained was to handle it as discreetly as possible.

Sometimes when she was buried in his arms she'd say to him, "This is my real life." His response would be to hold her closer. Though inwardly he acknowledged that his most blissful hours were those they spent together, he never put those thoughts in words. Ellie was tremendously important to him but at no time did he say anything which would lead her to believe she might become more to him than she was.

17.

As marriages went Bob and Sally Glynn's was no different from countless others—early crowded years, satisfying years when love burned brightly and problems melted away in the comfort of each other's arms. Though money was often short their dreams sustained them. Because Bob had a keen mind, set goals for himself and acted on them, the dreams slowly materialized and he moved ahead until they reached an enviably affluent level beyond which opportunity continued to beckon. At the same time, however, the very mechanism which brought them forward drove them apart. It seemed an inevitable progression and if their feelings for each other had lapsed into complacency, their relationship was harmonious and in social circles they were regarded as a not unhappy couple.

Sally was a bright, attractive, ambitious woman who had turned an early interest in art into an absorbing part-time career for herself, and Bob admired her for it though it widened the gulf between them. Her goals were strictly personal ones and if they concerned things of no great importance to him he made no attempt to curb her or to criticize. For her part she was careful to pay lip service to the life style his successful career afforded them and which she had no wish to relinquish. She had little interest in sex though she liked to give the impression she had and the mild deception reinforced the image created among their friends that theirs was a substantial and satisfying marriage. Actually the common ground they once shared had eroded over the years till little was left. The one firm bond between them was their children.

Scott, the older, was a serious reticent boy, good at his studies, only mildly interested in the sports his younger brother reveled in. Davie was the opposite, bubbling, boisterous, given to fervent enthusiasms that faded as promptly as they cropped up but he was a bright boy, quick to learn, and neither he nor Scott gave their parents any cause for concern. On the contrary, they were a source of deep pride.

The Glynns came from Denver, Bob the son of parents whose resources were drained away by the ill health of a younger child, a burden they coped with as best they could. Miraculously, when the boy reached his teens he mended and all the early problems disappeared. It did, however, leave the family permanently short of funds but Bob belonged to a generation of people who expected to work hard and it wouldn't have occurred to him to complain about his struggles to put himself through college, get a university degree and secure a foothold in the business world. That was the lot of most of his contemporaries and it was accepted as the norm. By the time he transferred to New York and connected with Consolidated Steel he had married the girl down the street and their two sons were born.

Bob traveled a lot and each time a foreign assignment came up he urged Sally to go with him. When the children were young she couldn't leave them but later an aunt of Sally's, widowed and childless, found herself uprooted and came to make her home with them. It gave Sally freedom to come and go as she pleased and in response to Bob's urging, she did go once to London with him and another time to Mexico City but she didn't really enjoy foreign travel and when further trips came up she begged off. They became used to being without each other, mostly a few days at a time, but frequently for longer periods. Then much would be made of his return, friends invited in for dinner and a busy round of social events embarked upon. Occasionally the thought crossed her mind that he might well take some woman to bed but as long as her security wasn't threatened, what difference did it make? Even if she knew it to be a fact she'd be foolish to make an issue of it and so she shrugged the thought away. Meanwhile the closeness they once enjoyed was becoming a thing of the past.

For Sally the years of early motherhood were the best of her marriage. The children's dependence on her gave her life purpose but as they grew older and their need of her lessened she was left feeling restless and vaguely unhappy. In her efforts to find something to fill the void she helped out at a small, newly established art gallery, the first of its kind to make an appearance in Greenwich. Art had interested her since her college days and though she lacked creative ability of her own, she admired it in others and she had excellent taste and judgment. Furthermore, most of the people involved in the venture were socially prominent and this was important to her. When the post of curator became vacant she was asked to fill it and because it was soon apparent that she was an able administrator as well, she took on other duties. She set up exhibitions and arranged for guest speakers and as these were things that kept the gallery solvent they carried considerable weight.

When Professor Martin Macaulay came down from Harvard to give a talk on prehistoric art he was prepared to face the usual daunting number of empty seats but to his surprise he spoke before a large and responsive audience. At the small private reception immediately following he was introduced to Sally as the person responsible. He was profuse in his thanks and before the evening was over he mentioned to her that he was in need of someone to do occasional research for him in New York in connection with a book he was writing. He wondered if she would be interested. Sally could think of nothing she would like more.

Bob encouraged her, glad she'd found an outlet for her talents, pleased to see her involved in something she enjoyed and did well. Though it widened the ground that already existed between them, he was proud of her accomplishments.

As her circle of friends in this new area grew, she did everything she could to present herself in the best possible light. There was no problem with her standing in the community which was at a gratifying level. Her home was beautiful, her husband and children smart and personable, even Aunt Belle, a gentle, unassuming old lady, passed with flying colors. The problem was Howard, Bob's younger brother.

Howard was a born loser, almost thirty but unable to hold any job for more than a few months. He'd show up from time to time, broke and needing a place to stay and there was no question of refusing him. Whether or not it was the result of his sickly childhood, he was lazy and unmotivated, content to live from hand to mouth, undisturbed by having to ask for handouts which he called loans and which he always promised earnestly to pay back but never did. He was a thorn in Sally's side.

She flatly refused to let him bring his friends to the house—people as shiftless as himself—but there was nothing she could do about the wreck of a car he parked in the driveway. He spent hours tinkering with it, assuring her that once he got it going he'd be on his way. Scott and Davie helped him and because he was good-natured and full of jokes, they loved him.

She had it out with Bob one night after he'd been there three months. I don't care how you do it, she told him, but he has to go. Howard had been talking about a fellow he knew in Phoenix who ran a movie house and who once said that any time Howard wanted a job he could use him. He thought he'd like to go out there and give it a try but the problem was transportation. His car was finished. However he told Bob he knew where he could get a good motorcycle for eight hundred dollars and if Bob could lend him the money plus a few extra dollars for expenses along the way, he'd get going. Sally bit her lip watching Bob hand over a thousand dollars knowing he'd never get it back but she admitted to herself that it was worth every penny if it kept Howard away. And one morning not too much later, after hugging the boys goodbye, he waved jauntily to Sally and roared off.

At first Sally stayed on in her job at the gallery but as the professor's work began to demand more time she relinquished it. She traveled regularly to New York and sometimes to Boston where she spent hours in libraries and museums, engrossed in her assignments. Though her duties consisted of little more than information-gathering she was skillful in what she did, going beyond it to suggest and recommend until the professor came to depend on her assistance in other related matters as well. It didn't matter to her that what he paid her barely covered her expenses. He was unmarried and inclined to be frugal. The work brought her into a small, exclusive world where often she rubbed elbows with people of immense distinction. She basked in the reflected glory. Once more her life had purpose and inwardly she gloated. Married to a successful man, successful in her own right, she had the best of both worlds.

18.

One of the surest signs of progress at the sanatorium was a move from the infirmary to a rest cottage, each named for the benefactor whose generosity built it. No money-back guarantees were given and no one dared think he was then home free but it was headway, a corner turned, the worst over.

Anderson cottage was set at an angle to the infirmary and slightly higher and Ellie had often watched its chimney smoke rising above the dense trees that surrounded it. Having studied it curiously for months her face lit up with pleasure when she was told that was where she was going and that she was ready to go.

Wrapped up against the rain and a blustery wind, she fought her way from the van along the path to the front door. Inside a fire blazed on a wide stone fireplace, snapping and crackling, filling the room with a fragrant piney aroma. A young woman sat with her back to it, cross-legged on a bearskin rug, drying her long blond hair. A cigarette burned in an ashtray on the floor beside her. She was a slender figure in an apple-green robe, her face as pretty and blank as a doll's. The commotion caused by their arrival—Charlie thumping suitcases through the door, Trudy groaning over the cardboard carton she clutched against her chest—had no visible effect on her. She sat with her head tipped back, one arm bracing herself, her free hand lifting her hair out from her shoulders in slow, languorous movements. Not until Charlie greeted her did she turn her head.

"Nona," he said, "this is Ellie Stuart, your new cottage mate." Nona murmured a few words with an air of studied aloofness.

The room, however, had a welcoming coziness to it. It was large and casually furnished, two couches across from each other at right angles to the fireplace, worn but comfortable chairs, shelves of books, the mounted head of an antlered deer over the front door where it peered into the room with sad, surprised eyes. At the far end was a dining area with small hallways on either side of it, each leading to two bedrooms.

Charlie, the moving job finished, lingered by the front door. He was a sociable man and he enjoyed chatting with the patients, drawing out the encounters as long as possible. With his hand on the doorknob he predicted a dry summer.

"A rainy spring like we've had," he said, "that means a switch to good weather. I've seen it happen that way time and again. And I've been here twenty-six years now, nearly twenty-seven. Brought my wife up here on a winter day when the snow was up to the rooftops. Worst winter they'd had in forty years they said. And when spring finally came they said it was one of the rainiest. Roads weren't paved then and cars got stuck in the mud as bad as they'd gotten stuck in the snow. Terrible rains. No let up. But there was a pretty summer that year. I'll never forget it." He paused and his face softened as some brief joyful memory came to mind. No one said anything and he opened the door partway as if to go. Some chilly air blew in and he thought better of it and closed it.

"Sunny days, warm nights," he went on, "and all this good air. She was so much better. She'd been dying down in Staten Island. Here she got up every day. We went out walking. We had a couple of rooms downtown and she even cooked a meal now and then. Things she hadn't been able to do before. It lasted five years. Five years we wouldn't have had otherwise. Of course, they didn't have the drugs then. You folks are so much better off today. There's no comparison."

His face held no trace of bitterness but if anything reflected content that she'd been granted those few extra years. How could anyone be thankful for such a pittance, Ellie wondered. In his place she would have stormed and sworn at fate. Why were people satisfied with such crumbs?

He opened the door again, holding it ajar, and once again some chilly air blew in.

"For God's sake, Charlie," Nona said, speaking between her teeth, her eyes narrowed. "Either go or stay. But close the damn door!"

He glanced over at her uneasily. "I'm sorry. I wasn't thinking. I'd better move along." And he and Trudy left.

That was typical of Nona. Irritable, impatient, indifferent to everything in which she had no personal interest. At first she hardly acknowledged Ellie's presence except to regard her critically as she ate her meals without complaint. The food was seldom to Nona's liking and often she sent things back to the kitchen half-tasted, ordering sandwiches and milkshakes from town instead. Her conversation emitted a continuous pained discontent and she found fault on all sides. The water wasn't hot enough, her porch was too shaded, the sheets had too much starch.

She was married, childless. She came from a small town in North Carolina where her family had settled three generations ago and where her husband was on the administrative staff of the town's prestigious university. He came up to see her shortly after Ellie moved to the cottage, a nice-looking, pleasant-mannered man, very much concerned about his wife's health. The doctors told him that a year at most would see her back on her feet but Nona greeted the news skeptically. When he remarked it seemed to him she was luckier than most she cut him off.

"Please," she snapped, "don't tell me I'm lucky!"

He excused her ill temper on the grounds of her health and treated her with a fondness she did little to deserve. Ellie constantly ran the risk of being put down and it made her uncomfortable. One afternoon as they sat together in the living room Ellie commented on an item in the sanatorium's weekly news bulletin which had just arrived.

"There's to be a picnic at Whiteface Mountain next Sunday for everyone on three hours exercise," she said. "Doesn't that sound nice?"

"My God, Ellie, you're easily pleased."

Then Tino Ramirez came on the scene and everything changed. He was a patient in a cottage on the other side of the grounds within five months of his discharge. They met at one of the tea parties held every Sunday afternoon during the summer in a parlor in the Administration Building. Nona had gone reluctantly. It was a waste of time, she remarked. Nevertheless she dressed carefully—white slacks that clung smoothly to her slim hips, a pale yellow sweater, a string of ivory beads.

The room was crowded and she stood a little apart, teacup in hand, a bored expression on her face but stunning in spite of it. She caught Tino's eye. He started to look away, looked back, then edged his way toward her until he stood next to her. They had never seen each other before and he studied her slowly, deliberately, half smiling. Nona stared back briefly but long enough to see his cool appraisal turn into manifest approval. He glanced down disdainfully at the teacups, his own and hers.

"A Martini would go better," he said.

A flicker of interest crossed her face. "How might that miracle be accomplished."

"I'm your man when it comes to miracles."

She responded with a faint smile. Putting a hand under her elbow, he steered her across the room, swaggering as he walked, their teacups left on a table along the way.

Ellie had never seen Tino before and she wouldn't have paid any attention to him except for the brazen way he looked at Nona. He had a husky build, dark shrewd eyes, a swarthy complexion and there was a certain crude sophistication about him. His clothes were expensive, a gold watch glistened below the cuff of his sleeve, a diamond flashed from his pinky. He was not the type one would expect Nona to be attracted to but when she returned to the cottage that evening just before nine o'clock her face was flushed and cryptic, her eyes speculative. They'd been downtown having drinks and dinner, she said. She reported it only because she was curious to know if she'd been missed.

From then on Tino began to show up at the cottage on a regular basis during the late afternoon visiting hours. Ellie didn't like him any better as she got to know him. He was born in Cuba and raised in Miami where by the time he was in his mid-twenties he'd made a lot of money in the real estate business. He now owned a marina which in addition to the usual services rented boats for daytime fishing excursions and chartered large sailboats for cruising in the Caribbean. He talked about weekends in Jamaica and San Juan, race tracks, casinos, expensive hotels and flashy nightclubs. He made it plain that the people he knew had money and the smirk on his face implied a lot of it came from dubious sources. His illness was a setback. The diagnosis of tuberculosis followed a visit to a doctor because of what he believed to be a cigarette cough but he was lucky. The disease was in an early stage, confined to a small area in his left lung and his cure was easily managed.

His advent into Nona's life sparked a complete transformation. Her moodiness and discontent vanished. The monotony that had so tried her patience gave way to dreamy silences and nervous anticipation. She spent her time preoccupied by her clothes and makeup, devoted an hour each day to dressing for Tino's visit. She'd watch for him from the living room windows with feverish expectancy and when he arrived, cigarette in the corner of his mouth, she stood waiting to greet him, to do his bidding whatever it might be. For one who had been so wholly self-centered, it came as a surprise to see her subservient and anxious to please.

Sometimes they'd go out on the grounds. Other times, especially if the weather was bad, they'd sit on the couch by the fireplace, Tino pressing her against the end, his knees widespread, his arm along the back above her shoulders. Often his conversation was crude and this amused Nona.

She'd smile slyly and give him sidelong looks while twisting a strand of her long pale hair round and round her finger.

Their behavior was embarrassing and Ellie and Carmen kept out of their way even though it meant staying in their rooms. Their bedrooms were on one side of the cottage, Nona's on the other. The fourth bedroom belonged to Nancy Tyler who was down at the general hospital having a resection and the door was closed awaiting her return.

More and more often Nona's room became the setting for Tino's visits. Sometimes the door was left open, sometimes not. One afternoon Tino arrived bringing sandwiches and containers of coffee and he and Nona retired to her room. They were still behind her closed door at six o'clock when the kitchen crew carried in the dinner trays. Ellie and Carmen ate their meal alone and spent a puzzled, uncomfortable evening in the living room. Tino was still there at nine-thirty when they put out the lights.

They stood a few moments outside their rooms talking in muted voices, not knowing what to think at such blatant disregard of the rules. Their prime concern was that Nona and Tino might be caught. Miss MacIntyre patrolled the grounds at night and chose cottages at random to drop in on. Even a minor infraction of the rule—a radio going after nine-thirty, a light still on—was treated as delinquency. It was impossible to predict her reaction were she to walk in on such a transgression.

"How can she be so stupid?" Ellie asked. "To take such a chance for someone like Tino."

Carmen shook her head soberly. "She's foolish, terribly foolish. Sooner or later they'll be found out if this goes on. And it's Nona I'm sorry for. She's the one who'll suffer."

Tino wouldn't. If caught they'd both be expelled but that would hardly matter to him. It was different for Nona. She had a husband who would expect an explanation. What reason could she possibly give for being compelled to leave?

But they weren't caught. The one evening Miss MacIntyre elected to check the cottage she found everything in order. Tino had visited in the afternoon and gone. Nona, Ellie and Carmen ate dinner together, lingered over it briefly and retired to their rooms. And that was how she found them when she walked in, stiff with authority, at nine o'clock. Nona laughed telling Tino about it the next afternoon.

"Good," he said. "That means she'll leave the place alone for awhile."

19.

It was an awkward state of affairs and it made Ellie resentful seeing Nona take over the living room day after day, acting without regard for anyone but herself and Tino. But neither she nor Carmen had any idea of how to handle the situation and so it continued.

Carmen was a gentle, unobtrusive person, always pleasant, always agreeable, though it seemed that much of the time she was sad. She was small and plump, her face round and devoid of makeup, her black hair wound into the plainest of buns at the back of her head. Small gold hoops went through her ears and, aside from her wedding ring, were her only adornment. She followed every sanatorium rule scrupulously, ate everything she was supposed to eat, slept and rested exactly in accordance with the regimen set up for her. In the evenings when she sat in the living room, she knitted or crocheted.

She came from Cali, Colombia, where her husband's family had many years ago set up a sugar exporting business. Her husband was now its head and under his management it had grown to three times its original size. From other members of the Latin community at the sanatorium it was gathered that the Ortegas were people to be reckoned with on their home ground, both socially and politically.

Once Ellie asked her how long she'd been married.

"Ten years," she said. "I was a bride at eighteen and here I am with no babies to show for it." She looked down at her fingers somberly as they plodded over the knitting. At the end of a long silence she added, "I had four miscarriages."

"Well then it isn't as if you never got pregnant," Ellie declared defensively. "Those things happen."

She shook her head firmly. "No, that isn't the way it's looked at in my country. It's my fault. They shouldn't happen."

Carmen arrived at the sanatorium in March. Her husband had made the arrangements for her admission from Cali and originally it was his intention to come up with her. A last minute business emergency, however, changed the plans and Carmen came up alone. She was careful to explain that it was more important for him to stay behind although as she went on to describe the journey. This was her first time out of her own country, three changes of planes to negotiate, and once at the sanatorium all the initial interviews and examinations to struggle through in her barely adequate English. Ellie wondered what business matter could have been so critical as to take precedence. It wasn't easy, she admitted, but people all along the way were kind and she insisted she'd managed very nicely. Fortunately her disease was found to be minimal and after a month in the infirmary she moved to Anderson.

Late one afternoon when Ellie was in her room resting, she came softly down the hall and tapped at the open door.

"May I come in?" she asked.

"Of course, Carmen." And Ellie sat up.

She'd just returned from a visit to the Medical Building and her face was radiant.

"Ellie," she said, "you won't believe the news they gave me. I'm pregnant. Four months pregnant."

"Carmen, how absolutely, positively marvelous!"

"I asked Dr. Trimble to call Julio in Cali and tell him and he said he would." Dr. Trimble was the director of the sanatorium.

It was a few moments before Ellie took this in. Why didn't Carmen call and tell her husband herself? She thought of the times she had dreamed of this happening and the dozen different, dazzling ways she'd make the announcement to Bob. Why would Carmen let someone else be the bearer of news of such magnitude?

The next night the phone rang. Cali, Colombia, calling Mrs. Carmen Ortega. It was Julio. He was so proud, so happy. The conversation, of course, was in Spanish and Ellie knew only what Carmen told her at the end but there was no mistaking the joy that had spread throughout the family.

"He's coming up as soon as he can get away," Carmen said. "He wants to make sure I get the best possible care. He said that at last he will have a son." Her smile was both timid and proud.

That was another thing. Why did Julio assume she would have a boy? It seemed to be laying the groundwork for reproach if the baby was a girl. Why would a daughter be so much less than a son? No dynasty was threatened. No royal succession was at stake. A child was a child. How could it possibly matter?

She thought of all the lighthearted hours when she and Bob played with this eventuality.

"I want a boy," she'd tell him, "exactly like you. Not a fraction different or I won't tolerate it."

He'd laugh and kiss her. "No, Ellie," he'd say. "I want a girl, a girl with all your sweetness and just the way you are."

And they'd tease and argue. "Girls are best," he'd say.

But Carmen didn't appear to think anything was wrong with Julio's matter-of-fact assumption that the baby would be a boy. Her delight at finding herself pregnant conquered any anxieties she might have felt about the infant's sex. Happiness transformed her and brightened her eyes and her smile.

20.

Julio Ortega arrived at the cottage by cab from the airport on a beautiful June morning, sunlight flooding the sky, the mountains outlined pure and sharp against it. The previous day Carmen and Ellie had picked lilacs along the road, exclaiming over their abundance, burying their faces in the softness of the blossoms. The flowers stood in stoneware bowls in front of the windows and their swooning sweetness filled the room.

Carmen had said very little about her husband but somehow Ellie pictured him as a successful businessman type, good-looking in a Latin way and cheerful, especially now with Carmen pregnant. She couldn't have been more wrong. He was a thin, testy man, frown lines permanently creased into his brow, two deep furrows plowed down either side of his mouth. He had a nervous habit of pacing back and forth and jingling the coins in his pockets. Carmen, wearing a pretty new blouse and a locket at her throat, brought Ellie into the living room to meet him and he bowed as they were introduced.

"Did you have a nice trip?" Ellie asked politely.

His eyes shot skyward. "Terrible." Handkerchief in hand he mopped his brow as if even the memory caused him to perspire. The planes were crowded and cramped, the food bad, the air bumpy. The airports were even worse. Airline employees were either incompetent or rude. Nowhere, apparently, was he treated with the deference he regarded as his due. Somewhat at a loss as to what to say next, Ellie asked him how long he was staying.

"I go back tomorrow."

"What a pity," she said. "Everything is at its best here now and there are nice places to see."

He shook his head impatiently. "I have no time for sightseeing. I was lucky I was able to get away for these couple of days."

Carmen, standing beside him, smiled gratefully. "There's really too much work for Julio," she put in timidly.

"Not at all," he contradicted. "It isn't too much work, it's too few people with know-how," and he tapped his forehead with his forefinger. "But where do you find them?" Apparently people like himself were in short supply.

There was an awkward pause. "I do hope you'll enjoy yourself while you're here," Ellie said and she excused herself and went back to her room.

Shortly afterward a taxi was called and they left. They returned that evening at eight o'clock and the rattle of Julio's Spanish filled the living room. All Carmen could be heard to say was "Si, mi amor." "No, mi amor." "Por supuesto, mi amor."

Then he left. Alone. Evidently they weren't going to spend the night together. But how could that be? They hadn't seen each other since March. Here it was June. Carmen would sleep in her narrow bed in the cottage and Julio in a downtown hotel? Ellie didn't know what to make of it.

Whatever Carmen thought she, of course, said nothing. She did explain, however, that Julio had brought his mother up from Cali with him and she would stay on. Having borne nine healthy children she was well qualified to supervise Carmen's pregnancy and that was what she intended to do. Carmen and Julio had spent the afternoon getting her settled.

The next morning Señora Ortega appeared at the cottage. She was a sour, lynx-eyed woman garbed entirely in black. Even the string of beads she wore was black and small black beads dangled from her ears. It would appear she might have been recently widowed but Carmen said later that she was in mourning for a second cousin. She spoke no English but she gave Ellie a cramped smile and offered her hand.

Poor Carmen with her soft eyes and gentle mouth. She stood defenseless between a pompous, peevish husband and a narrow-hearted mother-in-law. Only now, pregnant, was she of any importance and not for herself, but because she was to be the mother of Julio's child. Ellie pitied her from the bottom of her heart.

Every afternoon about four o'clock Señora Ortega arrived in a taxi and she and Carmen strolled for an hour on the grounds. The señora always came back to the cottage at the end of the walk, waiting until the dinners arrived when she'd lift the covers off the dishes to examine their contents. She scrutinized everything, even the soap used in the bathroom. Shortly afterward she brought a box of Colombian soap and for Carmen's sake Ellie used it.

Fortunately the señora was staying at a boarding house that catered exclusively to Latin Americans and this absorbed a great deal of her attention. Doña Alicia who ran it had brought her ailing husband to Saranac Lake from Ecuador twenty years ago and after he died she stayed on. With the small sum of money left her she bought a rambling three-story house not far outside the sanatorium grounds. She divided it into bedrooms, put in a large dining room on the ground floor and brought up from Guayaquil a succession of half-Indian girls to cook and clean. The venture was extremely successful and there were seldom many vacant rooms. Families of Latin patients came and stayed for varying lengths of time, made comfortable by the sound of their native language and the taste of their native food.

Carmen's pregnancy was not an easy one. She was sick most mornings and retched miserably behind the closed bathroom door. She stayed in her room until after breakfast was cleared away because the smell of food at that early hour sickened her. Complicating matters, of course, was the three-times-daily dose of PAS which she, along with all the patients at the sanatorium had to take. It wrought havoc with her easily-upset stomach and though Dr. Nichols was sympathetic he couldn't let her cut back more than a day a week.

Ellie once asked her if her mother-in-law didn't have anything to suggest for morning sickness. The señora appeared to be an authority on every subject which came up, particularly female disorders.

"No," Carmen said.

"Why not?"

She shook her head. "I had such morning sickness with my other pregnancies, I'm afraid she'd think I was going to miscarry again."

But then what was the purpose of her being here, Ellie wondered.

As far as Carmen's tuberculosis was concerned, however, she was doing well. She was one of the fortunate ones whose disease was confined to a small area in one lung and it was clearing up steadily. Dr. Nichols made it a point to see that her mother-in-law was kept advised and she appeared to be glumly satisfied. However, she never failed to mention whenever an opportunity arose that no one in the Ortega family had ever suffered from tuberculosis. The remark was another indictment of Carmen's shortcomings.

21.

It seemed that summer as if everyone was doing well. At the end of June Ellie and Carmen commenced eating lunch in the dining room down on the grounds and a month later dinner as well. Carmen's stomach was rounding out nicely now and happiness made her plain little face almost beautiful. Fernando, after six years, would be going home to Caracas the following spring. The final stage of his lung removal was scheduled for December. He, Professor Palmer, Amy Connor, even Mrs. Trevelyan whose illness was complicated by a heart condition—one by one they all started to appear for meals.

If one didn't know otherwise it might have been the dining room of an exclusive vacation resort. Recorded music, selected with taste, floated in the background. People, to all outward appearances in the best of health, were dressed casually but in fashion. There were ringed fingers, groomed hair, here and there a trimmed beard. Conversations were conducted in genteel voices and cups came to rest on saucers as gently as birds lighting on trees. Who would suspect that the lungs of these companionable people provided the files in the Medical Building with X-rays of every variation of tubercular disease? Who could guess that among the smooth young faces were some that a year hence would lie quiet in a grave?

The dining area was wide and high-ceilinged with a glass enclosed porch for the staff running the length of it. Beyond lay the magnificent vista of mountains, the most distant blue or lilac or velvety purple, changing as the light changed. Hills fitting into hills like Chinese boxes which open to reveal smaller and still smaller ones inside. On sunny days brightness from the great reach of sky flooded the windows but in gloomy weather and at nightfall the copper table lamps were lighted. Then the room, for all its size, took on a cozy air.

Nona and Tino had their own table for two in a far corner. Carmen joined the Spanish table. Foreign patients tended to congregate according to nationality and almost always there were two or more who spoke the same language. Georgio's case was the exception.

He was a Greek deck hand on a merchant ship who had been put ashore in New York after he was found to be suffering from tuberculosis. The emigration authorities sent him up to Saranac where a doctor recommended him to Trudeau thinking that among their foreign patients he might find a compatriot. At the time, however, there was no one on hand who spoke Greek and his English was negligible. He'd walk out on the grounds, wearing seaman's clothes, hands fisted in pockets, a solitary, outlandish figure, nodding or shaking his head whenever someone spoke to him. At meals he mostly ate alone.

Elsa who was the occupational therapist at the sanatorium discovered he knew a little German, a language she spoke well and she went out of her way to be friendly to him. Often she'd join him over lunch or dinner and she learned a few sketchy details about him. He came from an impoverished farming family on a small Greek island where the hand-to-mouth existence prompted him to run away to sea. When he was in his teens, and though the life was hard, it was far better than any he could otherwise have anticipated. He said he was thirty but he looked older. He had a leathery face with a pearly scar across his jaw, dark bushy hair and his forearms were tattooed. He was tough, work-hardened, semi-literate, but life had given him a tolerance for adversity and he accepted his present circumstances stoically. Elsa tried to have him included in whatever social activities took place.

She sat at the table Ellie shared with Fernando and Professor Palmer although by rights she could have joined the staff on the porch. She preferred to be with the patients, however, and as she spoke two or three languages besides German she liked to sit at one of the foreign tables occasionally and join in the foreign conversation. She was in her fifties, a handsome, fair-complexioned woman with long hair braided and set upon her head in a little diadem. Half her family was European and she'd spent much of her life in France and Switzerland. Her history of tuberculosis was lengthy, starting when she was twenty and since then, she once said, she'd spent some part of every few years in sanatoriums, most of them in the Alps. Occasionally she told about them.

"You have to remember," she'd say, "there were no drugs in those days. There was nothing for tuberculosis but the mountains and rest and a lot of heavy food. And oh my, fresh air! The colder the better! They used to think that cold air in the lungs would harden the lesions so they had us out on porches in zero weather. We lay there as snow piled up on our beds."

She spoke of a sanatorium outside Davos where it was mandatory for patients to lie out on porches regardless of weather. Not until four patients died of pneumonia one winter did the director retreat and make it a matter of choice.

"And those who didn't die kept coming back, just as I did. We'd see each other again and again. We were never cured. The months of rest at a sanatorium merely slowed things down, gave us a sense of well being that had no real foundation. But full of optimism, we'd pack our bags, have farewell parties and drive down out of the mountains to Paris or Barcelona or Naples or wherever we'd come from. And in six months or a year the cough and the fever would be back."

Professor Palmer, whose tuberculosis was also chronic and went back many years, stirred his coffee thoughtfully. "An

English doctor some years ago put it well. He said no patient should be regarded as cured of tuberculosis until he was safely dead of some other disease. It still applies today."

Ellie had never heard that said before and she flinched. Was this disease to lurk in her all her life? Was she never to be free of it? Must she always live in dread of an innocent cough, a fever arising from some harmless indisposition? Her heart lumbered unsteadily in her chest and she lowered her eyes to her plate but not before Fernando guessed her thoughts.

He waved his hand in a typical Latin gesture of dismissal. "They'll have the cure for tuberculosis in another five years. Maybe sooner. We're worrying ourselves for nothing. The day will come when we'll drink a glassful of something or other," and he lifted his water glass, "and pouf! We'll have no more tuberculosis. Or more likely it will be a new kind of shot for our poor hips," and he laughed and patted his much-abused rear. "But it will amount to the same thing. The end of tuberculosis."

Ellie looked across the table at him gratefully.

"Yes," said Professor Palmer. "I agree. The cure for tuberculosis is down the road but where? Will we all be around for it to do us any good?"

"Let's hope so," Elsa said and diplomatically she changed the subject.

Professor Palmer was seldom pessimistic On the contrary he was a cheerful, courteous man and Ellie was very fond of him. He used to stop by her room during her early days in the infirmary bringing a cartoon or a comic strip or with some silly story to tell and as soon as he had her laughing he'd leave.

"Don't go yet," she'd beg.

"I'll be back when I have something else funny to tell you," he'd say.

He came from a small town on the eastern shore of Maryland where, until his health failed, he taught history at a local college. He loved gardening and when he and Ellie got to know each other better he showed her snapshots in color of some of his flowers, especially his roses. They were magnificent and she didn't know roses came in so many glorious shades. Each January he'd receive in the mail a score of garden catalogues which he'd pore over, turning down pages and making pencil notations in the margins. He planned to change things around when he got home, he said. He'd take out his beds of dahlias and put in more roses. Sometimes he'd ask Ellie's opinion. What color did she think would go best next to the yellow. The silvery pink. No matter what she said his face would brighten at the images conjured up.

Ellie couldn't remember when she'd seen him as gloomy as he was that day at lunch and the mood persisted during the days that followed. Then his wife arrived on one of her rare visits. At lunchtime he brought her to their table where a few polite words were exchanged before they moved off to a nearby table for two. She was a mannish-looking woman dressed in a severe gray suit with a tailored shirt, and she had a loud, penetrating voice. Snatches of her conversation rang out above the subdued hum in the room.

"But I wrote and told you, Arthur, that there was nothing else to be done. There's no one to take care of it properly. Certainly I don't have the time or the inclination for gardening. So I had everything pulled up and now there's just lawn." Her words, blunt as a blow from a club, carried over with embarrassing clarity to nearby tables. "You might consider me for a change," she went on. "It'll make it a whole lot easier for me."

Elsa, Ellie and Fernando sat mute, each trying to find something to say to fill the awkward silence. Then Elsa skillfully took command, broached a new subject and the few unhappy moments ended.

But Professor Palmer was changed from then on. Not in any obvious, easy-to-recognize fashion but in lesser, more subtle ways. Never a talkative man, he became more silent. Always a man of deliberate movement, his step became slower. Lines deepened at the sides of his mouth and often, coming upon him unexpectedly, his eyes had a defeated look.

22.

Nancy Tyler, after a convalescence in the infirmary, returned to Anderson and that evening the four sat in the living room drinking coffee, Nancy in an armchair with a pillow at her back. She was a forthright, friendly woman, a down-to-earth sort, deceptively strong in appearance. She had short, thick, graying hair which she brushed impatiently away from her forehead from time to time as she talked about her surgery.

"It was no picnic, believe me. They pry the ribs apart to get at the lung. I swear mine feel as if they're not back in place yet." She held her cup at the level of her mouth and grimaced. "It's a good thing I didn't know beforehand what I was letting myself in for or I might never have gone through with it."

Carmen's face was full of sympathy while Nona looked on indifferently. She and Nancy had been acquainted for some months but their relationship was more an armed truce than

205

a friendship. Nona had little interest in the story of Nancy's surgery. In any event neither she nor Carmen were candidates for a resection and they took in her words objectively but for Ellie they had more impact. Dr. Nichols told her after her last X-rays that she should begin to think about surgery.

"You're doing okay," he said, "but it's a matter of preventing a break in the future."

Carmen rose and got the coffeepot to refill the cups. Ellie spoke for the first time since the recital began. "I'm supposed to be giving thought to a resection but I've already made up my mind and the answer is no."

Nancy looked disconcerted. "I didn't know they had you on the list. It isn't really all that bad, Ellie. I'm sorry if I made it seem so." Her expression was contrite.

"That's okay. I've heard all about it before. You didn't say anything I don't already know. But I've decided against it. I'd rather take my chances." It wasn't the pain which was only temporary. It was the scar.

"Anyway they may change their minds," Nancy said. "There are cases where it's been recommended but not done and patients have gotten along fine." She put her cup down and eased back in the chair. "With me it was different. I was running out of time."

Nancy came from Cincinnati where she started out as a kindergarten teacher. Her first bout of tuberculosis ended her career as well as her two-year marriage to an architect. All she ever said about her husband was that he was very ambitious and a sick wife was a handicap he wasn't prepared to cope with. She spent years off and on in sanatoriums in the middle west after which came a long period of good health. It led her to believe she was free of the disease at last but a year earlier she had a serious relapse which brought her to Saranac.

There were financial worries as well. Her family for years had owned a small general store just outside the city limits and while her father was alive it provided an adequate income. After his death, however, left in the hands of her mother and brother, poor management kept it in constant fiscal jeopardy. Her mother was improvident, her brother drank. Between the two trade dwindled and debts mounted and only when Nancy was on the scene could the store be counted on to stay out of the red. She finished her account with a simple, forceful statement. "I've got to get back home and take over while there's still something left."

Nona spoke for the first time. "When do you expect to be discharged?"

"The end of the year, if all goes well."

"I should be going then too."

"We'll miss the worst of the Adirondack winter. That won't be hard to take."

"I've seen enough snow to last me a lifetime," Nona said. "I want a whole new scene." She paused meaningfully. "I guess now is as good a time as any to tell you." Another pause. "I'm going to Florida." Nona smiled and stretched her arms languidly over her head. "Yes, Florida."

Nancy pursued it. "Just for the winter? Or are you and Paul moving down permanently?"

"No, not Paul and I. Tino and I. Tino wants me to go and I'm going."

Dead silence followed the announcement. Affairs such as theirs went on all the time at the sanatorium, unlikely alliances that arose out of circumstances and had no more meaning than shipboard romances. They ran their course and ended. It was seldom they led to any kind of permanent commitment and when they did there were usually grounds to assume the union had some reasonable chance of success. But Nona and Tino?

Nancy spoke. "Does Paul know?"

"Not yet but he will."

"You plan to divorce him?"

"I can hardly start a new life otherwise. I want to be free."

"And then you'll marry Tino?"

"Those are our plans."

Nancy pushed a swatch of hair off her forehead, her face grave. "I hope you know what you're doing, Nona. To divorce Paul and marry Tino is a pretty serious step to take. You haven't known Tino all that long."

"I've known him long enough."

"Your backgrounds are so different. That may not seem important now but it will as time goes on. Why rush into it? Why not wait awhile and be sure?"

Nona's eyelids narrowed. "I've spent eight months in this place. Eight dragging months. If there's one thing I've learned it's that life is short and time is precious." She spoke in an even, menacing voice. "I'm not going to waste a minute of it." It was the worst moment to pursue an argument.

Nancy knew that whatever she said would anger her further but she plunged ahead regardless. "If that's what you want, Nona, by all means it's yours to take but I just wish you'd give yourself more time. You could regret this for the rest of your life."

In a single exasperated movement Nona rose to her feet. "For God's sake," she exploded. "Since when are you an authority on marriage? You should be the last to talk." She paused, then spat out the final words. "It's my life!"

On that note the evening ended.

Each could have built a case against Tino. Nancy, her judgment mature, saw them as two people from totally different worlds with little common ground to sustain a relationship once the flames of physical love burned down. For Ellie it was Tino's personality that repelled her, his arrogance, the mocking smile, the swaggering walk and she wondered for the hundredth time how Nona could be held so totally in thrall. Carmen saw him as a fellow Latin, a type she knew well, a man for whom women were things to be used and discarded, as casually as worn-out shoes. She and Ellie stood talking briefly in the hallway.

"I don't know how she can be so foolish," Carmen said. "Tino will never marry her. It will never last. He'll leave her for someone else before a year goes by. I've seen these things happen again and again."

"I don't understand it." Ellie shook her head mystified. "She's always been so choosy. I didn't think anyone on earth would be good enough for her. And she picks Tino."

But nothing would have made the slightest difference. No words would have swayed her. If anything, skepticism merely strengthened her resolve.

23.

Nancy's return to the cottage brought with it a sense of order that was missing in her absence and Ellie and Carmen welcomed it. Tino no longer walked through the front door without knocking nor did he treat Nona's room as if it were his own. When they sat by the fireplace of an afternoon their behavior was fitting and Nancy's presence, of course, put an end to their nights together in the cottage. On that score, however, they simply resorted to other means. In spite of a sanatorium rule forbidding patients to have cars, Tino had a Chrysler which he kept in a downtown garage and which he used whenever it suited him. They would get passes, taxi into town, pick up the car and drive to a motel for a couple of hours. No one was ever the wiser.

Tino bought her a ring, a sapphire in a showy setting, unsuited to her thin hand, but she wore it with extravagant pride. Her wedding ring had been put away and anyone could draw whatever conclusion he wanted. Nona didn't care. She deferred to him in all things. Whenever there was a choice to be made his will prevailed. She consulted him about what to wear, reasonable enough on the face of it but suggestions soon became directives and the tone of voice changed. It became sharp, dictatorial.

"Put your jacket on, no, not the khaki, the blue," he'd say. Or, "Your white sweater looks better. Take that one off!"

In the dining room he'd fork a piece of meat off her plate and substitute something else. Often in the evening when patients would congregate in the parlors, she would go to sit down in a chair and he'd tap the back of another. "Sit here, Nona."

She took it all with unruffled calm. Blunt words, a curt tone of voice—what did it matter measured against their secret hours when he wanted her so fiercely? For those who remembered the way she used to be the change was striking. How easy it had been to annoy her, how savagely she reacted when crossed, how scathingly she disparaged everything around her. Now Tino set the standards. What he approved she accepted without question, what he disdained she dismissed with an echo of his own withering scorn.

There were occasions, however, when he was inexcusably rude. He would get into lengthy conversations in Spanish with one of the Latinos and he'd go on and on. Nona who didn't know the language would sit at his side silent and excluded. It was the same with the chess games. Chess was a favorite after dinner past-time at the sanatorium and many of the patients played. Tino was an excellent though aggressive player. He'd slam a piece down savagely, snatch up another, whoop at a misguided move and startle everyone within range. Nona for whom chess was a mystery sat beside him, her face tranquil. If she felt any resentment at being left out no hint of it was apparent. When the game at last ended she'd smile and sigh but often he'd immediately start another game with someone else. Never did she show the least sign of displeasure. She sat in docile devotion, her reward an occasional word or two, a hand placed absently on her arm for a brief few moments.

One day she announced she was going to learn Spanish. So many of Tino's Miami friends were Spanish-speaking, she explained, it would be nice for her to know the language. And so Señor Garcia, the Spanish teacher from town, started coming two afternoons a week to give her lessons. At the same time she said she wanted to learn to play chess and Elsa showed up at the cottage frequently to teach her the game.

Somewhere along the line she wrote Paul and told him she wanted a divorce. His response was swift. He arrived by plane one rainy summer day and he and Nona sat for a long time in one of the parlors. At lunchtime in the dining room their faces were stiff with strain and currents of emotion swirled around their table. Paul ate his meal baffled and angry, glancing at her from time to time searching for a clue to the riddle of her behavior. Nona sat back from her plate and picked at her food, looking like a willful child who is determined to get what it wants at any cost. Not once did she raise her eyes to her husband.

Before he left, Paul asked to speak to Dr. Trimble. The interview was brief. Dr. Trimble was sympathetic but the matter was not in his domain.

"All we do here," he said, "is attempt to cure their bodies. We have no control over their love lives."

The word that Nona and Tino intended to marry caused eyebrows to lift in surprise but the stir it created was brief. There was never a lack of titillating happenings to gossip about at the sanatorium and nothing held sway for long before another took its place. They were, however, more closely observed. They were always together, he the dominant male, she the compliant female and if their roles seemed excessive who was to criticize. They were happy, Tino breezy and bombastic, Nona flushed with pride, the sapphire on her finger time and again the focus of her dream-filled eyes.

24.

They dawdled up the sloping walk from the Medical Building, stopping from time to time along the way to catch their breath, both of them short-winded, Carmen from girth, Ellie from her collapsed lungs. A cold mist dampened the flagstones at their feet and formed beads of moisture on the underside of the iron railing running along its length. They leaned back against it, side by side, before tackling the last steep incline leading to the cottage.

They were returning from interviews with Dr. Nichols who had evaluated their latest X-rays and given each of them a favorable report. For another three months they were on firm ground, a little closer to the goal of recovery and a return to their normal lives. Curing, however, was like a steeplechase and the final outcome depended on clearing a succession of similar hurdles.

"He said that after the baby is born I can go home!"

This was the highlight of Carmen's news and the joy of it illuminated her face.

"That's wonderful, Carmen, I know you'd rather have the baby at home but I'm glad you'll have it here because then I'll have a chance to see it."

Carmen smiled in response. She was in the seventh month of her pregnancy and although she still suffered cruelly from morning sickness, all else was going well. The affected portion of her lung was almost fully healed.

"Just think, Ellie," she said once. "I'll leave here with a baby in my arms. And when I step off the plane in Cali I'll have a baby to give to Julio."

Her last weeks in these alien mountains were moving swiftly now, speeded by the vision of her triumphant return home. It had been worth it—the fear, the loneliness, the difficulties that came of being in a foreign country and having to communicate in a language other than her own. For the first time in the history of her pregnancies she was able to carry a baby this far into term. Whether it was the rest, the tranquility, the air that helped heal her lungs, whatever it was, give credit where credit was due. She would always remember this interlude gratefully. Nothing disturbed her now, least of all Señora Ortega's visits. The old lady showed up every afternoon as usual, meddlesome and critical, announcing her presence with cannonades of shrill Spanish to which Carmen never failed to respond courteously. Let her mother-in-law carp as she would, it didn't matter. Carmen at last was proving herself.

Ellie's news was exciting too and she was just as anxious to impart it. Some time earlier she'd had a letter from Joan saying that she and Frank planned to be married the beginning of December and she tacked on a compelling last couple of lines.

"How about coming down for the wedding? You should have some travel privileges after all this time. Please try!"

Ellie breathed a deep elated sigh. "Dr. Nichols said I could go to New York for Joan's wedding! Isn't that marvelous, Carmen? I'll be in New York again! I can hardly believe it."

But the most wonderful part of it was that Bob would be in New York then too and Joan's wedding was to be the occasion of their reunion.

His communications had been erratic, written mostly on postcards although sometimes he'd send a quirky little note adorned with pencil sketches of local scenes—an Indian woman selling baskets on a street corner, a llama with tassels in its ears, a line-up of Indian girls washing clothes in a stream, one flirting over her shoulder. They were sweet and clever but what she wished for were the love letters he didn't write. Then she'd remind herself of all the problems he faced, the demands on his time, and so reason away her disappointments and the little notes for all their brevity were read and re-read until they became limp from handling.

For her part she had written lengthy, loving, determinedly cheerful letters, assuring him she was doing well and backing it up with quotes from Dr. Nichols. She had the librarian get her books about South America and about Peru so she'd know something about his surroundings and could better imagine what it was like there for him. She even acquired a simplified Spanish grammar and, with Carmen's help, tried to learn some Spanish phrases to include when she wrote him.

Some time earlier her brother had sent her a postcard from Lima—a conquering general on a prancing horse amidst flower beds and walkways, gaudy, over-colored, the sky too blue, the grass too green. He was then working on the Grace Line ships that touched ports along the west coast of South America and he'd been back to Lima three times. "This town grows on you," he wrote. "You'd like it. It's got trolley cars." She smiled reading it. As a child she had a passion for trolley cars, probably because she and Larry so seldom had the chance to ride in them. She studied the garish picture minutely and marveled at the coincidence that put Bob and her brother, unknowingly and fleetingly, together in that faraway foreign city.

Then came the unexpected phone call from New York. Bob was back though only briefly. However, he intended to take a long break starting in November. And now at last it was all coming into place. They'd see each other again.

Underlying their buoyant spirits that day, however, was the sobering knowledge that in the struggle with tuberculosis nothing was certain. Months of steady headway could come to a halt for no apparent reason, setting the clock back, starting the whole dreary cycle over again. And although these thoughts were seldom voiced, they were riveted into the back of every mind. Don't count on anything. Don't be too sure. No matter how justified, optimism had to be qualified.

Amy Cannon was a case in point. It appeared her disease had finally been brought under control. She'd gone through surgery, months of bed rest, the slow return to activity. Two weeks ago a flare-up was discovered in the lung that all along had been quiescent. It had devastated her. The doctors then offered her one last resort.

There was going on in the scientific world at the time an aggressive search for the drug that would cure tuberculosis and it was steadfastly believed the cure would be found. The question was when. From time to time word of a possible breakthrough would sweep through the sanatorium and on two occasions a drug, still experimental, was offered to patients for whom all else had failed. Both proved to be ineffective. Then a third drug came out, more potent than the first two but more promising. Amy was asked if she wanted to try it. She did.

"What have I got to lose?" she asked one day as she and Ellie walked down to the dining room to lunch. She was bitterly discouraged. She answered her own question. "Nothing."

Ellie agreed with her and if she'd been in Amy's shoes she would have done the same. The experimental drugs tried out earlier were simple enough to take and held out a whole new vista of hope. Though they proved to be failures who could say that the next might not be the long awaited breakthrough?

25.

One afternoon Ellie sat on the couch in the living room studying her Spanish grammar and trying to memorize a list of words she had checked off for herself. She lifted her head hearing the familiar stomp of Tino's feet on the walkway outside, then a thump on the door and the door pushed open. Tino shouldered his way in, pulled off his jacket and tossed it on a chair. Carmen was out with her mother-in-law, Nona was down at X-ray and Nancy's door was closed.

"Isn't Nona back yet?"

"No."

He went behind her to the dining room table where a bottle of wine stood and she heard him pour himself a glass. She didn't stir. He came and stood in back of her and she thought he wanted to see what she was reading but all at once he leaned over and slid his hand inside the top of her blouse. She spun on him like a tigress.

"Don't you dare touch me!" She was on her feet in seconds.

"For chrissake, Ellie, why don't you grow up?"

"Stay away from me, Tino, I'm warning you!" She retreated a few steps and he followed, a leering smile on his face.

"Quit acting so innocent. Who do you think you're kidding? You've slept around. Why don't you give some of it away around here?"

"You're a pig, Tino." She spat the words at him. She got as far as the dining room table and stopped, afraid that if she went to her room he'd follow her.

"Come on, Ellie, relax," he said and his voice became insinuating. "I can teach you Spanish."

"I'll tell Nona about this. I'll let her know what you're like."

He laughed. "Big deal."

Just then Nona came up the walk and before she opened the front door Ellie got away to her room. She didn't say anything about the incident, nor had she any intention of doing so. By that time there were other straws in the wind.

In the front parlor one evening after dinner Nona and Tino sat across from each other over a chess board. There were six or seven others in the room as well, playing records, talking. Tino, in typical fashion, thumped a piece from one square to another. Nona studied the board, hesitated, made as if to move a piece, drew back and finally pushed her queen forward.

He clapped a furious hand to his forehead and got up from his chair, made as if to walk away, then sat down again.

"Holy Christ, how can anyone be so stupid!"

The words rang out and electrified everyone in the room. This was typical of Tino's behavior but never before had anyone seen Nona as the target. She looked as if he had struck her.

One morning in the Medical Building while waiting to get streptomycin shots, patients made idle conversation. Tino and Nona sat next to each other, Nona turned toward Mrs. Iglesias who was explaining to her some matter of Spanish pronunciation. Mrs. Iglesias was from Buenos Aires, a cultured woman whose husband was on the Argentine diplomatic staff in Washington. Just as Nona repeated a word that gave her trouble the conversation lulled and in the sudden silence her voice became painfully audible. Tino turned his head in her direction and laughed.

"You'd better stick to English," he said. "You'll never make it."

Nona made no reply, just tried to smile as if the remark was amusing, but Mrs. Iglesias looked at him with loathing.

The Melia sisters arrived at the sanatorium from Tenerife in the Canary Islands in September. Twenty-one-year old Luisa was diagnosed as having moderately advanced tuberculosis in the left lung and was promptly admitted to the infirmary. Marta, twenty-four, traveling with her as companion and chaperon, moved into Doña Alicia's boarding house and spent her days at the sanatorium, either in her sister's room or idling in the parlors.

Marta was indolent, impassive, sulky but most of all she was bored. She had dark eyes, very white teeth and a pretty bosom which she took pains to display to the greatest advantage. If the day was cool she wore a tight fitting sweater. If warm, a blouse with a neckline scooped out to the last permissible fraction of an inch.

One evening Ellie left the Administration Building to return to the cottage and for some reason she chose to go out through a side door. It brought her into a small courtyard dimly lit some distance forward where it joined the road. Two figures stood in the shadows to her right, the girl leaning idly back against the building, the man facing her, his flattened palm on the wall above her head. He turned at the sound of Ellie's footsteps. It was Tino and the girl was Marta.

Tino's visits to Anderson dwindled. Many afternoons Nona stood at the living room windows watching for him and he never came. On Nancy's birthday there was a party at the cottage with wine and cake and a dozen guests were invited. Tino came late, looking surly, he drank some wine, smoked a cigarette and announced he had to leave. "Tino, sit. Don't go yet." She put a hand on his arm. "You only just got here."

He looked around the room at the noisy, laughing guests—Fernando strumming his guitar, Georgio hunched over a wine glass, his pushed-back sleeves revealing tattooed extravaganzas on his forearms, Amy giggling on the floor at his feet, Nancy trying to blow out the candles on her cake. A thinly veiled expression of contempt crept into his face.

"I gotta be going," he answered.

"But why, Tino?" Nona persisted. "The party's just starting."

He brushed her hand away. "I said I'd show up and I did. What more do you want?"

Not everyone heard the exchange and those who did pretended they didn't. Tino shouldered his jacket on and left and shortly afterward Nona slipped away to her room. She seemed frailer and more and more often her face took on a distant, preoccupied look. They still ate together in the dining room and she still wore his ring. A semblance of the old relationship was maintained but no one was fooled. The end of the affair was in sight.

26.

Carmen's baby was due in November. At five o'clock one morning in October she knocked urgently on Ellie's door. Startled, Ellie turned on her light.

"Ellie," she said. "Will you call someone? I'm in so much pain. I think the baby's coming." Her face was gray and perspiration beaded her brow. Ellie leaped to her feet.

"Get back in bed, Carmen. I'll call down to the nurses' office."

Miss Rogers answered on the first ring.

"We need help," Ellie said. "Carmen thinks the baby is coming."

"Okay, Ellie." Her voice was calm as always. "We'll get somebody there right away. Have her stay in bed."

Back in Carmen's room she tried to reassure her. "It's all right. I spoke to Miss Rogers. Someone's coming right up."

Carmen lay back in bed, her eyes deeply shadowed and tears slid down her face.

"Is the pain so bad?" Ellie asked.

Carmen shook her head. "It isn't the pain. I'm afraid something's wrong. I haven't felt the baby move."

In minutes the sanatorium van, driven by one of the kitchen crew, was out front and Miss Rogers herself hurried into the cottage. With Ellie's help she got Carmen dressed and the van sped off to the hospital.

That morning at eight-thirty Carmen had a baby boy, stillborn. They brought her back to the infirmary two days later and in the afternoon Ellie went to see her. She lay as still as death, her rosary beads on the little table beside her, a box of Kleenex on the bed next to her hand. Not until Ellie spoke did she open her eyes.

"I'm so terribly sorry, Carmen. Please try not to take it so hard." What could one say in the face of so staggering a blow?

Carmen looked blankly at the wall beyond the foot of the bed and shook her head. Ellie went on. "You've got time for more babies."

She turned her head away. "There's no more time."

She was only twenty-eight years old. What made her so certain this was the end? But why had it happened, Ellie wondered. Surely there was a reason. She stayed on a little longer, sitting in uncomfortable silence, then left. Out in the hall she met Mrs. Cavanaugh, one of the older nurses, an old-fashioned, good-hearted woman. Ellie asked her what went wrong.

"I can't say for sure," she answered, shaking her head profusely "All I know is that a lot of women who've taken PAS during pregnancy have had miscarriages or stillbirths."

"Then why do they let them take it?" Ellie asked, indignant.

"There's nothing else they can do. Their tuberculosis has to be cured. They can get pregnant another time."

Ellie said nothing but thinking of Carmen's history she knew it wouldn't be as simple as Mrs. Cavanaugh made it sound. Did Carmen know why this had happened? Ellie went back to her room. She lay exactly as before.

"Carmen," Ellie said softly. "This wasn't your fault. It was the PAS." And she repeated the conversation she'd just had with Mrs. Cavanaugh.

Carmen nodded her head slightly at the end. "I know. They told me at the hospital."

"But it makes a difference." She was thinking of Julio and Señora Ortega. Once they knew they'd understand and show some signs of compassion.

"No, it doesn't make any difference."

"But you'll tell Julio?"

She nodded again, her face white and full of pain. "It won't change anything."

Ellie stood mutely at the foot of the bed but the silence widened until there was nothing to do but to leave.

The following week Carmen and her mother-in-law departed for Cali and Ellie and Fernando rode out to the airport with them in the taxi. Señora Ortega, her face like a thunder cloud, sat on one side of Carmen and Ellie on the other. Fernando sat up front with the driver. Because the señora spoke no English conversation was held to a minimum but before they parted Ellie asked Carmen to write.

"Please do, Carmen," she urged. "I'll be thinking about you and wondering how you are."

"I will, Ellie," she promised. "You've been such a good friend, I'll never forget it." She embraced her Spanish fashion, kissing both sides of her face, and then she followed her mother-in-law out to the plane.

Riding back with Fernando, Ellie asked him what he thought would happen.

"The Ortegas are very old-fashioned people and for a wife not to have children is a serious thing."

"But this wasn't her fault," Ellie said quickly. "It was the PAS. Mrs. Cavanaugh said so. It happens often she said."

"They've been married ten years."

"She's had four miscarriages. It isn't as if she never got pregnant. Maybe there's something that could be corrected. I wonder if Julio ever thought of that."

Fernando shook his head. "Maybe, maybe not. But anyway I don't think anything will make any difference now. The marriage will be annulled."

"And what will happen to Carmen?"

He shrugged. "Who knows? If she has a family she'll go back to them." He shrugged again.

Carmen's departure from the sanatorium where so many came and went caused little stir. While she still lay in the infirmary after the dead baby, her place at the Spanish table was taken by someone else. It was only to be expected—an empty chair at a table was at the disposal of anyone who wanted it. But there seemed to be a sad foreboding in the speed with which she was forgotten. The usual perfunctory expressions of sympathy were forthcoming, of course, but for the most part her exit was like a stone dropped in a pond, circles widening briefly and disappearing without a trace.

One of the books about South America that Ellie was reading contained descriptions of all its countries, a chapter apiece and because of Carmen, Ellie read about Colombia when she finished Peru. A single sentence caught her eye and colored all her mental pictures of the country. Noted for orchids and emeralds. So exotic an image was evoked that whenever Carmen spoke of her home in Cali Ellie assumed it was beautiful. Then one day Carmen showed her a snapshot and she was hard put to hide her dismay. Revealed were two bleak-looking buildings adjoining each other, the company offices and the other their home, and which was which would have been impossible to say except that over the door of the offices hung a sign with the company name. Carmen was quick to explain.

"Julio has always believed it important to make the home and offices one."

Ellie studied the photo in silence. The bare windows. The street of traffic in the foreground. So much for orchids and emeralds.

Remembering her at the airport the day they said goodbye, desolate and grieving for the lost baby, it was chilling to think of her return to that cheerless place, to that small-souled husband. Was it possible Fernando's words were true? That Julio would hold her accountable and annul their marriage? That in this day and age it was possible to put a woman aside because she hadn't borne a living child? Ellie hoped she'd write as she promised but she never did.

A red-faced girl with brawny arms scrubbed out her room and polished the furniture. New curtains went up at the window and the door stood open awaiting the next occupant.

27.

Wind blew the last leaves from the trees and the days shortened. Fields brown and forlorn awaited the first snows which with an even hand would hide the tattered remains of summer. The parlors with their cheery fires blazing became more than ever a favorite gathering place and during the permitted hours they were seldom empty.

Marta dallied there every evening, her tight sweaters more provocative than nakedness, her face imperturbable, her eyes watchful. Often at some point, Tino would walk through and five minutes later Marta would disappear.

One day word flew around that Tino and Marta had left the sanatorium—together. The first anyone knew they were missing was when Luisa in the infirmary held up a note and wailed that her sister had left her. The note was brief. Marta needed a change of scene. She was heading south with Tino for awhile. She'd be back.

And back she came. She returned in less than a week, alone and by train, her face inscrutable as ever. She took up where she left off as if nothing had happened. She continued her residence in Doña Alicia's boarding house though every Spanish tongue deplored the escapade and lashed out at Doña Alicia for permitting her to stay. Doña Alicia was as scandalized as anyone else but she was a prudent woman. She already had two vacant rooms. Why add a third?

At the sanatorium the pattern of Marta's days was exactly as before except of course that Tino was no longer there. Once when his name was mentioned she yawned.

Nona put a good face on things in the beginning and it seemed as if the whole misguided affair was safely behind her. She now sat at another table in the dining room and if she didn't contribute much to the general conversation over meals, she had never been particularly outgoing. She strolled the grounds every afternoon for an hour, seeking out the least traveled walkways and doing her best to avoid meeting people she knew. But who could blame her for that? In the cottage she was silent and evenings when they sat around the fireplace Ellie and Nancy did the talking while Nona's eyes were far away. But they believed she was over the worst of it and that time would do the rest.

The change came about gradually and started with her complaint of headaches. She lay in her room with a cloth across her eyes saying the light made the headaches worse. She used it as an excuse to have her meals sent up to the cottage and she no longer went down to the dining room. Days would pass without her ever stepping outside. She protested she couldn't sleep at night. Dr. Nichols had her down to his office twice to talk to her. There was nothing physically wrong and he urged her to see the psychiatrist in town to whom patients went with their emotional problems. She refused. Reluctantly Dr. Nichols prescribed sleeping pills.

Nancy worried about her and tried to reason with her. "If it's because you're concerned with what people think, forget it, Nona," she said. "People couldn't care less. It's all forgotten. It's water over the dam."

But that wasn't it. The problem went deeper and one day it came to light. She was due to be discharged in December and she told Nancy she had no place to go.

"I can't go home," she said in a rare burst of candor. "It's too small a town. I simply can't."

"That's foolish. Of course you can. Your parents are there. They'll be glad to have you. Go back to them."

Nona shook her head. "They didn't want me to divorce Paul. Oh they'd take me in. Sure, but they'd never let me forget what a fool I'd been. No thanks."

A short time earlier Kimmie Gardner had moved into Carmen's room and through no fault of her own aggravated the already tenuous state of affairs. She'd just become engaged. She was young and starry-eyed and she never tired of showing off her ring or talking about the wedding she planned. Nona could barely tolerate it.

The morning started like any other November morning, dark at eight o'clock, sleet tapping against the windows. Ellie woke hearing the truck from the kitchen groan up the hill and fight for traction on the icy road. Doors slammed. Charlie's voice and Lennie's. Heavy feet across the living room and a clinking sound as the rack of metal dishes was set down. A thump as the bundle of logs was dumped beside the fireplace.

Breakfast was the only meal the four ate together in the cottage, though Nona seldom joined them. Sometimes she appeared as the others were finishing and ate her meal silently. Other times, late, she drank a cup of coffee and smoked a cigarette. Once in awhile she didn't have anything at all.

The fire in the living room had taken off nicely and wrapped in a wool robe Ellie held her hands out to the blaze. Nancy came into the room, sleepy-eyed.

"Lord, what a wretched day," she said. "And I have to go out in it. I have a ten o'clock appointment at physical therapy this morning."

Kimmie appeared, hair tousled, cheerful. She looked out at the shiny crusted snow, tree branches bent under the accumulations of ice.

"I'll walk down with you, Nancy. I have X-rays this morning."

They ate leisurely, had second cups of coffee, and when Ellie finished she announced she was going back to bed. Nancy stopped her before she left the room.

"Nona has an appointment with Dr. Nichols at eleven this morning, Ellie. If she isn't up by ten-thirty will you check on her?"

Ellie dozed and when she heard Nancy and Kimmie leave a little before ten she stirred herself and rose. There was no sign of Nona so she bathed and dressed. It was a quarter past ten. She went to Nona's door and knocked.

"Nona, it's after ten. You have an appointment at eleven o'clock."

There was no sound. Ellie knocked again, louder.

"Nona!"

Still no sound. She turned the knob and pushed the door open. It went partway, then something blocked it. The curtains were drawn and the room was dark. She reached her hand around to the wall switch and turned on the light. Nona lay on the floor on her stomach, blocking the door, some of the covers pulled off the bed with her and lying across her legs. Her left arm was folded under her chest, the other stretched out as if in entreaty, or despair. The left side of her face was pressed against the bare floorboards, her skin the color of wax except for a lead-colored bruise across her forehead.

She was dead. Ellie knew it beyond question. Shock paralyzed her and she stood in the doorway motionless, staring down. Nona's long pale hair was spilled in confusion around her head and looked ghostly against the dark wood. Her pajama top had crumpled around her upper torso, revealing the fragile waist and the delicate bones of the lower ribs. The fingers of her narrow hand were curled and stiff. The sight left on Ellie's mind an image so sharp and durable it was to haunt a decade of unrelated dreams.

On the bedside table stood an empty water pitcher and a half empty glass. The drawer of the table was open. Inside, in one of the boxes PAS came in—a hundred packets at a time—were two remaining sleeping pills, her wedding ring and the sapphire in its glittery setting. How proudly she'd worn Tino's ring. What meaning she'd placed on its bestowal and what promise it held for her. Who would ever know her pain when she realized that for Tino it was a transient gift given in return for transient pleasures? Ellie turned out the light and closed the door.

In the living room she went first to the windows to see if there was anyone she could summon for help but on that frigid morning with thin, icy sleet pelting down no one was abroad. She dialed the nurses' office. The line was busy. She paced the living room and dialed again. Still busy. She called the infirmary and Miss Bodelle answered.

"Miss Bodelle! It's Ellie, in Anderson. Please send someone quickly. I think Nona is dead!" Her voice sounded strange and she realized shock had tightened the muscles of her throat.

There was momentary silence as the words hit home but in her years of nursing Miss Bodelle had heard everything. She said with customary calm, "We'll get someone over right away."

In minutes Dr. Nichols arrived accompanied by a young visiting doctor and Ellie led them to Nancy's room. They opened the door, stepped inside and softly closed it behind them. The sanatorium van pulled up out front and Charlie unloaded a gurney which he maneuvered up the slippery walk and through the doorway. Miss Bodelle and Mrs. Cavanaugh followed close behind him.

"You're alone here, Ellie?" Miss Bodelle asked.

Ellie nodded. "Nancy and Kimmie both had appointments at the Medical Building this morning. They left before ten."

"Mrs. Cavanaugh will stay with you."

Even as she spoke Mrs. Cavanaugh untied her headscarf and removed her coat and boots. She led the way to Ellie's room and had her lie down, and while the grim routine that attended death went on a couple of walls away she sat and talked of small inconsequential things.

Nancy and Kimmie learned something had happened to Nona while they were still down on the grounds but had no idea what actually transpired. By the time they got back to the cottage Nona's body had been removed and her door closed. Together the three sat in the living room, stunned and disbelieving, while Mrs. Cavanaugh did her best to maintain an attitude of objectivity for their benefit.

"These things happen," she said "from time to time" and then went on to talk about something else. But she stayed through lunch and naptime and didn't leave until five-thirty when Dr. Nichols appeared. Surprisingly he announced he was taking them out to dinner. Much as they would have liked to speculate as to the reason there was no opportunity for he stood by the fireplace waiting while they scurried around getting dressed.

Dr. Nichols was a skillful conversationalist, adept at steering talk in directions he wanted it to go. A lot of things were discussed that night over drinks and dinner but neither tuberculosis nor death was among them. When they got back to the cottage at eight o'clock they found that in their absence all of Nona's belongings had been removed, her room scrubbed, the bed made with a brand new pink coverlet and the door stood open.

That awful day. The dreary, freezing day that Nona died. What irony that in a community of people, everyone of whom would have given all he possessed for an added year of life, she threw her life away. Ellie and Nancy sat across from each other in front of the flickering fire, no other lights in the room, Kimmie in bed. They went back to the start of it all, the heady beginning, Nona transformed, the few fervid weeks that moved so swiftly into a doomed progress where each step foretold the next, its end as fixed as summer's passing. Nothing on earth could have changed the course of events. But Nona needn't have died.

"Why did she do it?" It was the question Ellie had asked herself all that day. "I can't believe she cared so much about Tino that she couldn't live without him. Not after the way he treated her. What was it, Nancy? What do you think?"

"No, I don't believe either it was because she couldn't live without Tino. The whole affair was never anything more than an infatuation even though Nona thought in the beginning that she was in love for the first time in her life. I think it ended when Marta came on the scene. I think that's when she realized that she'd made a great mistake. The problem was the hang-up she had about what to do when she left here. The only place she had to go was back to her parents and that was something she couldn't face. I told her to go to Charlotte or to Raleigh, get a job, start a new life. But she'd never worked, she had no skills and she said she had no money."

"But how foolish not to go home. No one would have cared." Ellie had seen enough by then to know that everyone was too preoccupied with his own affairs to concern himself for very long with someone else's.

"That's true, but she couldn't see it that way. She wouldn't listen to anything anyone suggested. No one could help her. Dr. Nichols tried. Dr. Trimble even had her up to his office one day." Nancy shook her head. "It was useless."

Tino's image rose up in Ellie's mind and bitterness consumed her. Tino with his overbearing manner, his rudeness, the everlasting orders. Sit here, Nona. Wear your blue jacket. Eat this, not that. And Nona, adoring, submissive, obeying his every command without protest as if all these injunctions were proof that he cared. The swift spiral downward. Nona waiting in the parlor while he dallied outside with Marta. Her stricken face the day it was learned they had gone off together. Ellie had never come to like Nona very much but that someone so worthless was the cause of her death filled her with pain. She wondered if Tino would ever find out what had happened and if he did what his reaction would be. She could see him—a blank stare, then narrowed eyes and a shrug of the shoulders to absolve himself of any trace of blame.

The fire burned lower and the room grew chill. The sleet had stopped but a wind arose and a tree branch tapped at a window like a beckoning ghost.

28.

Nona's death was headline news at the sanatorium for a few days, blazed about and speculated upon, then something more immediate caught the general interest and its gossip value waned. At the cottage, however, it wasn't so easily put aside. All her belongings had been shipped back to North Carolina but little things, overlooked or too trifling to bother about, called to mind her white face, the lost eyes, and because they were of so little consequence they were somehow the more pathetic. Her hoard of Vogue magazines, an untouched box of chocolate turtles on a shelf, blond bobby pins, pearls from a necklace she broke one day and didn't bother to retrieve. The cleaning girl picked up the scattered beads.

"Whose are they?" she asked.

"No one's," Nancy answered. "You can have them if you want them."

One by one she put them in her apron pocket.

At last there was only the empty room. Whether intentionally or from lack of need it wasn't immediately filled and it continued to be referred to as Nona's room but finally, stripped of everything that had given it identity, it became anonymous and its haunted history faded.

"What will you wear?" Amy asked.

Ellie had long since decided. Her jade green corded silk with a standup Chinese collar, worn only once before. She described it.

"It doesn't sound very dressy to me. Not for a four o'clock wedding and a reception at a Park Avenue hotel."

A buffeting wind scoured the walkways and they leaned into it, sometimes turning and walking backwards against it.

"You can borrow something of mine if you like," Amy went on. They reached her cottage. "I've got a lot of new things! Come in and I'll show you! You might see something you like."

"No Amy, thank you. I like my dress. I don't want to wear anything else."

"Well come in for a minute anyway. You might change your mind."

Reluctantly Ellie followed her into the cottage. Most of Amy's clothes were chosen for her by her mother and they were expensive and in good taste. Nothing she owned prepared Ellie for the wild assortment of acquisitions Amy proceeded to pullout of her closet. A cheap purple sequined blouse, a multi-colored beaded blouse, flimsy underwear in theatrical colors, a black shiny skirt split up the side, gold shoes—the kind of things seen in the windows of the trashy stores around Times Square. A tangle of jewelry lay scattered on her dresser along with bottles of violent perfumes. She swooped up a rope of glass beads a yard long.

"Isn't it gorgeous?" she asked, and she tossed it over her head.

Ellie nodded dubiously.

"No, Amy…it's just that… When are you going to wear these things?" She looked around at the gaudy display. Clothes more inappropriate, more out of character, would be hard to imagine. Where could she possibly go in them? Nor were they suited to a climate where most months of the year woolens and boots were worn. She said she was going home for the holidays. Did she plan to wear them there? What would her parents' reaction be were she to appear in such garb?

"I'll wear them whenever I want," she declared. "Why not?" Her exuberance changed in a split second to deadly earnestness.

"You know, Ellie, I've never in my life had party clothes. I was never able to go any place where I'd need them. I've spent days dreaming of the things I'd wear if I went to a formal. Or a nightclub. Or a big fancy party. Then I thought why dream about them? Why not just go ahead and get them?" She marched to her closet and hauled out a trailing thing on a hanger with tissue paper over it. "Wait till you see this!"

Uncovered it was a long narrow dress, salmon pink, strapless, adorned from top to bottom with rows of trembling fringe. She regarded it with the admiration reserved for a coronation gown. Holding it against her she admired herself in her dresser mirror. All Ellie could see was the lovely ruddy gold of her hair against the hideous pink and involuntarily she winced. Amy laughed.

"Oh Ellie, I thought you'd understand. Maybe it's a little dramatic but it's a fun thing. All these things are. Haven't you ever bought something just because you wanted it? Does there have to be a reason for everything?"

It didn't make a lot of sense to buy clothes you couldn't wear but maybe that was all it amounted to—things bought for the fun of it. A not inexpensive form of play considering the extent of the wardrobe but with parents who had money and who indulged her least whim a possible explanation.

Ellie was curious. "Where did they come from?"

Amy opened a drawer and pulled out a mail order catalogue. Most of the patients did their shopping by mail and were targets for all manner of advertising material, the greater part of which they threw out. The catalogue she handed to Ellie came from an obscure town in New Jersey with a box number for an address and an unfamiliar name. It offered the cheapest kind of clothes and accessories.

"I haven't finished yet," she said. "There are some other things I want to get." She took the catalogue back and flipped through the pages, halting to study a sweater here, a handbag there. Suddenly she put it down and looked at Ellie conspiratorially.

"I'll tell you something I haven't told anyone else. But first I want you to guess. Guess who I've been dating."

Ellie didn't know she was dating anyone. "Fernando?"

"Oh Fernando," she said disdainfully. "Of course not. Fernando hasn't any money. He can't take anybody out." She waited while Ellie tried to think who it might be.

"I give up," she said finally.

"Georgio."

"Georgio?" Ellie couldn't have been more taken aback.

"Yes, Georgio. Why are you so surprised?"

What could Ellie say? She couldn't think of anyone more unlikely for Amy to go out with. Georgio, who barely spoke English. Whose background was light years away from hers.

"He's very nice," she went on. "People around here look down on him because he's a sailor and he's Greek. But they're wrong. He's a really nice person."

"I don't look down on him, Amy. I just never thought he was someone you'd want to go out with."

"You say that because you don't know him. We have all kinds of fun together." A pause. Then came her announcement. "We go to the Cave."

The Cave was a notorious little dive on the river at the end of town reached by a flight of stairs that descended from the sidewalk. Once in awhile somebody went there out of curiosity and would come back with stories of what it was like but it was no place for the discriminating. It catered to brawling types, drunks, women on the loose. And there were rooms overhead which could be rented by the hour. To go there once was admissible. To go there on a regular basis was to put oneself in question.

"Why the Cave, Amy? There are nicer places to go."

"The Cave is more fun."

Standing amidst the glitter of spangles and beads, the riotous pinks, purples and scarlets, she looked past Ellie, past the confining walls of the long-familiar room. Her gaze was turned inward and it was as if she saw images that pleased and stirred her.

Puzzled and ill at ease Ellie rose. "I'd better go. It's after five."

Amy didn't answer at once. An odd, secret smile lingered on her face and it appeared that only with effort was she able to come back from wherever her visions had taken her.

"You're sure you wouldn't like to borrow something?"

"Thanks, Amy, but my own dress will be all right."

"How about some jewelry? Or the black net stockings?"

"No. Thanks very much. If I change my mind I'll let you know, okay?"

"Sure, Ellie, that's fine. And remember I'm not making this offer to everybody. Only special people."

Walking up the path to Anderson Ellie wondered who else knew about this strange behavior and if it struck them as ominous as it did her. Something had happened to Amy. She'd changed. Somewhere along the line basic elements of her personality had shifted.

29.

That Friday in December was a gala day, Elsa easing her car down through the mountains heading for New York. Dentist-bound, she had least reason to look forward to the expedition but ever-amiable she was as cheerful as her passengers. Snow lay deep on the flanks of the hills, deeper in the valleys but gradually it disappeared until as the land flattened out there was nothing but mile after mile of bare, brown fields marked by an occasional small cluster of farm buildings. The day was clear and cold and their rooftops were silhouetted sharply against a blue immensity of sky.

The sum total of happy anticipation within the car was like air in a balloon, swelling, surging, lifting as the miles slid past, inducing Johnny Bern to burst into song from time to time. He had a good voice for a seventeen year old and he knew the words to all the hit songs. Sometimes Susan Connor, Dr. Connor's wife—pearls, perfume and a beaver coat—who joined the party at the last minute to Christmas shop, read snatches of department store ads from the New York Times folded on her lap. In a pleased southern voice she disclosed where she intended to go and what she wanted to buy.

"We'll only be there a day," Elsa laughed. "Not a week."

"You'd be surprised what I can accomplish once I've made up my mind."

As for Ellie, it had finally arrived, the day she'd waited for, the day she'd pulled out of her mind like a jewel to illumine lackluster hours. She clasped the knowledge to herself as if it were tangible and the anticipation of being with Bob again burned inside her like a flame. He was looking forward to it as hungrily as she. Tonight they'd be together after all the months of separation, of living on letters and phone calls. Sitting up front next to Elsa, she was all but unaware of the road which spun out before them except that every hour it brought her closer to her destination.

By mid-afternoon they were on the outskirts of the city and at what Ellie always thought of as the magic hour—offices closing and winter dusk deepening to dark—they were in Manhattan. Nothing had changed. The clogged traffic, prodding horns, the towering buildings lighted in crossword puzzle fashion, gleaming store fronts, smartly dressed people hurrying by. She might have been away only a week instead of a year and a half.

Elsa left her outside the Marguery, a fashionably unobtrusive hotel she and Bob selected because the wedding reception was being held there. She stood for a moment on the sidewalk, the better to take it in and excitement mounted within her. Accustomed as she'd become to the strolling pace of everyone at the sanatorium, she'd forgotten that people walked so quickly. She gave the uniformed doorman a radiant smile which he returned widely as he spun the revolving door.

Upstairs in her room she unpacked slowly, listening for the phone to ring. Five o'clock, five-thirty, six o'clock. They'd spoken the night before to confirm the arrangements and Bob's words as well as hers were filled with anticipation. It was a year since they were last together. He said he'd call her before he left Wall Street to make sure she was there. What could be keeping him. A last minute meeting? Possible but not likely.

By seven o'clock she was concerned and she was hungry. She'd eaten an egg salad sandwich at the roadside restaurant where they lunched but that was at noon. Reluctantly she left her room and in the lobby she told the clerk at the desk she was expecting a phone call and to have her paged in the coffee shop if it came through. Anxiety, however, robbed her of her appetite. Sitting at a table with a Danish pastry in front of her she ate only half of it, took some sips of coffee and pushed her cup aside. Nobody paged her, nobody called. She went back to her room.

At ten minutes past eight the phone rang. It was Bob and her immediate reaction was a surge of relief.

"Ellie, I know you've been worrying but I haven't been able to call before. It's been a bad day."

Relief become alarm. "What's wrong?"

"There's been an accident. Davie."

It was moments before she was able to speak. "What happened?"

It seemed that after months of silence Howard returned from the southwest, showing up at the house that afternoon. Davie was just home from school and begged for a ride on the motorcycle. Howard was tired, glad to be in out of the cold, but he finally agreed. A couple of miles out of town on an icy stretch of road he lost control and skidded into a guard rail, pitching Davie several feet forward into a tree.

Bob's voice was strained. "He's pretty badly banged up, poor kid. I hardly knew him when I saw him."

"Bob, how awful, how simply awful. Where are you?"

"In Greenwich, at the hospital."

"What do the doctors say?"

"He's got a fractured skull and back injuries. It's too soon to tell for sure, but it's possible that the damage to his spine might be permanent."

"Oh no!"

"There's a good team working on him. The best. He came out of surgery a little while ago so we'll just have to wait and see how it goes."

"Is Sally there?"

"Yes, she was in Boston. She got here about an hour after I did. They called me at the office from the emergency room."

"What about Howard? Is he hurt too?"

"He has a broken leg and a lot of bruises."

"Oh God, Bob, this is terrible. I'm so sorry, sorry for Davie and for what this is doing to you and Sally."

"I know you are, Ellie, but I don't want you to worry. Let's just hope everything'll be okay."

"I pray it will."

"Look, Ellie, I want you to go to the wedding tomorrow just as planned and I want you to enjoy yourself."

She didn't answer.

"You must go, Ellie. It's such a disappointment that things turned out this way but we'll make up for it once Davie is out of the woods. Don't make it worse. Make the most of this little while that you're in New York. You've looked forward to it for so long. Besides they're expecting you at the wedding."

"Yes, they are," she admitted. "I called Joan earlier and told her I was here." All right, she'd go to the wedding but as for enjoying herself? There wasn't a chance.

"I'll call you tomorrow and give you whatever news there is. Now please don't worry."

Stricken, Ellie sat where she was on the edge of the bed, her hand still on the replaced receiver, unwilling to release her hold on the means which brought Bob's presence into the room. The breakdown of the longed-for reunion—a year of yearning for this hour—left her numb and it was minutes before she was able to think beyond that overwhelming disappointment. Yet there was another reality she was obliged to face, one which most of the time she pushed into the recesses of her mind and ignored. Bob had another life apart from her and its ties were strong and its commitments deep. He might be the center of her entire world but she was only a part of his and circumstances could quickly relegate her to second place. Was there any more conclusive evidence than what had just happened? She looked around at the luxurious room they were to share—the brocade drapes, the rose taffeta spread, deep chairs, handsome appointments—let her mind dwell briefly on the cancelled joy, and recognized that the crushing disappointment was a trifle by comparison.

The wedding was a beautiful affair but Ellie moved through it blindly. It took place the next day in a nearby church that was once a neighborhood landmark but was now a relic of times gone by, outdated as a horse and carriage, outflanked by skyscraper steel and buildings of glass and granite. Its rituals, however, remained unchanged and the vows, the rings, the rice, the extravagance of flowers were no different than a century ago. There were more flowers on the tables at the reception, bowls of pink and purple asters, and at the entrance to the room the glowing bride and groom were embraced and congratulated amidst crescendos of talk and laughter.

Many of the guests Ellie didn't know. Those she did greeted her in happy surprise. How marvelous she looked! Was she back for good? No? Surely she soon would be!

Ellie nodded agreement. It wouldn't be much longer. Probably another two or three months. No one who saw her, a slight figure in jade green silk, Spanish earrings glinting above slender shoulders, smooth and poised, would have guessed the wintry climate of her heart.

Joan frowned in concern when Ellie explained Bob's absence and Frank instinctively put an arm around her. They listened as she reported the few details of the accident Bob had given her. It was too soon to know the extent of the injuries or what the outcome would be.

"Don't assume the worst, Ellie," Joan cautioned. "people recover from all kinds of ghastly things. You'd be surprised if you knew." She remembered her nursing days. "And children are tougher than you think."

A waiter moved among them offering glasses of champagne. Frank handed one to Ellie, then Joan, and took one for himself.

"Let's assume the best. Let's drink to a happy future for all of us." Gallantly he addressed himself to Ellie and he touched his glass to hers and then to Joan's.

"Yes, Ellie, we must. This is your first time back in New York in how long? A year and a half? What a damn shame this had to happen. Please try to enjoy yourself."

But the festivities couldn't end soon enough to please her and she was one of the first to leave. Back in her room she sat by the phone and waited for it to ring. Bob called at nine o'clock. His voice was grave. Davie's condition had stabilized but not much more than that could be said. It was now simply a matter of waiting.

"How was the wedding?"

"Beautiful."

"I'm sorry I couldn't be there. I hope you told Joan the reason why."

"Of course and she sends you her best. She says try not to worry. She's sure Davie will be okay. She says children mend fast."

"He has up to now, for what that's worth."

"Will you call me again tomorrow and tell me how he is? I'll be so anxious. I'm leaving for Saranac in the morning so will you call me at the sanatorium tomorrow night?"

"Of course, Ellie. I'll give you whatever news there is. I'll call you when you get back."

She longed to be able to comfort him but even if the miles between could by some wizard power be made to vanish he would still be beyond her reach. No way could she approach him, unthinkable that a mere secretary would intrude at such a time. No, she had no place in his world. Its inhabitants were for the most part total strangers. Her single memory of Davie was the bare-legged laughing youngster on the beach the afternoon of the cocktail party, throwing sticks for his dog. Her manifest image of Sally was scarcely more tangible—a smart, self-possessed woman whose distant manner held others at bay.

And what of Sally? What had this calamity done to her? Did that steely composure break under the strain? Did she turn, weeping and disheveled, and seek the solace of her husband's arms? Ellie pictured the scene as if she were an intruder in the hospital hall, catching a glimpse through a door ajar of two figures locked in the immemorial posture of shared grief. Out of their mutual pain might not love come alive again? With clenched hands and far-off eyes she weighed the chances of a healing between them and their original love rekindled. If that turned out to be she would lose him beyond recapture.

Images formed and faded in Ellie's mind all during the long ride back the next day. It was a cheerless trip, in stark contrast to the blithe trip down. Elsa's tooth had been extracted leaving her jaw swollen and painful. Susan Connor was moody, vastly disappointed in New York stores.

"There were just simply masses of people, hordes of them, pushing and shoving and so rude." She didn't get to do nearly as much shopping as she planned. Her pretty face was petulant and the sugary voice had an aggrieved edge to it.

There were only the three of them. Johnny Bern was staying on an extra two days in New York.

The cold increased as the hours passed, the melt on the roads re-froze and by dark a savage wind swept through the looming mountains, rocking the car and sending icy fingers in around the windows. Ellie was scarcely aware of it. Her mind was locked into a single train of thought. What lay ahead for her and Bob? She tormented herself with visions of a long slow recovery or worse—Davie left handicapped. The back injuries still couldn't be satisfactorily assessed. Her blood froze at the thought of a permanently disabled child. What then would the future bring? She forced herself to remember Joan's words. Kids are tougher than you think.

Around a curve of road the first lights of Saranac Lake gleamed faintly. It was seven o'clock and the long trip was almost over. Bob would call tonight and Ellie prayed that the news would be good.

Back at the cottage there was a message for her beside the telephone. Bob had called. Davie was dead.

30.

The curtains were drawn against the waning afternoon with its grim sky and stark trees, a day painfully like the day before when Davie's white casket was lowered into the frozen ground. For an hour Sally had stared out at the bleak view until Aunt Belle, her eyes red from weeping, came and lit lamps and prepared the room for evening. Now she stood with her face buried in her forearm which was pressed against the wall. Tears had given way to dazed disbelief. A week ago this day he had raced up the stairs, stuffing his mouth with cake, banged around his room looking for whatever it was he wanted and raced down again. Young, bursting with life, no day was long enough to exhaust his boundless energy. The waste, the blind cruelty of his death.

The front door opened and closed. Bob's voice and Scott's followed by silence. Then she heard Bob enter the room and felt his arm across her shoulders in a gesture of comfort. She flinched.

"It didn't have to happen." She said it again and again, rocking her head back and forth in despair. "It didn't have to happen."

All the pain, the torrential grief, was channeled into a single outlet—rage against Howard.

"Why did he have to come back? Why didn't he stay in Phoenix? It would never have happened only for him."

Bob's grief was as deep as hers. He had still not come to terms with the pitiless speed of events. The few crumbs of hope they'd clung to and magnified had faded hour by hour and at the end the doctors admitted there was never any real chance Davie would pull through.

He stood beside her, his arm still across her shoulders, wanting to comfort her as he would have done in the early years when they loved each other. Her feelings were not all that hard to understand. He remembered those first anguished hours and his own fury, cold and contained but fury nonetheless. Wherever Howard went incompetence and failure followed, now tragedy. But Bob was incapable of sustaining anger on such a scale and as it leveled he saw the episode in clearer light. Howard loved the children and he did no more than acquiesce to Davie's wish. Why the accident happened no one would ever know. He'd driven thousands of miles without a mishap. Why, on a short stretch of icy but sanded road, going at a moderate speed, he'd lost control, no one, least of all Howard, could say.

As Aunt Belle told the story Davie came home from school and was delighted to find his uncle in the house—sprawled in a chair in the living room, shoes off, feet up on the coffee table. The boy gave him no peace until Howard agreed to take him for a spin on the motorcycle. True, he'd had two bottles of beer—little bottles, Aunt Belle explained—but he was sober. She wouldn't have let them go if he wasn't.

"He didn't want this to happen anymore than we did," Bob said quietly. "It doesn't do any good to blame him."

"He's never appeared on the scene but that he hasn't disrupted our lives one way or another."

"Sally, it was an accident."

"He was drinking."

"He wasn't drunk."

She spun around, her face contorted with grief. "Why are you taking his part? Defending him? If it wasn't for him Davie would be alive today!"

"Good God, Sally, do you think he wanted this to happen? He was injured too."

"Yes," she said and her voice was acid with scorn, "a broken leg. And Davie died." She buried her face in her hands and sobbed. The paroxysm over, she wiped her sodden eyes and spoke in a measured voice. "I don't want him in this house again, Bob. I don't ever want to see him again."

Howard was still in the hospital, due to be released in a day or two. He'd need a short while to get his things together before moving on. He told Bob he wanted to go to Miami. A couple of fellows he knew worked at the dog track down there and he thought they might be able to help him get a job.

"Look Sally, he's almost ready to leave the hospital. He wants to go down south. Can't we let him stay here for a couple of days until he gets his bearings? It won't be any longer than that."

"I told you, I don't want him ever to set foot in this house again."

She shook her head compulsively. Once more her face contorted into a spasm of misery and fresh tears fell.

Friends of theirs who lived nearby offered Howard their guest room when he left the hospital and shortly afterward Bob drove him down to New York. At the bus terminal he bought him a ticket and they moved outside to wait for the Miami bus to commence boarding. It was a bright cold day, filled with sounds of snarled traffic and the roar of departing buses, foul with exhaust fumes. Christmas decorations and people carrying packages in holiday paper were reminders that the Christmas season was in full swing.

From the time they were children Bob's feelings towards his younger brother were mixed with pity. In the early years because of his poor health and later, as he saw him flounder from one inconsequential job to another, he knew he'd never amount to anything. He was gentle, well-meaning but one of the world's losers. He'd never be any different. Seeing him now, a crutch under his left arm, a battered suitcase at his feet, his clothes seedy, Bob felt again the old sweep of compassion.

Howard was talking and tears streamed unashamedly down his face.

"What can I say, Bob? I've wished a hundred times it was me who died. I loved Davie. I couldn't have loved him more if he was my own son. I hope some day you and Sally will be able to forgive me."

Bob's pain was too great to enable him to answer so he merely shook his head. What difference did it make if Howard was to blame or not? If Sally ever forgave him? What difference did any of it make? Nothing would bring Davie back.

The Miami bus started to load. Howard put his free arm around Bob's shoulder, tears still running down his face. "I'm sorry, Bob. I can't tell you how sorry I am."

"I know you are, Howard. It's all right." Bob put a wad of folded bills into his hand. "Take care of yourself."

31.

The winter sleigh ride was a tradition at the sanatorium, a carry-over from its early days when the chief means of transportation during the long snowy months was a horse-drawn sleigh. More sophisticated wintertime activities had since taken its place and its popularity had dimmed but no one was willing to break that small link with the past and abolish it. The sleigh was kept in the barn of a local farmer whose family had proudly performed this service for the sanatorium patients for a couple of generations which was another reason, it was felt, to continue it.

"You're going, aren't you, Ellie?" Fernando asked.

He and Ellie were standing in front of the bulletin board outside the dining room where an announcement of the sleigh ride was tacked up in prime place. A pencil on a string for signing up hung beside it.

"I don't know, Fernando. I haven't made up my mind yet."

She had no wish to do anything. Davie's death left her fearful and unsettled. A note came from Bob written shortly after the funeral saying only that he would call her as soon as he was able and each day started with the hope he would phone. When he didn't she would picture that grieving household trying to adjust to its devastating loss and rebuke herself for being unrealistic. How could she expect him to think of her at such a time? Constantly she brooded over whether the tragedy had ended their intimacy or if some day it would be resumed. Time alone held the answer and she had no choice but to resign herself to uncertain speculation. "Come on, Ellie," Fernando urged. "You don't go any place anymore. It'll be fun, you'll see."

"I'll think about it."

"Elsa's going. Amy's going."

So that was it. Amy was going. He was as smitten with her as ever although her behavior had become more and more unpredictable. Sometimes she treated him affectionately. Other times she took pleasure in making him look ridiculous though she was less inclined to do so in front of his friends. For that reason he sought to rally them around.

"All right, Fernando, you win. I'll go."

He had never seen snow, much less a sleigh, until he came to Saranac Lake and the idea of a wagon with runners instead of wheels pulled by a horse was totally new to him. Snow itself continued to fascinate him. He would stand at a window as if mesmerized, watching the flakes float down and blot out the ground, inch upward at the base of trees, cushion steps and railings, bend tree branches earthward. No repetitions jaded him. His pleasure was as keen in March as it had been in October. But not once in his years at the sanatorium had he been well enough to go on the sleigh ride. On each occasion he'd been ill, the first couple of years near death, and in subsequent years bedridden or in surgery. This time he would make it, but barely. The following day he was scheduled to go into the hospital for the last stage of his lung removal.

The evening was glacial and snow squeaked under boots as muffled, laughing figures ran across the road and climbed into the sleigh. Everyone was on hand except Amy and when time passed and she didn't appear there were exclamations of annoyance. Fernando who stood on the sidewalk waiting for her looked again at his watch.

"She said she'd be here at seven-thirty." It was now a quarter to eight. "I'll go see what's keeping her."

Amy's cottage was only a short distance away and eyes followed him as he trudged down the road and turned up the lighted path. The front door opened, he disappeared inside and a few minutes later reappeared. Alone.

"She's not there, she's out for the evening," he explained when he rejoined the others. His disappointment was obvious but he made a valiant effort to hide it. No one said anything and he climbed into the sleigh and they took off.

The ride was a fairy tale journey, a pale moon gleaming amidst a diamond glitter of stars, stretches of black forest alternating with white blanketed fields where the dim shapes of mountains crouched in the distance. Silence except for the clip-clop of the horse's hooves and flutters of harness bells. Buried deep in piles of ancient furs, each individual was as snugly warm as if encased in a cocoon. A flask of brandy was produced and it went the rounds from mouth to mouth. By the time it was empty there was a lot of tipsy laughter and the bearded driver of the sleigh turned around in his seat to beam down at them indulgently. Fernando made some half-hearted attempts to join the fun but mostly he was silent.

Back at the sanatorium as they were saying their goodnights a taxi passed them and pulled up in front of the path to Amy's cottage. It might have gone unregarded if it hadn't been for Amy's laugh, a clear, high peal in the icy air. Heads turned and the lamplight revealed her clinging tightly to Georgio's arm as she picked her way over the packed snow up to her door, laughing again in response to something he said. Georgio was in a thick windbreaker and stocking cap. Amy wore her mink coat, a gift from her parents the year before. And the gold shoes.

A look of pain crossed Fernando's face but in a moment he regained his composure. The goodnights went on from where they left off and when Ellie looked for him he'd gone. His cottage and hers both lay in the same direction and she took it for granted they'd walk together.

"Wait for me, Fernando," she called and he stopped. Catching up she fell into step beside him and they walked together in silence. Finally for want of something to say she asked him how long he thought he'd be in the hospital.

"Not long." He lifted his shoulders indifferently.

"The first time was the worst. The second not so bad. This time shouldn't be anything. I'll be back in a few days."

"I'll come to see you."

"You don't have to."

"I know I don't but I want to."

His face softened a little then. "All right, Ellie. Thank you. I'll look for you."

The next afternoon he waved a casual farewell as he climbed into a waiting taxi for the ride to the hospital. Ellie and Kimmie and a student nurse blew him kisses with their mittened hands as he drove off.

32.

Thursday afternoon as soon as naptime ended, Ellie dressed and boarded the little shuttle bus that for a couple of hours each morning and afternoon ran back and forth between the sanatorium and town. She got out on Main Street in front of Gordon's General Store where the day before she'd discovered a gift to bring Fernando. Christmas was only two weeks away and stores had all their holiday merchandise on display. Nothing she saw seemed to be right until in the back of Gordon's, past counters piled high with candy canes and Christmas tree ornaments, she came upon cages of birds and an aquarium of fish. Fernando's long years of illness had forced him into the role of spectator and given him a taste for the undemanding diversions of the invalid. A bowl of goldfish. What better choice?

Ellie selected a small glass bowl with an arch of pink coral in the bottom of it and she pointed out to the man who waited on her two speedy orange fish with plumy tails. He scooped them out with a little net and they took off in their new home with fanatic purpose. She smiled thinking how Fernando would exclaim over them.

"If you're going to carry this any distance," the man said, "we'd better wrap it well. You don't want to have frozen goldfish when you get to your destination."

"I'm only going as far as the hospital," she replied, "and I'll be in a taxi. They'll stay warm till I get there."

Nevertheless he set the bowl snugly in a cardboard carton, stuffed layers of newspaper around it, handed it to her and she left the store. Outside the day was deteriorating. Although it was not much past four o'clock it was already dark and street lights were coming on. The temperature which had been plunging since midday was now in the teens and as she got in the taxi the first flakes of a new snowstorm started to fall. They picked up momentum rapidly so that before they got to the hospital the driver had to turn his windshield wipers on.

The hospital was about two miles out of town on the road to the airport, an unpretentious stone building, decades old, set at the end of a slowly rising drive. Holly wreaths with red ribbon bows hung on the inside of each of the double glass doors and pots of poinsettias lined the sides of the marble stairs that ascended to the main hall. A desk stood at the top where usually a nurse presided ready to answer visitors' questions. No one was there but she knew Fernando's room number and with the cardboard carton clutched against her chest she turned down the hall.

The door to his room was open, the room empty. Ellie looked in and recognized Fernando's ancient robe on the chair and the flattened-down slippers by the bed. Puzzled and uncertain she stood in the doorway. A nurse came down the hall, a stout woman with neat pale hair and Ellie asked her where Fernando Carmona was.

The nurse studied her a minute. "Are you a member of the family?"

What an odd question to ask, Ellie thought. "No," she said. "I'm a friend of his from the sanatorium."

The nurse lowered her voice. "I'm sorry to have to tell you but he died a half hour ago." She looked truly regretful.

Ellie stared at her in disbelief. "I talked to him on the phone this morning. They told us at the sanatorium that he was doing fine."

"It happened suddenly. He started to bleed and it couldn't be stopped. I don't know anymore than that. The doctor's report will come out later."

Dazed, Ellie turned and went back down the hall. A table holding a lamp and a small artificial Christmas tree stood against the wall at the end. She put the box with Fernando's goldfish upon it and started to walk away but paused for one last look down the empty corridor to his room. She half believed someone would come out of it and say, "He's here! It was a mistake. He's back!" There was only silence.

A nurse now sat at the desk at the head of the stairs and Ellie, tears spilling down her face, asked if she could use the phone to call a taxi.

"There's no need. The hospital taxi is on its way back from town. It should be here any minute."

She stood in the hall waiting, crying, and people passing by looked at her curiously. To avoid the stares she went out on the drive to the road and started to walk, her thought being to intercept the taxi as it came back. Thick snow with a wind behind it now swirled down in earnest. It fell on her face where it melted and mingled with the tears. I'll look for you at four o'clock, Ellie, he said. Don't be late.

She couldn't take it in that he was dead. He was to go home in the spring after six years at the sanatorium. Recovered at last after eleven years of illness, all he suffered in that long struggle, the pain and discouragement he'd borne with such fortitude, all of it was for nothing. All of it ended here today. She couldn't stop crying and her leather glove smeared the tears across her face when she tried to wipe them away.

She looked for the lights of the promised taxi but there was no sign of them. In fact, not a car passed in either direction. At one point she stopped, wondering whether to continue or turn back but when she faced the other way the wind out of the north hit her and took her breath away. If she returned she'd have to battle it at every step. She walked on. The road was lighted and a sidewalk ran along the edge but it was much colder now and she shivered. She pulled the hood of her jacket tight around her face and pushed her hands under her arms for warmth. There were no landmarks to tell her where she was or how far she'd come, just white empty fields and straggles of skeletal trees, occasionally a lighted house, mute and distant.

Fernando and his guitar. His puzzles and his book of magic. Illness had kept him a child with all a child's love of games and tricks, all a child's sweetness. But at last the protracted childhood was ready to be left behind. He was going back to school and learn a trade, he said, and his dark eyes glistened. He intended to make something of himself, pay his family back and give them cause to be proud of him. He wanted to marry and have a family. He'd like to marry an American girl and Ellie knew from the way he said it he was thinking of Amy. A week ago in a genial mood Amy told him she'd write. All the beguiling plans and hopes ended in a single hour in these distant snowbound hills. He'd never see his home again.

"It isn't fair," Ellie said to the silence as she walked, "it isn't fair." The words stirred a memory of a long ago afternoon, of herself speaking them to protest her impending banishment. "It isn't fair," she'd wept on that day. And Bob's answer. "Nobody ever promised that life would be fair."

The snow deepened and made walking more difficult. There was still no sign of the taxi. It was senseless not to have waited at the hospital and she swore at herself for her bad judgment but she was committed. She knew when she got to the railroad tracks she'd be two thirds of the way to town but she must have walked for an hour before they came in sight. After that houses appeared along the road, then stores and finally at the start of Main Street in front of a bar and grill, a taxi was parked. It was the hospital taxi, the driver and a couple of his cronies inside fortifying themselves against the weather.

At six-thirty she got back to the sanatorium. Kimmie was in her room and Nancy still at dinner. She got out of her wet clothes, put on flannel pajamas and her woolen robe and sat on the bearskin rug in front of the fire, chilled to the bone. She was still rubbing her icy hands and feet, trying to warm them, when Nancy came in, letting in a flurry of snowflakes with her. There was a look of stunned disbelief on her face.

"We heard about Fernando. I guess everyone knows by now. What in God's name went wrong! What did they tell you at the hospital?"

Ellie shook her head. "I don't think they knew yet. I got there right after it happened. The nurse just said he started to bleed and they couldn't stop it." Tears slid down her face.

"There's to be a service for him at the chapel tomorrow after dinner. Then his body goes down to New York on the night train. And from there back to Venezuela." She pulled off her outer clothes and sat down heavily on the couch. "Just the other day he told me about the party his family was planning for him when he got home." Ellie said nothing, just stretched her hands out to the warmth while the silence deepened.

"When did you get in?" Nancy asked finally.

"A little while ago."

"Did you have dinner?"

"No." And she told her about the taxi that never showed up and walking from the hospital back to town.

Nancy looked at her aghast. "What on earth made you do such a thing? And on a night like this. Why didn't you go back to the hospital?"

"It was stupid. I wasn't thinking of what I was doing when I started out and when I wanted to turn back I couldn't on account of the wind. It nearly blew me off my feet. Besides I kept thinking the cab would come."

"We have cheese and crackers. And there's coffee. That's enough. But first I want to get warm. I'm so cold."

"I think we could both use a drink."

She rose and going to the cupboard where a bottle of bourbon was kept she poured some in each of two glasses and handed one to Ellie. She held hers up in front of her for a moment before drinking as if about to speak but then thought better of it.

Everything that could be said had been said. There was nothing to add.

Long after Nancy went to her room Ellie sat by the dying fire, too tired to go to bed, her head aching from the day's tears. She'd wept as well that day for Davie, for Bob and for herself, for the anguish of the unforeseen, for all the sorry endings. So much grief in such a little while. Sorrow upon sorrow. Carmen, Nona, Fernando. The history of suffering in that wounded place was weightier than its mountains, darker than the deep untrodden forests. Ghosts peopled the fog that lay in the hollows and in the mists that hung over the lakes. They were everywhere, a procession of them, ghosts of the exiled, the guiltless, the innocent who moved in a failing line back down the years. By now Fernando had taken his place among them.

33.

The draped casket stood in front of the altar rail, on top of it a sheaf of lilies bought with money collected in the dining room at lunchtime. Beyond it the altar fitted into a space no bigger than a monk's cell and held a polished brass crucifix flanked by candles whose flames trembled each time the door opened. The faint sweet scent of incense from a Sunday mass lingered in the chilly gloom, elusive, routed finally by the smell of damp heavy clothes and blasts of frigid air as people entered and took their places.

The chapel lay back from the road on the far edge of the grounds, half-hidden by thick growth, and because it was built soon after the sanatorium opened it was constructed of the same rugged stone that fashioned the earliest buildings. The surrounding trees partially enclosed it, dwarfing its steeple and the modest cross atop. The studded double doors, never locked, were on the same small scale. The shadowy interior was lit by an economical dozen light bulbs down each side but a bolder light glowed behind the altar where the pebbled surface of a slender arched stained glass window reflected the gleam of candles and glinted rose, cerulean blue, purple and yellow ocher.

The pews were narrow, few in number and all were filled. Most of the patients who sat at the Spanish table in the dining room were there and Doña Alicia, bent over her rosary, was in the front row. Elsa sat across the aisle with Dr. Lundy, head of the Biochemistry Laboratory where Fernando sometimes helped wash beakers and decanters, while Ellie was squeezed in next to Dr. Connor whose face was grave. Amy came in late and stood at the side. She was wearing rhinestone earrings. Remembering the night of the sleigh ride and the pain she caused Fernando, Ellie hated her.

She didn't feel well. She couldn't get warm. All that day she had chills and she'd debated with herself at dinner whether or not to attend. In the end she decided she couldn't let Fernando go without this much of a farewell, but now in the cold chapel she shivered from time to time and wished she was back in the warm cottage.

Father Cheney of St. Michael's Catholic Church in town wearing a white vestment over a coarse gray sweater, conducted the brief service. He'd done it many times before and the words came easily. Prayers were murmured while the candles fluttered, their flames skewing and recovering. The heads that inclined over gloved, folded hands lifted to watch holy water sprinkled on the lilies. Then it was finished and four men from the funeral home, heavy parkas over black suits, thick laced boots, lifted the casket to their shoulders as lightly as if it contained the body of a child. While everyone filed out they carried it down to the hearse waiting in the road.

It was snowing again, thick, soft flakes that in moments shrouded the coffin's polished lid with a last gentle blanket of white. Fernando would be pleased, Ellie thought, if he knew. Memories of him, quick and vivid, brought her to the brink of tears again but Dr. Connor walked beside her and she didn't want him to see her crying. She got control of herself but he noticed she was shivering.

"Are you all that cold, Ellie?" he asked

"I don't know what's wrong with me. I can't seem to get warm today."

"Do you have any brandy in the cottage?"

"We have bourbon."

"Take a shot of it when you get in."

34.

The next morning Ellie awoke with a raw throat. She told Miss Alexander about it when she came to make beds and later the nurse returned bringing something for her to gargle. The following day the rawness extended down into her chest and it was painful to swallow. She stayed in bed and had her meals in the cottage but the soreness persisted and a cough developed. "It's only an ordinary cold," she explained to Dr. Nichols when he stopped in to see her. "It's no different from any of my previous colds." She said this as much to convince herself as to convince him. "I had a worse cold last spring, remember?" He didn't say yes or no, just listened to her chest with an inscrutable expression on his face and afterward prescribed medication.

In the beginning it didn't seem to be anything out of the ordinary. Everyone was subject to minor respiratory complaints and they generally caused no lasting harm. Ellie had had her share of them. This time, however, the cold lodged in her chest and lingered and instead of getting over it a fever developed that climbed a little higher each afternoon at dusk. A stitch in her side, vaguely uncomfortable at first, began to cause pain whenever she took a deep breath.

Dr. Nichols stopped by the cottage every couple of days to see how she was doing and frowned at her elevated temperature. She didn't tell him about the stitch in her side and anyway it seemed less painful which she took to be a sign of improvement. But one night, after a restless feverish day, a series of racking coughs tore through her chest and a rush of blood filled her mouth. Sitting up in bed she stared at the wad of stained Kleenex, unwilling to believe what she saw. It seemed like a re-run of those days in New York when her disease was making its first serious onslaughts. She was badly frightened. On Christmas Eve, bundled up in blankets against a flighty wind that clawed at the frozen trees, she rode back to the infirmary in the sanatorium van.

"Just for a few days, Ellie," Dr. Nichols said. "We want to keep closer tabs on you." He was as non-committal as ever. Nothing in his manner indicated he thought the situation was anything more than routine, but Miss Bodelle looked at her with troubled eyes.

That evening Bob called.

It was the first time Ellie had spoken to him since Davie's death and at the sound of his voice her heart raced. Day after day she'd waited for a call, trying to imagine where he was, what he was doing, trying to sort out the changed circumstances and what, if any, place she would have in them. Her mind circled monotonously around the possibility that mutual grief would bring husband and wife together again, restore their early love, the bond between them strengthened by their loss. She saw herself put aside, part of a closed chapter in which her name shared the finality of Davie's.

His voice had a soberness never before detected and though it didn't surprise her it filled her with foreboding. Yet his concern at finding her once more in the infirmary put ground back under her feet. She was still important to him and quickly she sought to put his mind at rest.

"It's nothing, Bob, really. Just a cold. "

"Just a cold? And you're back in the infirmary?"

"It's on account of the holidays. So many people are away. It's easier for everyone if I'm here instead of at the cottage." It wasn't the truth but it was part of it.

"This isn't much of a Christmas for you, Ellie."

"I don't mind. It isn't important." She paused. "Oh Bob, it's so good to hear your voice. I keep thinking about you, wondering about you. I felt so bad that I never had a chance to tell you how terribly sorry I was about Davie. I couldn't believe it at first."

"We couldn't either in the beginning."

"I just wish there was something I could do or say."

"No Ellie, there's nothing." Pain threatened to distort his voice.

"This must be an awful Christmas for you and Sally."

"It is, but we have to go through the motions for Scott's sake."

"How is Scott doing?"

"Pretty well, I guess, but it's hard to tell. He seems bewildered more than anything else. He's going away to school next month and that should help. It's something he's been looking forward to for a long time."

"How is Sally?"

"Fair. It's been a terrible time for all of us. Sally is going to start working again after the holidays and I think that will help. I'll be getting back to work too."

"Will you be going down to Lima again?"

"Yes." There was a long silence. "That's more bad news."

"More bad news?" Ellie froze.

"They want me down there permanently. They want me to head up the new office."

"But that's not the way it was supposed to be."

"No, it wasn't."

"What made them change their minds?"

"Office politics more than anything else." He made no attempt to conceal his bitterness. The vice presidential slot he'd hoped for and felt certain would be his vanished when an outsider was brought in to fill it. The man was a long-time friend of Knox's recently retired from a military career. Knox took great pains to commend Bob for the fine job he'd done in setting up the Lima headquarters, and when he made the announcement publicly he stated that there was no one on hand whose knowledge of the South American markets could match his. Privately he added that he'd have a new title, a boost in salary and a living allowance.

Stunned, disbelieving, Ellie protested. "Surely they can't ask you to go down if you'd rather not."

"It isn't a matter of choice. It's take it or leave it. It's as simple as that."

"I don't know what to say," she faltered. "I never dreamed anything like this could happen. Surely there was some other way." Improbable alternatives surfaced in her mind. Knox would decide against it after all and Bob would stay on in New York. Bob would be taken on by some other prestigious New York firm. And as a last resort Ellie would go down to Lima and be with him. But there was Sally.

"What does Sally think of it?"

"She isn't happy about it but I guess she'll make the best of it. We haven't talked about it in any depth yet."

Ellie's wild alternatives faded to be replaced by silence.

Finally she asked, "Will I see you again?"

"Of course you will, Ellie. Whenever I get to New York."

"Will that be often?"

"As often as I can manage it." He meant his words to be reassuring. He'd do all he could to be with her whenever circumstances permitted. He loved her. But his own world had caved in on him and he hadn't yet had time to come to terms with it.

Ellie never remembered the rest of the conversation. The words that followed, both his and hers, were lost in a blur of pain. She saw at last that love wasn't enough, that a dream realized had more to do with practicalities than passion.

35.

Many patients went away for the holidays and the sanatorium took on a deserted look but for those who remained a determined gayety prevailed. Each room had a small, decorated Christmas tree, a miniature version of the mammoth spruce fresh out of the nearby woods that sparkled with lights at the nurses' station in the hall. There was holly on dinner trays, eggnog, cookies in the shape of Santas, mistletoe tied to light fixtures and on Christmas night children from one of the local churches, mittened hands shielding candle flames, stood in the snow outside the windows and sang carols. Rules were relaxed and patients partied in each other's rooms.

Nancy had been discharged and went home to Cincinnati. Mrs. Iglesias returned to her husband's diplomatic post in Washington, in both cases their disease pronounced arrested. Professor Palmer died on Thanksgiving Day, his death the end of a rapid decline that started in summer, as if at that point he quit the battle he'd fought for most of his adult life.

Elsa stopped by to visit, knocking first on Ellie's open door. She found her sitting up in bed, a book on her lap, indifferent eyes on the dim mountains beyond the window. She turned at the sound and Elsa was taken aback at the sight of her bleak face. She'd heard Ellie was in the infirmary on account of a cold. Was it something worse? She studied her as they talked.

"We miss you in the dining room, Ellie. When will you be going back to the cottage?"

Ellie shrugged as if it didn't matter. "I'm still running a temperature. They want to take X-rays after the holidays and I suppose it depends on how they look."

"So many people have colds at this time of the year. I shouldn't think it's anything to worry about."

"Probably not."

Elsa could be depended upon to say the right thing in any situation. She was a woman of great good sense, traveled, literate, attractive. Once Ellie had asked her why she never married.

"Not getting married is my biggest regret," she said, "but my health was too precarious. I was never in the clear for much more than a year at a time. What could I have offered a husband in those circumstances? How could I have cared for children when I was forced to spend months and sometimes years in a sanatorium. At times it seems as if I've spent most of my life contemplating mountains."

But today she was intent on being cheerful. "You young people here now are so much better off than we were. The disease at last is understood and there are weapons to fight it. In my day there was nothing but guesswork. It's a wonder so many of us survived."

"Some of the weapons leave much to be desired."

"You mean the surgery?"

Ellie nodded.

"It isn't that bad, Ellie. Not when it's the difference between being cured or not being cured. How I wish we'd had that option when I was young."

Because of her history Elsa was a staunch advocate of the surgical techniques that then supplemented the drugs and the sanatorium rest cure and she considered it unwise to pass up any of them.

"One of these days they'll discover the cure for tuberculosis," Ellie said, "and all this that we go through now will be obsolete. Think how you'd feel with your back all carved up and then they discover it wasn't necessary."

"I wouldn't like it, I agree. But for now that's all there is. A cure will be found but it may take years. Who can afford to wait?"

By the time she stood up to leave she could come to no conclusions about Ellie. It would be easy to say she was suffering from holiday depression, a common affliction among patients but there was something more. Since the trip to New York Ellie had made no mention of the man who was so important to her. In the past she'd done so frequently. To Elsa the omission was disquieting. Coupled with her cough and fever there was cause for concern.

To Ellie nothing now mattered. Nothing could fill the void she now faced. How foolish she'd been, how blind, dreaming the days away, seeing herself recovered and back in New York, imagining that she and Bob would pick up exactly where they left off, that everything would be the same. She took what comfort she could from telling herself that circumstances alone were to blame. It wasn't as if Bob tired of her or stopped loving her. That, however, was the meager comfort she always disdained.

The Christmas mail brought a letter from her mother with the news that she was planning to be married. She'd met a marvelous man, a retired Navy Captain, positively one of the handsomest men she'd seen outside of Hollywood, and there was to be a quiet wedding in April. They would live in Palm Springs and how glad she was to be leaving Florida.

'It's gotten very tacky,' she wrote. 'You can't imagine the hordes that have descended on us, crowding the beaches and littering the streets. One hardly knows where to go anymore for a restful afternoon or a civilized meal. I won't be sorry to see the last of it. It distresses me more than I can say to find you still at the sanatorium. If I had

known in the beginning that it would take years for you to recover I don't think I could have endured it. What a blessing it is that we don't know the sorrows that lie ahead of us. I am grieved too that you won't be able to share in the happy occasion of my marriage but I want you to promise to come visit us in California just as soon as you are able. I know you'll love Everett. He's really a darling.'

Ellie put the letter aside. It didn't surprise her that her mother was getting married. In fact, she'd expected her to do so long before this. She hoped she'd be happy. As for paying her a visit, Ellie permitted herself a small cynical smile. She could imagine her mother's consternation were she to write and tell her she was planning to come out.

Mrs. Stuart swept through her social world, scattering invitations as she went, all of them meaningless. "You simply must come and spend a few days with us!" she'd say. Or "Stop by for a drink, please do!" "Come in for a cup of tea, anytime!" Not one of the entreaties, voiced with such charm of manner, was meant to be taken seriously. Even Larry, who got home so infrequently, incurred his mother's displeasure once by calling her from the dock area in downtown Miami, saying his ship had just tied up and that he'd see her in an hour. "Really Larry," she told him, "this is a dreadfully inconvenient time. You simply must give me more notice."

No, a visit to her mother, new husband or not, was something Ellie didn't think likely in any foreseeable future. She pushed the glib invitation into the recesses of her mind and let herself drift back to the ever-recurring contemplation of her shattered future.

36.

F ew patients stayed away long. Most began to straggle back after Christmas and by New Years only Amy and Georgio were unaccounted for. They came back together the next day, Georgio carrying a suitcase, Amy in thin shoes and a sleazy coat. Amy hadn't gone home. Georgio hadn't spent the holidays with a Greek family in Trenton. They'd left the sanatorium separately the day before Christmas Eve but met in town and rode the bus down to New York as they planned beforehand.

A taxi let them out in front of the Medical Building in late afternoon just as the nurses on the day shift were going off duty. Amy, expressionless and full of purpose insisted on seeing Dr. Trimble. Airily she introduced Georgio as her husband of a week and explained that they had come back to the sanatorium merely to pick up their belongings. They planned to go back to town to a hotel until they could find an apartment for themselves. Dr. Trimble offered no resistance but suggested that since it was getting late they stay at the sanatorium overnight and get their things together in leisurely fashion the next day. If it meant being separated from Georgio, Amy said, she wouldn't hear of it and only when they were offered the room at the end of the hall used by the nurses for their rest periods did she agree to the arrangement.

Georgio confirmed their marriage and produced their marriage certificate while Amy twirled a dime store wedding ring around her finger. Her account of the occasion was blithely disjointed, Georgio's hard to follow because of his poor English. The picture that came through, however, was of the pair of them wandering through the muddy morning streets of lower Manhattan, Amy in a silver dress that hung below her coat to her ankles, Georgio steering her into cheap bars to celebrate. On Amy's face was a smile of madonna sweetness as she remembered the day.

Miss Rogers helped them settle in. The suitcase held a few of Georgio's things and all that remained of Amy's finery—a peacock-embroidered skirt and a lavender satin negligee trimmed with boa. Everything else was stolen, Amy said.

It seemed they stayed first at the Waldorf Astoria, a place she'd heard her parents talk about, but it was very expensive and after two days they moved out locating finally in a rundown, anonymous hotel near a bus station where the rates were low. But the maids had helped themselves to everything she owned, she claimed, first her jewelry then her clothes even the dress she got married in.

"But it doesn't matter," she said, summarizing the recital, and she waved a hand in breezy indifference. "I can replace everything."

Miss Rogers eyed the sleazy coat. "Where's your mink?"

"Stolen."

"Did you report any of these thefts?"

"It wouldn't have done any good."

Privately Georgio told a different story. She had given her things away. First a rope of pearls, then a gold belt, then a nightgown, until the maids discovered they had only to admire something and she'd present them with it. All her belongings had gone in that fashion.

The mink coat was different. That had disappeared the evening before. It happened in Grand Central Station while Georgio was buying tickets for their return on the night train to Saranac. Amy said she had to use the ladies room. She put her coat down on a bench and when she came back it was gone. If not for the woman at the Travelers Aid desk who saw they were in difficulties—Amy coatless and shivering in the cold station, Georgio searching the waiting room—it would have been more serious. They hadn't enough money left to buy anything, even a sweater, by way of replacement. The woman telephoned a local church where a coat was produced from a bin of donations in the church basement and sent around by messenger but that was not until hours later and by then they'd missed their train. They dozed on benches till morning, ate candy bars for breakfast and got the day train to Saranac.

Georgio had shaken his head in bewilderment, stumbling over words in an effort to describe her behavior.

"Something happen to her," he said. "I tell her it's no good she give her clothes away but she don't listen. She have no sense. She act crazy."

Amy declined imperiously to go to the dining room for dinner, insisting that trays be brought to their room. They were finished with the sanatorium, she declared, and she was full of plans for the next day when they'd clear out and move downtown but by morning her mood had veered sharply to a deep depression. She wept and wrung her hands. She accused the nurses of spying on them, claimed their room was wired to pick up not only sound but her very thoughts. She threatened suicide.

Amy's mother arrived that night, her father a day later. They had no idea she was given permission to go home for the holidays and were incredulous to learn she'd not been in Saranac. Amy had phoned them from New York just often enough to forestall their calling her and they had no reason to believe she was not spending the holidays at the sanatorium.

North of Saranac, near Plattsburg, a small private rest home had opened a year before. It was exclusive, expensive, noteworthy for its discretion and it catered to patients with emotional illnesses as well as faulty lungs. In Amy's case there was another complication. She was three months pregnant.

However, all would be handled smoothly, no problems were anticipated. The devastating toxic reaction of the experimental drug she'd been taking had temporarily unbalanced her mind. Time was needed to leach it out of her system. No one was able to say, of course, how speedily that might be accomplished.

37.

The holidays were over. The Christmas decorations and lights came down, rules went back in force and the sanatorium shifted into its accustomed routine. Winter had tightened its frigid grip on the land. There was seldom less than a foot of snow on the ground while back in the woods it was piled four and five feet deep. Icicles lengthened. The sound of the snow plows was as familiar as the whistle of the morning train and one never knew when another storm would come marauding out of the north with all the clearing of roads to be done over again.

Dr. Nichols stood at the foot of Ellie's bed and held an X-ray up against the light from the window.

"There's a break at the site of the original lesion," he said and he pointed out the area with a pencil. "It's a setback, no question about it, but the good news is that it doesn't appear to have spread."

Ellie nodded, absorbing the information mutely. She was sitting up in bed, knees hugged to her chest.

"You have a couple of options, Ellie," he continued. "You can go back on bed rest and we'll see what your X-rays look like in three months' time. Or you can have surgery. I'd opt for surgery if I were you. I think at this point it's your best bet." Silent, subdued, she didn't answer but instead turned her head to gaze out on a gray landscape where the mountaintops were scarcely distinguishable from the clouds.

"You don't have to decide now but consider it. I know how you feel about surgery but I'd just like you to give it some thought."

"I will. I'll think about it."

Her mind was made up. No surgery. What was the point when there was no longer any urgency to get well? Maybe Dr. Nichols was right. A resection might now achieve the result that a year and a half of drugs and bed rest had not. But to what purpose? What did she have to go back to? No, she'd go through the familiar months of infirmary routine all over again—exercise doled out in fifteen minute portions, frigid hours on the porch—and whether ultimately she was cured or not, what did it matter? Maybe she'd become one of those sorry figures who stayed on for years in cottages on the grounds, abiding by rules that no longer applied, fashioning from their imagined invalidism a design for living. The truth was they had no place to go and lacked the courage to make a new start. Whatever happened she didn't care.

Meanwhile nothing had changed. Patients were discharged, others died, new patients arrived. Recovery was still a slow, uncertain process. No miracle cure had yet come forth to blaze across the horizon. The experimental drugs which were hailed each in turn as the long hoped-for breakthrough were all failures. One caused a ravenous appetite with a consequent enormous gain in weight and the girl who took it wept, not only that it did nothing to halt her disease but that her once-slim figure had become grotesque. There was the drug Amy had been given which put her in a rest home for the mentally disturbed, no one knowing if or when her mind would return to normal.

Lacking anything more specific, doctors, nurses, staff and everyone involved with patients could be relied upon to recite from time to time that age-old axiom. Make up your mind to get well and the battle is half won. Ellie didn't dispute it. There were examples enough of its proof. But she shrugged it away. Her life had once been rich and full of promise. Now it was meaningless and whether she got well or not it hardly mattered.

38.

Professor Macaulay, a man temperamentally incapable of hasty actions, was deep in thought. The matter was of serious personal consequence and every aspect had to be carefully examined. At age fifty-six he had just received the highest honor of his career. The sudden death of the learned Dr. Hinsley-Breck, for many years an associate director of the Metropolitan Museum of Art in New York, had left the post vacant and Professor Macauley had been chosen to fill the place. The position carried with it not only enormous prestige but a handsome salary as well and he intended to make certain that nothing which would ensure his success be left undone.

Which brought him to his present dilemma. Unquestionably a wife would be an asset. He had only to think of the indefatigable Mrs. Hinsley-Breck, a wily old lady with sparse gray hair—presiding at teas and gallery openings, relieving her husband of a multitude of irksome duties, shielding him from importunate underlings—to recognize the importance of the role a spouse could play. Fleetingly he regretted his single status. However, it was not too late. He could still marry.

But whom?

The professor's blood ran tamely through his veins, his passions spent in his work. There had been a brief, ill-advised marriage in his youth but once free of it he'd remained single finding no compelling reason to do otherwise. Until now.

From the start of his cogitations the image of Sally Glynn—though already married—kept slipping into his mind, not for any romantic notions but because he could think of no one who would more ably fill such a role. Most important was her value to him in his work. She handled his assignments with skill, she was quick, resourceful and she had an almost intuitive grasp of his wishes. The very qualities which made her so effective had in the last year or so caused others to seek her out and this disturbed him. He couldn't afford to lose her. In addition she was attractive, socially oriented, young enough to win him envy but not so young as to expect an amorous husband. On that score, however, he imagined he might enjoy some pleasant dalliance from time to time provided it was not too frequent.

Until now he had never given much thought to Sally's personal life but examining what little he knew of it he wondered just how sound her marriage really was. From the beginning she seemed to have unlimited freedom to come and go as she pleased. Then there was the tragic death of her younger son some months before which he knew affected her deeply. One of her ways of coping with it was to lose herself in her work, taking on assignments which demanded more and more of her time. Her husband was away a great deal and it rather surprised him—especially since the boy died—that when he'd return she asked for no change in her work schedule but continued to put in the same number of hours, even accepting out-of-town stays in Boston. Was the marriage as tenuous as it appeared to be on the surface?

Over the next weeks the professor took pains to show her small attentions and whenever an opportunity arose, his hand rested on hers a trifle longer than necessary. He discussed with her at length the dimensions of his impending new status, the doors it would open, the people of note he would deal with, the scope of the charmed circle he would inhabit. The professor was not a particularly observant man except where his work was concerned. Had he been he would have observed an increasingly thoughtful look on Sally's face.

39.

A decided coolness in Sally's welcome on Bob's return from Peru was the first indication of a shift in the balance of relations between them, a balance which had grown increasingly precarious since Davie's death. It was more than the usual matter-of-fact way she had of greeting him after an absence. The aloofness in her manner that even in one who was seldom demonstrative was undisguised. She was waiting at the airport and kissed him perfunctorily when they met but driving the distance to Greenwich, with rain spattering the windshield, her conversation was strained. It was late, Bob had eaten on the plane, Sally had had a sandwich at the terminal and once home they sat in the living room with coffee cups beside them.

Her announcement that she wanted a divorce was low-key and she stated her case in careful words. It was, of course, the transfer to Lima that forced a decision and she added reason to reason to illustrate how impossible such a move would be for her. Scott needed a parent within reach in case of emergency and he needed a home to come to on holidays and vacations. True, Aunt Belle was here but Aunt Belle was old and in need of increasing care herself. There was the Peruvian climate, a far cry from the seasonal climate she was accustomed to and preferred. There was the language which she didn't speak and doubted she could learn. She recalled how sick she'd been in Cuzco and used it to condemn all Peruvian food. And certainly there was no denying the fact that they'd grown apart and that their marriage had become little more than a matter of convenience.

Bob listened in silence. It was true that their relationship had deteriorated, markedly so in the last few months. Her bitterness toward Howard was unyielding and Bob's refusal to hold him responsible for the accident smoldered between them. The transfer to Lima after the high hopes of advancement in the New York office was the final straw. He couldn't claim to be surprised but he wondered why she chose this time, so soon after Davie's death, to make such a decision. More to the point, what had she to gain? Sally was level-headed, shrewdly aware of the material advantages she had as his wife. She had a life style that suited her and all the freedom she wanted to come and go as she pleased. What made her decide she would be better off on her own?

Lamplight glimmered on her polished nails as she lifted her cup to her mouth, sipped and set the cup down. Smoothly— as if she'd rehearsed the words beforehand—she continued, pointing out how widely their interests differed and how few things remained that they shared. Now with Davie gone, she paused because the mention of his name was painful—with Scott away at school there was no reason to keep up the pretense.

"You wouldn't have to live in Lima, you know. You could stay on here and go down from time to time—or not at all—whatever suited you."

Her mouth tightened and she shook her head. "I thought you'd agree."

"I'm thinking about Scott. Our splitting up right now is bound to affect him. He's still not over Davie."

"Scott's practically an adult. Mature for his age. He'll take it in stride."

"I don't know. I wouldn't bank on it. He's a sensitive boy. Things have always hit him harder than we expected."

"As a child yes. But he's old enough now to understand."

"Don't you think it might be better if we hold off, at least for awhile?" Bob's concern for Scott was genuine.

Again she shook her head, this time more emphatically. "We'd only be postponing the inevitable. It's going to happen sooner or later."

It was apparent she was determined to prevail and she had thoroughly prepared her case. Did she suspect he was unfaithful? If so, she had never given any indication of it and it was not now any part of her argument. Only in passing did she speak of Professor Macaulay and then in connection with her work. She said nothing about the unexpected turn their relationship had taken.

In the discussions that followed there were no acrimonious exchanges, no rancor and at the end in a tone of voice more superficial than sincere, she expressed regret that their marriage had failed—but then so many did these days, she sighed. It was almost a sign of the times. The details, the financial arrangements, the time schedule, all of it was amicable, orderly and would proceed without undue haste. Sally prided herself on being civilized and everything went exactly as she wanted it to go.

Professor Macauley having been apprised of the coming change in Sally's marital status lost no time in pressing his suit. It was hardly necessary since it was Sally's objective. She believed that the new life she would embark on with the professor, in addition to the prestige it would offer, would help heal more quickly the grief of Davie's death.

As for Bob, free of the guilt he sometimes felt in the unsettled relationship with Sally, he was now free of it and could begin to envision a future which held the promise of happiness.

He told Ellie by phone from New York of his meeting with Sally and her wish for a divorce. Ellie was stunned into silence at this barrier lifted. Bob planned to see Sally's lawyer as soon as possible.

As for Ellie, she told him she must talk with Dr. Nichols and tell him she would have the resection surgery which at that time was so staunchly believed to prevent a relapse. She wanted desperately to feel it was so, that none of her former reasons for refusing it were given justification. After more discussions, Dr. Nichols spoke to the surgeons and the date for surgery was set.

40.

Ellie never dreamed there could be such pain. She lay in a sea of it, sinking from time to time into merciful oblivion but rising again to the surface where waves of it gnawed at her bound back. A nurse stood by the bed.

"We'll give you something for the pain in a little while," she said. "But not right away. We want to take your blood pressure first."

She sank into the clement darkness only to come back once more to the lighted room and the agony. A knotted rope was tied to the foot of the bed, the end of it close to her hand. Each time it swam into her vision it puzzled her, grotesquely out of place on the white counterpane in that stark, white room. To her drugged mind it seemed to have some mysterious importance. Ah yes, it was the rope they used to lash her with, left there as a reminder. And she drifted away again.

One summer when Ellie and Larry were children their parents took them to Spain and she remembered walking with her father through a vast building filled with pictures in Madrid. Some of them frightened her. It all came back with singular clarity—the great, domed room, small individual lights illuminating what seemed to be miles of paintings, her father's reassuring hand holding hers. One picture was of a thin-faced monk with just such a knotted rope around his waist while in front of him a man knelt and begged for mercy. The figure of the man faded and Ellie saw herself kneeling on the stone floor.

She felt the sting of a needle in her arm and after awhile the pain subsided but she became aware of thirst, a thirst so all-consuming her parched mouth could barely form words.

"Can I have a drink of water?"

The nurse shook her head. "It will make you nauseous."

Later however, she brought a bowl of ice and held a piece to Ellie's mouth. Sinking, drifting, her eyes would open at the feel of the coldness against her lips and the white, uniformed figure would be beside her. Then her face shimmered away and Bob's face came into focus in its place and he held ice to her mouth and there were tears on his cheeks.

She pondered this gravely as she slipped away again but when she came back he was still there. His hand enveloped hers and she tried to smile at him. He bent forward and kissed her forehead.

"You can have a drink of water now," he said and he held a glass with a straw in it to her mouth.

"When did you get here?" she asked him that evening.

"Not until noon. The train was late due to flooding down the line."

"We've had so much rain this spring."

"Maybe this is the last of it."

"I kept trying to remember that you were coming but each time I did I thought I was dreaming."

"You've had a rough day, kitten."

"How long can you stay?"

"Till Thursday. I'm to see Sally's lawyer on Friday and next week I have to go back to Lima."

She reached for his hand and closed her dreaming eyes. "It's hard to believe this is happening."

Each day Ellie was stronger and before Bob left she had improved enough to sit in a chair in the hospital lounge, her back resting gingerly against a feather pillow. Beyond the windows bare trees stood against a bleak sky but the breeze that stirred their branches had none of winter's ferocity and the ground beneath was beginning to thaw.

"Tell me about Lima," she said to him. "What's it like?" Wonder about this foreign city now consumed her.

"It's very Spanish. You were in Spain. It's very much the same."

"But I was small. I really only remember that every day was sunny and there were flowers everywhere."

"There are lots of flowers in Lima and there are tiled courtyards with fountains and walled gardens and balconies and grilled windows. It's very pretty actually. There's an olive grove in one part of the city they say was planted in Pizarro's time and houses have been built there at random among the trees. You might like to live there."

"Can we live in a house with a walled garden?" That struck her as particularly intriguing.

"We'll live in any kind of house you want, kitten."

She never thought of herself and Bob as belonging any place but in New York but now she looked ahead to a whole new life in a city she could scarcely imagine. It would have been frightening except that they'd be together, married some day not far off—her heart stalled at this dazzling eventuality—and the strangeness would be another excitement.

"Are you sure you won't pine for New York?" Bob teased. "There's no Fifth Avenue, no Bergdorf Goodman."

"Of course I won't!" she answered indignantly. "Anyway we'll be coming back to New York. It isn't as if we're going to stay in Peru forever." She caught her breath in sharply. "Oh Bob, won't it be heaven?"

"I think you'll like living there for a while." As if she wouldn't! With faraway eyes she smiled but another thought struck her and the smile faded.

"It all depends on what my next X-rays look like and if I can leave."

"No, Ellie, not if, when. Whenever it is we'll start from there."

Next day they kissed goodbye and Bob left. For the first time since Davie died he was able to look beyond his loss and see a future that held the promise of happiness. As for Ellie, happiness shimmered around her like a halo.

41.

In the cool brightness of an early summer morning—X-rays taken the day before—Ellie walked down the road to the Medical Building and up a flight of stairs to Dr. Nichols' office. He greeted her with a smile so approving she knew beforehand what he would say. Still, the message was electrifying.

"The X-rays look good, Ellie. You're okay."

She used to think that when she finally heard those words she'd fling her arms around the neck of the person who spoke them. Instead she sat in the chair in front of his desk, hands clasped in her lap, eyes fixed on his face, as still as stone, so dazzled to be free she didn't move a muscle or utter a sound, as if deliverance were a fragile thing that yet might be undone.

Professor Palmer used to say that curing tuberculosis was like trying to force a way through moving water and often she thought how apt that was. He never reached the farther shore. She did.

"To be honest," he went on, "I'd like to see you stay on over the summer but under the circumstances we'll let you go whenever you're ready. Just remember you're not out of the woods yet. You still have to take things easy. You've got to make a very gradual return to normal activities."

"I will, Dr. Nichols, I will." What wouldn't she have promised in return for her release?

It was finished at last. She was cured. She was free. Dazed with joy she returned to the cottage and that evening she relayed the news to Bob in Lima. She could hear the satisfaction in his voice but he wasn't nearly as surprised as she expected him to be.

"I was sure this is what you'd tell me, Ellie. I knew the day would come. It took a long time getting here but it finally arrived."

They talked about the things that needed doing in connection with her departure from the sanatorium and the move to Lima.

"Why don't you plan to be ready to leave the end of the month? By then I should be able to get away long enough to come up and get you."

"But you don't have to come up to get me, Bob." She was struck with surprise. She never dreamed he'd make a special trip from Peru to Saranac Lake just to bring her down. And there was no need. "I can go by myself."

"No," he said, and he said it very firmly. "I won't let you. There's high altitude flying between Panama and Lima. You're just over lung surgery. Maybe you won't have any problems, probably not, but one never knows. I don't want you to come down alone."

She still protested. "Honest, Bob, I'll be all right. I feel wonderful, really."

"No, Ellie, we're not going to take any chances, not after waiting all this time. You just sit tight. I'll stay in touch and as soon as I know when I'm able to come up I'll give you the word."

That was the way they left it. In a transport of delight she began to get her belongings together.

42.

One day shortly afterward exciting news reached the sanatorium. It was learned that Dr. Lundy had been singled out to receive a prestigious award for his research in silicosis, work he'd managed to complete while maintaining a busy schedule as head of the Biochemistry Laboratory. The occasion was the Tenth International Conference of Research Scientists to be held at the University of Argentina in Buenos Aires the middle of June and of the four people so honored Dr. Lundy was the only American. He was well liked at the sanatorium and there was genuine pleasure on all sides at this recognition of his achievement.

A reception was held for him the day before he departed and the parlors were crowded with well-wishers. Dr. Lundy in his usual modest fashion stood a little aside as if the party were for someone else, smiling and protesting all the expressions of esteem. His wife and two pretty daughters stood with him. Mrs. Lundy was a small, plain-looking woman but she had a smile of extraordinary sweetness capable of giving her face an illusion of beauty it didn't possess in repose.

Ellie congratulated Dr. Lundy, then turned to his wife and asked if she were going with him.

"No," she replied. "I'd like to and I'd like for the girls to go too but school isn't out yet and it's best for us to stay home. We'll wait and hear all about it from Ben when he gets back." She smiled and her unexceptional face became beautiful.

Next morning at the airport his family and another group of well-wishers saw Dr. Lundy off and pictures of the departure, everyone smiling and waving, were in the local newspaper.

Eight days later the front page of that same newspaper blazoned the news of his death. The Pan American airliner in which he was returning disappeared over the Atlantic off the east coast of the United States and all aboard were presumed lost. The four-engine Boeing left Buenos Aires for New York at 8:00 PM Tuesday, arrived in San Juan, Puerto Rico, ten hours later and was on the final leg of its flight. The last message sent by the plane included an ETA for Wilmington, North Carolina. There was nothing to indicate the plane was in difficulties. It carried a flight deck crew of four, three cabin attendants and sixty passengers, twelve of them American citizens. The Coast Guard searched a wide area where it was believed to have gone down and later found some pieces of wreckage but no bodies were recovered.

The town staggered under the news and at the sanatorium Dr. Lundy's colleagues were mute with shock. Heads shook in disbelief. The loss of so knowledgeable and dedicated a man could not be easily measured. The flag in front of town hall flew at half mast and a memorial mass was offered up at St. Michael's Church on Friday morning at eleven o'clock.

Ellie shared a taxi into town with Elsa, the two of them riding in self-imposed silence. All along the black-topped road, past houses with tidy gardens where lupine and delphinium bloomed, they heard the church bells ringing and in the clear air of that sunny June morning the sound reached far into the hills.

At the church the pews were filled with people who had known him, many of them the same people who had been present at the reception given for him less than two weeks before. Elsa leading, they took places near the center and watched as Mrs. Lundy and her daughters moved down the aisle to the front. Family members from the mid-west had come in to be with her and one of them, an older man, walked beside her, his hand under her arm. She wore a dark, unadorned dress and her face, without the illusory beauty of her smile, was plain and sad, her eyes red-rimmed.

How awful, Ellie thought, to have no body, no grave nothing for the mind to rest upon but the endless night at the bottom of the sea. How terrible an image it would become for her, the immense and empty ocean.

The church bells, now directly overhead, pealed out again, loud and insistent. They tugged her thoughts away from death and nudged them into the future. Everywhere in South America there are church bells, Bob had said, every day you hear them. And she tried to imagine the streets she soon would walk, the shape her life would take in that faraway country. This day or the next he'd be here. Any phone call might bring the sound of his voice and set in motion the beginning of her real life. The church bells ceased and in front of a soft blaze of candles the priest, wearing the vestments for the dead, began the mass. With all the mourners Ellie knelt and stood and bowed her head but her thoughts were far away and the prayers she murmured were crowded out of her mind by the words of Bob's last letter.

"I have to go down to Santiago, Chile, next week but only for a few days. From there I'll head back to New York and I'll call you as soon as I get there. I found a house for us with a garden wall."

A house with a garden wall. Once Ellie asked Bob what kind of flowers grew in Lima and he said all kinds and when she insisted he be specific he mentioned poinsettias and calla lilies, bougainvillia and hibiscus. They floated through her dreams. She pictured a house, shimmering white, with delicate iron traceries barring the windows and a flower-smothered wall that would enclose them and shut the world away.

On the altar a bell tinkled and a cloud of incense wafted upward, filling the church with its ancient sweet aroma. Mrs. Lundy's small figure in the front row was straight and unmoving, head lifted to follow the ritual taking place before her as if she would memorize each genuflection, each cross described in air.

Again Ellie's thoughts drifted. "We'll get a car and drive down to New York," Bob had said the last time they talked on the phone. "It's a beautiful season of the year and I want you to see some of our own country before you leave." Ellie was delighted.

"We'll spend a few days in New York too, Ellie. I know how much you'll like that."

"Oh Bob, how perfectly marvelous. How long do you think we can stay?"

"You'll have shopping to do for one thing. And we ought to see a show or two while we have the chance. And I know you've got a list of places you want us to revisit. Do you think a week will do it?"

"Of course. Whatever you say. Oh Robert, it'll be heaven."

A final blessing and the mass ended. The priest stepped down from the altar and went to where Mrs. Lundy knelt and took her hand in both of his. There was a quiet exchange of words and Mrs. Lundy, eyes downcast, nodded. Then her relatives grouped themselves around her and with her daughters close behind, she was led up the aisle.

Outside the church bells pealed again, clamorous, urgent, filling the air with sound that drifted through the peaceful streets and echoed faintly along the black-topped road as it commenced its slowly-rising ascent to the sanatorium.

43.

That afternoon just as Ellie was on the verge of leaving the cottage to walk for an hour the phone rang. Her heart leaped, as it did now every time a call came through. It was Joan. Ellie thought at first she was calling from New York and was astonished to learn she was in a pay booth a few miles south of Lake Placid. She was five months pregnant. They'd just bought a house in Manhasset and were in the process of settling in. What was she doing here? In fact that was the first question Ellie asked.

"Frank is with me," Joan said. "We just wanted to get away from everything for a couple of days."

Either the connection was poor or she wasn't speaking directly into the mouthpiece because Ellie could hardly hear her. "We're coming by to see you. You'll be around, won't you?"

"Yes, of course. That's great, Joan. This is such a surprise."

"We'll be there in about an hour."

Ellie sat on the low stone wall in front of the Administration Building waiting for them and at about five o'clock they drove in. Smiling, she got up and went to meet them. Joan's face looked strained and Ellie wondered if something was wrong. Frank too appeared serious and his greeting was subdued.

"Can we go inside where it's cool and sit down?" Joan said. "It's been awfully warm driving."

"Of course."

Turning, Ellie led the way into the building and on through to an empty parlor but neither Joan nor Frank made any move to sit. By now she was thoroughly alarmed.

"Is something wrong?" She looked from one to the other.

"Yes, Ellie, there is," Joan said, "and I wish to God I didn't have to tell you."

Ellie's heart began to thunder in her chest. "What is it?"

"It's Bob." Joan paused. "He was in the accident. The Pan American Boeing that went down."

It was as if the earth stopped turning. Wide-eyed, disbelieving, she shook her head.

"Bob's in Lima," she said.

"No, Ellie. The plane left from Buenos Aires. He was in Santiago, Chile, and he found that if he took a Panagra flight over to Buenos Aires, he could connect with the Boeing leaving that evening and get back to New York three days sooner."

Ellie still wouldn't credit the words. "How do you know?"

"We saw his name on the casualty list in the papers and I called Consolidated Steel. They gave me the story."

She handed over a little bundle of newspaper clippings held together with a paper clip. The top one listed the dead.

Robert Glynn, age 42, American citizen, leaves a wife and son.

Ellie felt the blood drain from her head. Her heart beat with smothering violence. Joan's face, the windows, the mountains beyond, all of it reeled, spun—faster and faster and faster. Then the darkness came and closed in on her.

44.

Time takes no note of grief or joy. The hours and the seasons pass the same for one as for the other. For nearly a year Ellie lay in the infirmary, suffering from a puzzling, sporadic fever. For some months it was suspected of being caused by a flare-up in her lungs and she was kept on streptomycin and PAS but a series of X-rays showed her lungs to be clear. She had no more disease.

The fever persisted and could be attributed to no recognizable illness. Her temperature would hover at a hundred for a week or more, drop back to normal, then creep up again. Sometimes when Dr. Nichols looked perplexed and the nurses fussed over her she imagined she might die and the thought comforted her, and when each morning she woke, weeping from dreams too sad to endure, her solace lay in the belief that it would soon end.

One day before Mrs. Lundy left to return to the mid-west, she came to the infirmary. She stood at Ellie's bedside, her face desolate, her manner apologetic as if her presence might be disturbing.

"They told me you weren't well," she said, "and I was sorry to hear it. I hope you'll start to feel better soon."

Ellie nodded vaguely.

"We're going back home next week and I couldn't leave without telling you how sorry I am. I'm as deeply sorry for you as I am for myself and the girls."

Tears trembled at the corners of her eyes as she spoke and slid down her face. She wiped them away with a handkerchief held ready in her hand. Ellie tried to answer but no words came. She was hollow and sick and she could do no more than turn blank eyes on her, reach out and touch her hand. Mrs. Lundy stayed only a few minutes and left.

After she'd gone Ellie thought about her and the curious bond they shared. Ties as immediate as those of blood bound them—a drowned forest at the bottom of the sea, bones intermingled in the sand. And Ellie wondered if those who die together are linked in some way, like travelers who set out together on a long journey. Like travelers would they discover they'd had the same destination—a place called Saranac Lake, a sanatorium called Trudeau?

Would Bob ask, "Did you know a girl named Ellie Stuart?"

"She came to my farewell party."

"I loved her very much."

Imagining the words it came to her that they fell automatically into the past tense. How faint the hope that after death love would remain intact.

In a pitiless void the days passed. Summer. Autumn. Then winter came. The fever persisted and Dr. Nichols, baffled, ordered her to get up morning and afternoon.

"You can walk in the hall or sit in the alcove but I want you out of this bed twice a day."

When the worst of the winter was over he had her walk out on the grounds morning and afternoon and oddly enough, it was during that period the fever disappeared.

After Amy Cannon's disastrous experience no further experimental drugs were offered to patients at the sanatorium. It took ten months for her mind to regain its equilibrium, a year and a half before she was free of recurring depression. Divorce ended the impossible marriage but she was left with a retarded child to raise. Meanwhile the search for the cure continued and reports of success sprang up every so often from undetermined sources. So many rumors and so much distorted fact spread through the sanatorium that no one paid much attention anymore. But the day came when the news was neither hearsay nor distortion. The miracle drug, tested and proven, was a reality.

Ellie and Fernando used to joke and tell each other how it would be, one outdoing the other in describing the celebrations they imagined would take place. Fernando's had a strong Latin flavor—statues lifted from altars and carried through streets, flowers and fireworks. Ellie's were more banner headlines in newspapers and a D-day type of affair. They were both wrong. The day was as unremarkable as any other day.

The news slipped quietly from one to another, faces thoughtful, voices restrained. Mrs. Randell who had the room next to Ellie came and stood in her doorway.

"They've got it. The new drug for tuberculosis. It's official." She pushed her hair back from her forehead with a weary gesture of her hand. "I'm glad, of course. But after ten years it's a little late in the day for me."

Hers was an old familiar story. A husband who had tired of waiting, found another woman and asked for a divorce. Their two children were turned over to her sister, unmarried and partially crippled as the result of an automobile accident. She was raising them.

Tommy Blair, the Canadian boy down the hall said, "Three years ago I would have been cheering in the street. But now?" He shrugged his shoulders. His place in his father's law firm had been taken by his younger brother who in spite of his shortcomings, was sent on business trips abroad and drove a new car every year.

Who was there to rejoice? Could any of them, marking the lost years, counting the dead, impoverished by love's end—

could any of them be glad? Would any of the newly afflicted, given that magic dose, say to himself how lucky I am, how blessed? Would all of those still sound, when their day came, remember the way it used to be and give thanks?

"But think," said Miss Bodelle, "you no longer have to fear a breakdown. You'll never have to go through all this again." She spoke to cheer them but there was a rueful note in her voice as if she too looked back to a day when the world would have been a shining place had she not been afflicted.

And in a strange separate category were those for whom the miracle drug spelled disaster. They were the people, once patients, who cured and had no desire to go back where they came from, the people for whom the dislocation of their lives became a design for living. They stayed on at the sanatorium, abiding by rules that no longer applied, measuring time in sanatorium terms—before nap time, after nap time, before lights out—magnifying every sneeze and sniffle, persuading themselves they had no choice but the womb-like security of the sanatorium. Some of them worked a few hours a day. Others did nothing. All lived in cottages on the grounds or in the warren-like rooms on the top floor of the Administration Building.

These people were among the hardest hit. Having long ago severed all ties with home and family they had no place to go. Millie, the librarian, slit her wrists with a razor in a furnished room in Pittsburgh. Mr. Zigler, a courtly sixty-year old who for years had lived for the evening bridge games, drifted down to Albany where he was found wandering the streets one freezing winter day, coatless, and committed to a mental institution. All of them believing that to the grave they'd be coddled and secure, were lost when their world vanished overnight.

Dr. Nichols, remembering a son who died of tuberculosis at the age of eighteen, was subdued. He came into Ellie's room in late afternoon and stood at the foot of her bed.

"You know they've got the cure?"

"Yes. I heard this morning."

He sighed deeply and walked to the window where he stood looking out at the mountains, drowned this day in springtime mist.

"After all this time they finally got it. Isoniacid. You can cure in weeks now. You can cure in a cellar." He turned back to the room and suddenly he seemed old. "It means the sanatorium will be closing. All of them everywhere will. We're the victims of our own success." He paused. "What are you going to do, Ellie? Do you have any plans for the future?"

She shook her head dully. "I haven't thought about it," she said. It was a problem she knew she'd have to face but she kept putting it out of her mind.

"You can type, can't you? You did secretarial work, I believe." Ellie nodded. "Would you like to take a job here for awhile? We need some help. Nothing's ever been done about the Biochemistry Laboratory and there's a file full of papers that need sorting out and typing. If you'd like to take it on we could use you. You'd just work mornings. I think you're up to that."

She wanted to say no. She didn't think she could bear, ever again, to sit at a desk and a typewriter. When the day came for her to take a job it would be in some totally unrelated field. But Dr. Nichols stood waiting for her answer. He was kind and he wanted to help her. "All right. I'll do it."

"Good. The first thing is to get you moved out of here. I'll see Miss Bodelle about putting you back in a cottage. As soon as you're settled, talk to Steve and he'll get you started."

Dr. Connor had taken over the running of the Biochemistry Laboratory after Dr. Lundy's death, his interest in medicine more scientific than clinical, but because of the changes in the wind, it operated on a limited basis. Its main concern was to get its affairs in order pending a consolidation of its work with the work of the laboratory in town.

Ellie met with him one morning in the laboratory's small office, a room crowded with hand-me-down furniture and lined with shelves piled high with dusty periodicals. He showed her the file drawers and the papers that needed organizing and the next day she started. Each morning thereafter she sat at the ancient desk, working her way through mazes of material and typing on a rusty, rackety machine. An elderly laboratory technician worked in one of the back rooms and most days Dr. Connor showed up for an hour or two.

He gave her a lift downtown one afternoon and before she got out of the car he asked if she'd go to a movie with him some time. Ellie turned in surprise.

"Didn't you know?" he said. "Susan's gone back to Memphis. We're getting a divorce. I thought everyone knew by this time."

"No, I didn't. I'm sorry."

He shrugged. "She was never happy here. This place depressed her. The long winters. All the sick people."

Ellie looked at him attentively, curiously, for the first time in many months and realized that he'd changed. His face was thinner, the gray eyes shadowed, and it occurred to her that some place along the way he'd become uncharacteristically sober. But now he smiled a little.

"What do you say, Ellie? A movie sometime?"

"I don't know, Steve. I'm not very good company."

"Will you think about it?"

"Maybe." And she thanked him for the ride and got out.

But nothing came of it. Right after that she had to start looking for a place in town to live. The cottages were emptying fast and the sanatorium expected to close its doors by the end of the year. No new patients were arriving, of course, and it was just a matter of letting the patients in residence go when it was best for them.

In what was once a boarding house a couple of blocks off Main Street, Ellie found a three-room apartment. The rooms were too large and they were divided one from the other by thin, unsteady partitions. The kitchen had once probably been a bedroom and the porch, useless and obsolete, appropriated the light. But it served. It was near the lake at the end of town and sometimes in the afternoons she'd walk down and sit on one of the benches.

Steve found her there one day and his face brightened. He wore a thick, white turtle-necked sweater and the autumn-scented breeze ruffled his hair.

"You're just the person I wanted to see!" he exclaimed.

They'd seen each other just that morning at the laboratory and Ellie looked at him questioningly. "How about a ride to New York?" he proposed. "I'm driving down Thursday and coming back Sunday. Ride down with me! How about it?"

It was as if an iron hand seized her heart, constricting its beat. New York. Pain still attended the memory. She stared out at the sun-dappled waters of the lake while Steve stood with his foot on the bench, his arm braced on his knee, looking down at her and waiting for her to speak. Slowly she shook her head.

"Thank you, no. I don't think so."

Disappointment showed in his face. "Are you sure?"

"Yes, I'm sure."

"Okay, Ellie." He took his foot off the bench and stood a few moments, reluctant to go but without reason to stay. "Let me know if you change your mind though, won't you?"

"I will."

He started to walk away and Ellie thought of something and called him back. "You could do me a favor if you would."

"Sure."

"There's a woman in Greenwich Village who has a cat that used to be mine. Would you go see if she still has it and bring it back? She can't keep it anymore."

A note had come from Mrs. Spencer, poorly written in pencil, saying she was having trouble with her eyes and she was afraid she'd have to get rid of all her cats. She wanted Ellie to know in case she was able to take Dulcinea back or find another home for her. She's a very nice cat, she'd written. The note came two months ago. Maybe it was too late. Maybe she'd already got rid of her.

Steve's face softened. "I'll be glad to."

"Her name is Dulcinea. I'll bring the woman's address to the lab tomorrow."

At nine o'clock Sunday evening Ellie's doorbell rang and looking out before she answered it she saw Steve's car in the drive. He stood at the door, smiling, a brand new cat carrier in his hand out of which came faint meows of protest. Taking it from him she opened it on the floor of the living room. Dulcinea arose from within, slowly, cautiously, and just before she jumped out Ellie took her in her arms. She looked exactly the same—her gray fur glistening, her sea-green eyes as bright as gems, and around her neck she wore her red collar and the little silver bell.

"Thank you, Steve. Thank you so very much." She held her tight against her breast.

"Lucky cat," Steve said.

Two years later Ellie and Steve were married. By that time he was on the staff of the laboratory downtown where Ellie also worked after the sanatorium closed. Steve was involved essentially with the transition underway from decades of research in tuberculosis to other avenues of study, a change which brought new goals into being and offered new promise. The laboratory staff was small in the beginning but it grew as the work burgeoned. Later a handsome building was constructed just outside of town to house what was by then a significant operation.

Neither of them had any desire to leave the area and when Steve received an offer to join a prestigious research facility in Los Angeles at a considerably higher salary he turned it down. Shortly before they'd bought a house on the shore of a small, secluded lake and had no wish to go elsewhere.

The years have brought changes to the town but they have been modest ones and the inhabitants have been spared the fate of losing their identity to a welter of clover leaves and shopping centers. When the sanatoriums closed there was a general exodus and for a time it was a ghost town. Empty stores and houses with For Sale signs were everywhere. Fire brought down the old wooden hotel on Main Street and for years the site remained vacant, as ugly as a missing tooth. The open porches, once of such trembling importance were sealed up and where the occasional one was left undisturbed it was used for potted plants in summer and storage in winter.

Rail service ended. No longer did the hordes of sick, coming from everywhere, converge on the town in the belief the cold piney air would cure them. No longer did those cured return to homes left years before to pick up the threads of disrupted lives, nor others go back to lonely graves in the cemeteries of distant cities. The railroad station became a haunted place, its windows boarded up, its lines a little out of plumb, the steep roof sagging. The grass once neatly trimmed came back each summer untended and turned into an unkempt tangle. Weeds grew between the railroad tracks.

Little by little new uses were found for some of the many sanatorium buildings throughout the area and new people came and settled. The old hospital out on the road to the airport was rebuilt. A new hotel rose up in the center of town. Shop fronts were modernized and restaurants elbowed their way into likely locations. There have been other changes as well but the character of the town was never lost. It is as tough and indomitable, as discerning and giving, as ever it was during the long years it befriended the sick.

For miles around the mountains rise in splendor, clouds drift above the peaks. Their flanks are clothed in summer green, their pebbled streams run free and in the enormous silence of the dawn the slopes are drenched in beauty. The valleys teem with memories. How many bitter tears nourished this soil? How much despair darkened the brightness of the hills? The day is past, the record ended. The grief this land once witnessed can never be renewed and in the rush of years will all but be forgotten. Those who remember no longer protest. Time tamed them. Painfully they learned there are questions which must never be asked. Because they have no answers.

The End